§§§

His chuckle was hoarse as he ran his fingers down her torso. "We did it your way last time. Now it's my turn." He teased her lips, not giving in to the warm cavern that lay just beyond, preferring to let his mouth travel down her neck, across the V of her dress, before slipping the straps off her shoulders. His nose and cheeks moved against the red lace bra, tantalizing the smooth skin underneath. While his head occupied her upper body, his hands pushed the dress down. Jolie managed to do the rest, and soon she was partially nude.

"So beautiful," he sighed as his right hand joined his mouth and undid the front clasp of her bra.

§§§

Indigo Sensuous Love Stories

Genesis Press, Inc.
315 Third Avenue North
Columbus, MS 39701

Copyright© 2002 by Edwina Martin-Arnold.
Jolie's Surrender

ISBN: 1-58571-071-7
Manufactured in the United States of America

First Edition

Jolie's Surrender

by

Edwina Martin-Arnold

Genesis Press, Inc.

I would like to thank my husband. Writing love stories is a whole lot easier when I've been involved in one for fifteen years. Next I would also like to thank Jen, Gil, and Connie who have provided constant support since they've been born. Last, I would like to thank the friends and family who have listened to my ideas ad nauseum and have always given me good feedback. Also, if you would like to get in touch with Edwina Martin Arnold. She can be reached at www.edwinamartin-arnold.com.

Prologue

Jolie Smith was barely twenty years old. Much too young to know about death, but now she feared that she would know it intimately. Waves of agony assaulted her as she struggled against the knowledge. She held her cramping belly and prayed that God would spare the tiny life growing within. "Mamma," she cried.

"Shush, baby. Help is on the way. It's going to be all right." Gentle fingers passed over her forehead. "I hear the sirens now."

"Mamma!" She grabbed the hand soothing her forehead and held on tight. "Please, Mamma. I don't want to lose my baby."

Her mother put her head in her lap. "As there's a God in heaven, I don't want that to happen either."

Her mother stayed beside her as the piercing wail grew louder. It reached a crescendo, and then stopped. Doors slammed and raised voices drew close, yelling orders. She cried for her mother when the men brushed her aside. Strange hands grabbed and poked, and then she looked down and saw the blood.

That's when she began to scream. The sound started in the pit of her belly, and worked its way through her soul before erupting from her mouth. It was a sound that only a mother can make when she's hit with the loss of her child. Even if it was a child she had yet to see. Disquieting and chilling even to the seasoned paramedics. It was a cry that once heard could never be forgotten. Jolie screamed it until she blacked out.

Chapter 1

Fifteen years later.

"Good Lawd!" someone from the crowd yelled. "That kid is jumping rope! He's actually jumping rope with a basketball!" Alvin Guillory watched the boy with the reddish brown hair in amazement and had to agree with the excited fan's observation. The kid would lightly tap the ball with his right hand, and it would glide under his slightly raised right foot as if the ball were tethered to his hand. Then, he'd tap it with his left hand, and the same thing would happen with the left foot. The boy's foot rose above the floor with just enough clearance for the ball to squeak past. He'd walk forward a few paces, and then back, all the while keeping the rhythm of skipping rope.

I'll be damned, Alvin thought. Pre-game warm-ups, and the kid's already impressing me. He'd never had a boy make him look twice within two minutes of seeing him. "I may be looking at someone special," he whispered.

"Damn right you're lookin' at someone special." Frank MacDonald gave him what was supposed to be a shoulder nudge, but it was more like a shove coming from his big frame. "Big Mac ain't never lied, dog," he pointed to himself. "Wait 'til this game here starts. You about to see some stuff you ain't gonna believe. Tyrese Smith is the real deal

Holifield with corn rows."

Smith. Such a common name, yet it still had the power to evoke old memories in Alvin. "I hear you, man, I hear you." He glanced at his companion. Mac's deep, raspy voice went with his bald, round head and thick body. He had no neck and Alvin thought of him as torso man. His clothes could have made him a regular on Miami Vice. Apparently Mac didn't know the show had been cancelled. He was living off the reruns. His shirt and pants were loose and drapey, and even during Seattle's rainy winter, he wore sandals with no socks, showing off the bracelet glittering on his ankle. It went well with the gold earrings that adorned both his ears, and the three gold rings that blinked from his fingers. Too bad his meticulous attention to dress didn't extend to his grooming. The webs between the meaty digits of his hands were usually chalky white with ash, as well as his ankles.

The buzzer signifying the end of warm-ups sounded, and both men turned their attention to the court. As a former NBA player and an associate head coach at Washington Agricultural and Mechanical University, Alvin had seen a plethora of talent, yet this kid gave him chills. He was a maverick, a rule breaker. Oh, not the rules of the game. He didn't double dribble or travel. No, Tyrese broke the rules of gravity, the laws of momentum. He went against the grain in unbelievable ways.

Alvin watched the epic battle between Tyrese and his defender. He knew the defensive mindset, and he gathered that the poor guy defending Tyrese was frustrated, confused, and in awe. All good coaches told their players, "Watch the midsection. If the offensive player's chest goes right, he's going there, also." Not so with this kid. His body would go one way and with an ambidextrous flick of the wrist, he'd send the ball the other way. Before the defender could react, Tyrese would be gone at the hoop, laying it up with either hand.

"See, dog," Big Mac tried to explain in his own eloquent way, "the ball ain't big to Tyrese. It's attached to his hand like a yo-yo. He controls it like a puppet." He demonstrated, moving his hand up and down.

Alvin tuned out his companion as he focused on the kid. According to the typed sheet of paper that served as a program, he was six foot five inches and a hundred eighty pounds. Tyrese was razor thin, a lean exclamation point, and boy, did he make a sharp statement.

Alvin continued to watch the game, along with everyone else in the crowded high school gymnasium. The Garfield Huskies and Rainier Beach Titans had a fierce rivalry that had been energetically maintained for over fifty years. The Huskies had dominated for the last decade, but now the Titans had a secret weapon, Tyrese Smith.

"Look at the defense, dog. I don't think Ty's man has scored. He's shut him down!" Big Mac elbowed him.

"Uh huh," Alvin uttered, keeping his eyes on Tyrese.

"Man, you owe me big time. I could've shared this gold mine with any coach in the Pac ten, but yo, dog, I gave you the heads-up first. But you know I got to share this with the rest of my contacts? All's fair in love, war, and hoops, dog." Mac laughed and playfully thumped Alvin's back.

Alvin nodded. He knew it was a matter of pride for people like Mac. They liked the prestige that came from being associated with good players. Spreading the word about Tyrese first, would bring Mac kudos for years to come.

"Hey, dog, do you know why you're so special?"

Alvin shrugged his shoulders.

"'Cause I like what you cats are tryin' to do up there. Black coaches at WAM! Two brotha men running the show! I wanted to share Washington State's next top recruit with you. Ya feelin' me, dog?" Mac rolled around in his seat like a spinning top that was about to stop moving and tip over. "Forget the state, this kid could be the top recruit in the nation when I get the word out, right here in Seattle, Washington."

Alvin nodded his head in full agreement. If Tyrese continued to play like this, he'd have his pick of schools. Also, Alvin was very thankful he was the first to know, and he told Big Mac so. With some recruits, it was crucial to get in there early and establish a relationship before the kid became overwhelmed by the process. Phone calls, letters, and intrusive media attention could take their toll on the most savvy of kids. If the boy liked you and saw you as a beacon in the hellish maze, he might just pick your program at the end of the day.

"How did you two brothas end up there?"

He wanted to tell Big Mac to shut up until halftime, but no sense in offending the brother. As a summer league coach, Mac saw lots of young players. "Rock Softli and I played together at UCLA. I went to the NBA after school, and he went straight into coaching. When I blew out my knee," he unconsciously rubbed his patella, "I couldn't make those cuts like Tyrese and I had to stop playing."

Chuckling into his hand, Big Mac said, "Shoot, dog, you could never switch directions like that kid. No one can."

Alvin laughed with Mac. "Anyway, Rock was the head coach at WAM by then. He asked me to come and join him." The halftime buzzer sounded. Alvin turned to Mac. "So what gives? How come this kid's a senior, it's the middle of basketball season, and no one's heard of him?"

Big Mac had a flair for the melodramatic that could sometimes be nasty. "Ya see, dog, there was tragedy in hoodville. Ty's originally from Seattle but he moved some-where near Compton, California, with his parents 'cause of his dad's job. He was playin' in a recreational league when some of our young warriors decided to have a battle in the bleachers. Guns started blastin' and Ty and a few of his teammates were hit. Ty's wound was minor, but two of his teammates didn't make it."

"My God." Alvin shook his head.

"I know. Horrible but true, dog. Ty refused to play organized ball again. That is, until I saw him playin' rat ball down at the park. I turned on the charm and became the master of persuasion. Next thin' you know, Ty is tryin' out for Rainier Beach."

Though Alvin inwardly grimaced at the man's callousness, his smooth face showed no signs of his personal dislike for how Mac relayed the information.

"So, he didn't play on your team?"

"No, I'm sad to say he didn't, man. It took me six months to get the kid to play for a team anywhere. I just got 'im to try out for the Beach two weeks ago, during the Christmas break. Their coach told me he'd check Ty out, but no way was he gonna let 'im join the team mid season. Shoot, after seein' 'im for five minutes, he was beggin' 'im to play, dog. This here is the first game in January, and the kid's startin'."

"So, the kid's a baller with issues." It was more of a statement than a question. Alvin wasn't put off by the fact that the kid had challenges. Most did nowadays. But in order for the kid to be a successful college player, Alvin had to be aware of the problems, so he could help him deal with them.

Big Mac rushed to assure him, "No, no, dog," he touched his shoulder. "Ty left the battlefield right after it happened, three or four years ago. His older sista's been raisin' 'im."

A woman's face from his past burst through his mind. When they'd been together, she'd had a three-year old brother, which meant that he'd be about Tyrese's age, but her brother's name was Randy. Still, the hair color was similar.

"Sis has done an incredible job. Got the kid counselin' and some other mess. Ty has a 3.9 grade average, and he's takin' those college courses."

A dream come true, Alvin thought. A kid I don't have to jump through hoops to get ready for the college entrance exams.

"And Al," the low conspiratorial tone made Alvin look at Mac "big sis is quite a looker. She has a cute little dimple that winks at you sometimes, and her skin's like warm caramel. Heats me up just lookin' at her." Mac rubbed his chin, "And baby got back, front, and everythin' else to make a niggah salivate. I'm seriously thinkin' 'bout tryin' to get with that. Ya know, make a Big Mac sandwich." He chuckled into his hand.

The woman he knew had such a dimple. It only appeared when she laughed, or was angry. Alvin shook his head and smiled lightly. "That's a pretty horrific thought, Mac."

"Dog, you just jealous 'cause you know I got skills with the gentler sex." Mac leaned in and whispered again, "And one more thang about sis, she ain't no tiny woman. Oh, she ain't fat, but she's tall with a little muscle, so she could handle a big brotha man like me."

Alvin laughed outright, then said, "You're right, Mac. It'd take quite a woman to handle your big butt. What's big sister's name?"

"Jolie. Ya know, pronounced like Joe and Lee together. And hey, hey, hey, speak of the devil, here she comes," Big

Mac gestured with a quick head lift towards the aisle.

Shock was too mild a term for what Alvin was feeling. More like a cluster bomb going off all over his body, annihilating his insides. He tightened his gut and prepared to deal as the woman he'd been imagining walked towards them. So the boy's last name and hair color hadn't been a coincidence. Jolie was even more beautiful than he remembered. Her thick auburn hair was pulled back into a ponytail that disappeared down her back. Flawless pecan skin surrounded honey-colored eyes that searched the bleachers for an available seat. She wore khaki pants and a blue polo style shirt with some insignia he couldn't quite make out. Despite the casual attire, her carriage was regal as her hiking boots advanced up the stairs. As she drew closer, he was able to read the logo embroidered on her top. It said Woodland Park Zoo above an image of a tree that sheltered a zebra, an antelope, and a lion. Of course Jolie would work for a zoo, he nodded his head knowingly, she'd always loved animals.

With wide eyes, he sat up straight in his seat near the aisle, and his large hands gripped his knees. Jolie was going to pass right beside him. It was inevitable that their eyes would meet.

His companion made sure of it. "Hey, Joe Lee. How ya doin'?" He reached across Alvin and waved at her.

"Oh hi, Big Ma..." The words died on her lips when she saw Alvin. Jolie had known this moment was bound to happen with both of them now living in Seattle. It had bothered her when he'd first moved back a year ago, especially when he'd called her. Jolie remembered hearing his voice and freezing. She couldn't decide if she was scared or mad, but she knew one thing, she didn't want to talk to him, so she'd hung up. He hadn't called again. Jolie thought she'd prepared herself for the horrible eventuality of a chance encounter. Apparently not. As she stared into his face, she knew nothing could ready her for this.

He was still as handsome as ever. Clean cut. He sported a small rounded 'fro that was blended at the sides. He wore very light sideburns that framed his face and faded into the etched brown of his cheeks. The sideburns went well with the mustache coloring his upper lip. His black pullover shirt disappeared into black slacks, and it was just tight enough to highlight his lean upper body as he sat up straight.

Jolie clutched her fingers into a fist to still the slight tremor. She refused to wipe away the moisture she could feel popping out on her face. The old deodorant commercial burst into her head, never let them see you sweat. All the emotions mixing around in her body were generating an enormous amount of heat; so, if she wanted to follow the advice of the commercial, she knew she had to leave. She turned to continue up the steps, but Big Mac's voice stopped her.

"Hey, wait, Joe Lee. I want ya to meet this guy. He's a coach at WAM!" Big Mac was so loud that a few people turned to stare.

"I know him. Believe me, no introduction is necessary."

"Hi, Jolie. It's been a long time." Alvin watched as long lashes brushed high cheekbones when she briefly closed her eyes. He looked at the dimple. She sure wasn't happy, so its appearance must mean that she was upset. Knowing that didn't stop Alvin from remembering how he used to caress the dimple with his fingers, lips, tongue.

God, his voice still moves me, Jolie acknowledged. It was like a purring cat. Jolie could hold one to her chest all day long, feeling the softness and the constant quiver that sank down to her heart and just made her feel good. The natural resonance of his voice affected her the same way. How was that so when the man had wounded her so deeply? Her reaction made her even madder. "Not long enough," she spat.

The harsh words drew Alvin's eyes to her pursed lips. They were full and rich like the blackberries he used to pick as a kid. Alvin was so lost in observing her, he didn't respond as Jolie lifted her well-defined, dimpled chin before continuing up the stairs.

Big Mac, a master of the obvious, said, "I don't think the lady cares for you, man." His voice was full of questions.

Alvin had no intention of telling him that Jolie was his first and only true love, and that he'd been too naïve, too selfish to cherish the gift. Instead, he'd driven her away. Time, basketball, and other women had yet to erase the memory and his regret. He'd returned to Seattle determined to win her back. He'd kept tabs on her enough to know she wasn't married. The cold click in his ear when he'd called made him hesitate. Her behavior back then and just now made him ask the same question. Why is she so angry?

"Well, it's alwright if ya don't feel like sharin', but let me tell you somethin', dog, and I hope you're listenin'. If you want to recruit this kid, you better make it right with sis. The two are as tight as my head and shoulders." Big Mac demonstrated by stretching and rolling his non-existent neck.

If Alvin hadn't been recovering from shell shock, he would have laughed heartily.

$$\clubsuit\clubsuit\clubsuit$$

By the grace of God, Jolie made it to the top of the bleachers where she sat down. She'd had no intention of sitting that high up, but the shock just kept her moving until she ran into the brick wall, then gingerly eased herself onto the wood plank. Halftime was almost over. The players were warming up, waiting for the buzzer to start the third quarter. Jolie's eyes focused on her brother. She'd spoken to Tyrese briefly before starting up the stairs. He'd given her the thumbs up and smiled big to let her know he was all right. Pride helped ease the numbness that still resonated through her body. Tyrese was truly putting the tragedy behind him.

Jolie's wary eyes darted to the back of Alvin's head, and then quickly shifted away as if she would turn into a pillar of salt if she stared too long. "Has it really been fifteen years?" she whispered to herself. Seeing him made it seem like yesterday. She was back in high school, drooling over him like every other girl her age within a fifty-mile radius. He was still gorgeous; the hollowness of boyhood had been replaced with the fullness of manhood.

Jolie closed her eyes and allowed the memories to wash over her. She recalled her jitteriness when he first approached her in the lunchroom cafeteria. It was during their senior year, and they'd both been aware of each other, but they traveled in different circles. Jolie hung out with the more academic minded students, and being a basketball star, he was always surrounded by jocks and cheerleaders. She hadn't realized until he told her much later, that her natural beauty was an immediate attraction, and he'd been aware of her since the tenth grade. On that day, Jolie had been talking with her friends in the crowded high school lunchroom when he first approached. Leaving his clique staring, he'd boldly crossed that great invisible divide in the dining hall to sit with her and her friends. He had slowly tossed a basketball between his long, thin hands as he walked.

"Hi," he said, sitting across from her and looking directly into her eyes. "My name is Alvin."

"Hello," she whispered back, completely amazed that he was talking to her.

"You're Jolie, right?"

She nodded. Her friends were whispering, giggling, and

smiling like fools. The whole thing was horribly exciting and embarrassing at the same time.

Alvin glanced at her girl friends. He rolled the ball around. "I hope I didn't take someone's seat."

"Oh, no!" they rushed to assure him.

Excitement gathered in the pit of Jolie's stomach when he turned back to her and smiled. There was a tingle she didn't quite understand at the time. Underneath the table, she pressed her knees together to keep them from knocking. She had a death grip on her cookie and couldn't look at him directly.

"Is that a good cookie, Jolie?"

She nodded her head and took a small bite.

"Chocolate chip?"

"Yes, double chocolate chip," she managed to say as she met his eyes.

"Hum, it looks good." Alvin's eyes were focused on her face. "Very good."

Instinctively, she knew he was talking about more than the cookie. Wide eyed, she stared back at him. "They're delicious. Would you...?" She'd meant to reach into her lunch sack and get him one; however, she became transfixed when he rose from his seat. Ball on the table, hands on top of the ball, he slowly leaned up and over it. Jolie watched his dark head come forward. She drew an unsteady breath as he moved closer. His full lips opened and white teeth took hold of the cookie. His lips eased around it, biting off a large piece. A tremor coursed through her when the soft flesh brushed her hand as he moved away. The bite probably took three seconds, but it seemed like three years to Jolie. She forgot they were in a crowded lunchroom. It was just him, her, and her wildly beating heart. His tongue passed over his top and then lower lip, removing the crumbs. He sat back and put the ball in his lap.

"You're right. It is tasty." His voice was slightly husky and his mouth tilted into the barest of smiles. "Well, I just wanted to formally introduce myself, Jolie."

She loved how he said her name. It didn't sound like two men's names because the J was soft, more like the sh sound, and the O was left open instead of clipped to an ending. When he pronounced it, Jolie felt special.

"Thanks for sharing." He nodded at the cookie, which was still clutched between her fingers. Ball under his right arm, he walked back across the hidden lines with the sounds of her friends clamoring over her ringing in his ears.

The next day at the same time, he was back, basketball in hand. This time she was ready for him. She ignored the 'everyone in the cafeteria is looking' feeling as she watched her friends move over, so he could ease his big body down beside her. He wiggled in comfortably and turned to hit her with that devastating smile full of even, white teeth.

She ignored the skip in her chest. "Let's talk," she said in a firm voice, which surprised him. "Follow me."

"Excuse me, ladies." He got up and left the lunchroom with her. She didn't turn to see if he abided by her wishes. She stopped in a small cove created by the lockers. Her confidence amused and attracted him even more.

"Just because you're good at fondling an orange ball doesn't mean I'm going to run after you like you're Svengali."

"Who's that?"

"I saw it in an old movie last night. He's some guy, I think he's Russian, anyway he hypnotizes women so he can take advantage of them."

Alvin held the ball with two hands in front of his chest, and squeezed it with his elbows out. "First, I don't fondle the b-ball. I handle it. I only fondle pretty young things like you." He enjoyed her blush. "Second, you don't have to sit at home watching T.V. tonight because you can go out with me; and, if you're lucky, I just might fondle you."

She rolled her eyes before saying, "Can't." He stared at her blankly. She liked the reaction, the fact that she could startle him. "I have a previous engagement."

He put the ball under his left arm. His lips tightened and a slight frown was beginning to cross his forehead.

She smiled at him. "You can come if you'd like. I'll pick you up at four–thirty"

He had practice from two-thirty to four o'clock. A half an hour was enough time for him to shower and dress. "Okay, I'll see you outside the gym."

"Great." Grinning, she backed out of the cove, turned, and left.

He stood there, rolling the ball around in his hands, smiling like a simpleton. As she walked down the hall, she heard him say, "Where the hell are we going?"

Jolie sat on the bleachers and glared at the back of Alvin's head. "Jeez, what a fool I was. Taken in by lips on a cookie." She gripped the hard wood of the bleachers. She'd been head over heels in love only to be dumped and pregnant a year and a half later. A shadow crossed over her face, making her blink.

"Hi, Jolie," the soft voice said.

She looked up and saw a pretty, brown-skinned girl. "Oh, hi, Robyn. Have a seat," she patted the space next to her.

"I'm glad you made it. Ty thought you'd have to miss tonight."

"No way! This is his first game. I was determined to see it. I left work early and I should have been here before the start of the game, but there were two accidents on the interstate. I nearly pulled my hair out trying to get here."

"Ty'll be so glad you made it." Robyn unconsciously rubbed her stomach.

"How's it going? May I?"

"Sure," Robyn nodded.

Jolie rubbed her big belly.

"The little tyke is kicking me all the time."

"Oh," Jolie responded to a movement. "That's wonderful."

"Yeah, it sure is," she covered Jolie's hand with her own. "Thanks for being so great to me about this."

Jolie remembered a time when she hadn't been happy about her brother's girlfriend being pregnant. But now she'd adjusted to the idea. At least they were both getting an education. Tyrese was a senior in high school, and Robyn was a freshman at a local community college.

The third quarter began and like everyone else in the gymnasium, Robyn's eyes zeroed in on the soon-to-be father of her baby. Jolie also focused on Tyrese long enough to make sure he was doing okay, but then the past lured her back.

She remembered pulling up to the gym's side door in her beat up VW Bug at four–thirty exactly. Alvin got in and tossed his workout bag in between his feet on the floor, "So what's up? Where are we going?" She flashed him a beaming smile that stunned him with its brilliance. Wherever they were going, she was happy about it.

"You're about to experience the wonders of life at its earliest stage."

He stopped trying to wiggle his knees out of his chest in the small car and stared at her.

"I work for a vet. We're about to help a stallion and mare breed tonight."

He was silent. "So much for my getting bred tonight," he griped in a low voice.

She'd heard him, but decided to pretend she hadn't. "Hey, are you all right? Do you want me to take you back?"

"No, I'm okay. You just caught me off guard. Why do they need a vet to do that? Doesn't it come naturally?" He raised and lowered his eyebrows suggestively.

She glanced over at him and laughed at his antics. "You know how you guys can get on a girl's nerves? Sometimes, the mare can get feisty and kick the you-know-what out of the stud. The owners of both horses want to take every precaution, so my boss and I are going to be there just in case there are injuries."

Alvin sat back, apparently resigned to being up close and personal with his knees for the rest of the ride. After a time he said, "You know, this isn't the typical first date?"

"I know." She stopped at a light and hit him with the smile once more.

After a time, Alvin spoke again, "How far away is this place? We're in the boonies."

Jolie didn't look at him as she concentrated on going down the one lane, dirt road. She chuckled and said, "They don't breed horses in the city, so you have to go to the country." She risked a quick glance at him before saying, "We're in Spanaway, about forty miles from Seattle. There's a large horse breeding community out here." Jolie drove around the main house and pulled up to a large barn in the back. There were several cars already parked there. "Good, my boss is already here." She turned to him with a whisper of a grin on her lips, tilted her head just a tad and asked, "You ready?"

Alvin looked back, seemed to hesitate, and then leaned forward, angled his head and lightly kissed her lips. "Yeah, I'm ready for whatever you're offering."

As she watched him untangle his body and ease out of the car, her hand rubbed her fluttering stomach. It was doing something she'd never experienced, but she'd heard all her friends rave about it. Butterflies! That brush from his lips had turned her insides into churning mush. Somewhat in a daze, Jolie grabbed her bag, left the car, and led the way into the barn.

"What in the world are they doing?" Alvin whispered in her ear. The horses were rubbing and touching each other's body.

Jolie pulled a small black sketchpad from her bag and busily outlined the two horses. She looked up before whispering back, "Teasing. This is just the tail end of the process. The mare's been teased all week, but not by this horse. He's new at this, so a more experience stud has been getting her ready."

"Oh, he's a virgin? You wouldn't have to worry about that with me."

The whispered comments made her feel flushed. Her boss looked over his shoulder and smiled. Jolie and Alvin were leaning against the back wall, and her boss was up closer to the action, so she doubted that he'd heard Alvin, but the fact that he'd looked at that moment added to the heat coursing through her body. Jolie cleared her throat and continued speaking as if he hadn't made the previous remark. "It actually takes a pretty talented horse to be a good teaser. He has to be gentle and manageable, but still aggressive enough to make the mare receptive."

"Ohh. It sounds a lot like flirting to me, or maybe foreplay. What do you think?" He looked at her sideways. Jolie was struggling not to appear embarrassed and drawing furiously. He glanced down. "Hey, you're pretty good."

"Thanks. I like sketching. It's a hobby." Jolie shifted her feet and looked at the horses again.

He let her off the hook and turned to the animals. "Why is he chewing her neck?"

"Nipping, not chewing. If he was actually hurting her, the handlers would stop him." They watched as the mare nipped back, and the two rubbed their necks together.

"Oh, I see," Alvin said. Jolie's long hair was in a ponytail, and he glanced longingly at her neck. She caught him and gave him a shy smile. They both turned back to the animals. After a time, he said, "Why does he keep sniffing her...well, you know, her..."

"Private part?" She enjoyed the fact that now he was the one feeling awkward. Jolie stopped drawing and put the pad back in her bag. She wouldn't be sketching this.

"Yeah, and why does he do that thing with his lips when he's, you know, back there?"

Jolie lifted her hand to stifle a chuckle before answering, "The curled, fluttering lip thing means that he likes what he's smelling because she's ready for action." Jolie almost said, "See how he's ready." Embarrassment stopped her from mentioning the quickly emerging penis.

She felt Alvin looking at her and knew he was aware of the horse's aroused state. Jolie maintained a stone face, as if she saw this sort of thing everyday. She was beginning to wonder if her impulsive action to invite him had been a mistake. Animal breeding was nothing new to her after working on a farm for five summers straight and now working for the veterinarian. She didn't think of animal mating as making love; it was just an instinctive process to produce babies. Animals didn't get hot for each other like people. Their cycle came around and they bred. But watching the horse with its huge member about to mount the mare while a gorgeous hunk was standing beside her made her think about what it would be like to be naked with Alvin. How would he kiss? Oh not that little peck in the car, but a real, open-mouth kiss! How would his chest feel pressed up against hers? Her thoughts caused the tingle she'd experienced in the lunchroom to return. She was hot. She shifted her feet and lifted the collar of her T-shirt to catch some of the air flowing through the barn.

Alvin looked at her and smiled. Jolie began chattering in a low voice to cover her discomfort. "This mare is experienced, but as I said earlier, the stallion isn't. So don't be surprised if he tries to mount her from the side. An inexperienced mare would kick or strike at him. However, Molly is gentle. She won't beat him up if he makes a mistake." Alvin nodded.

The stallion didn't go for a side mount, but once he did assume the position behind the mare, he slipped off her back. The mare snickered a bit, but she didn't seem to be upset. After a few more sniffs, the young stallion tried again, and was able to finish to everyone's satisfaction. Two farm hands began washing the animals' genitals.

Jolie whispered, "Stay here. I'll be right back." She assisted the veterinarian in a thorough examination of both horses. They'd survived the process with very minor nicks and bruises.

When she came back to him, he said, " That was neat." She gazed at him quizzically, and then reached into her bag. She ripped a picture from the pad. "Would you like to have this?" she asked in a quiet voice.

Alvin looked at the picture featuring the horses nuzzling each other's neck. "It'd mean a lot to me. Thanks, Jolie."

Jolie released a large smile and began leading him out the barn. As they walked, Alvin said, "I like watching you work." He shrugged his shoulders. "It's not about sex or anything. It's just all right that you do stuff that most kids aren't doing." He smiled at her over the roof of the bug. "It's cool."

It was a real compliment, and she felt it deep within the essence of her being.

ξξξ

Jolie choked on the memory and coughed herself back to the present. Robyn lightly tapped her back. "You okay?"

"Yes, thanks, I'm fine now." No one was on the court, so Jolie asked, "Is the game over?"

Robyn gave her a slight smile, and tilted her head.

"Those were some thoughts you were having. You were in another world, Jolie. The third quarter just ended and the fourth is about to start. There's a full quarter left, and Ty is tearing them up."

Jolie laughed. "Okay, I'm paying attention now." True to her word, she refused to let the past take her again. She focused on her brother and was soon swept up in the vibes. The air pulsated with expectation. Everyone wondered what the kid would do next. No one leaned back, or slouched inattentively in their seat. They sat forward, waiting, anticipating that Tyrese would do something special. It didn't take long for the ball to find itself in Tyrese's capable hands. He didn't disappoint when he delivered a no look dart that bounced between the defender's spread legs. His teammate scored an easy two. The crowd reacted as one, reeling back and forth as shouts of, "Did you see that? Oh, man, that was sweet," rippled among them.

Big Mac's endless chatter competed with what was happening on the court. "Ya know what it is, Al? I've figured it out. The extraordinary is ordinary to Ty. What we think is hard is kindergarten stuff to 'im."

Nodding, Alvin acknowledged Big Mac's point. Tyrese moved at a pace far beyond his peers. He was like a Concorde amongst crop dusters, an eagle amongst pigeons, a phenomenon amongst the mediocre. Tyrese had to slow his game down so others could catch his passes. If his teammates weren't on constant alert when he had the ball, they'd feel the pain of one of his lightening bolt passes

25

drilling them in the chest.

The end of the game was fast approaching. With ten seconds left, Rainier Beach was up by fifteen points. Tyrese stood dribbling the ball in between the half court line and the three-point line. When the clock was down to three seconds, he let loose with a jumper that needed air mail postage. No one was surprised when the beautiful arc ended with a loud swish through the net.

Big Mac reeled around on the bench, bumping Alvin solidly with his girth. Fist to his mouth, he blew air through a small hole, creating a hissing sound. "Wow, dog. Did ya see that there? This cat is too funky! He's got skills!"

Alvin nodded his head. He half listened to Big Mac while he watched Rainier Beach celebrate and waited for Jolie to come down the stairs. Both coaches walked by and nodded or said hello, acknowledging that a major recruiter was there. Alvin responded in kind, knowing that he'd probably be calling only the one from Rainier Beach. As the rest of his teammates headed for the locker room, Tyrese made a beeline toward Alvin, who reared back and felt the wind as the kid zoomed past him. Tyrese and Big Mac shouted greetings as he flew by. "Yo, dog," Mac was tapping his shoulder. "That's his girl up there with his sister." Alvin turned and saw Tyrese hugging a pretty young girl. "She's in a family way, if ya know what I mean?"

He heard the girl say, "Yuck, Ty. Go take a shower. You're getting me wet." However, she seemed to be grasping him just as tightly as he held her.

Jolie watched, chuckling, and Alvin was able to observe her unnoticed. Studying her, Alvin felt compelled to speak with Jolie, even though he didn't have the slightest clue what he would say.

Alvin turned back around when he heard Tyrese tell Robyn, "Wait for me, baby. I'll take you home." Then he ran down the stairs, taking two at a time, and disappeared into the locker room. Alvin stood and turned to go up the steps.

Big Mac's voice stopped him. "Yeah, dog, that's right. Ya better go take care of that situation if you want this kid."

The words irritated him. "Look, Mac, let's get one thing straight right now. I would never try to get with her just to get to the boy. That's underhanded and unethical, not the way we run things at WAM."

Alvin's harsh tone was completely lost on the big man. It just bounced off his hefty shoulders. "Whatever **ya** say, player. But why don't you mosey on up there?"

He did just that after one last glare at Mac.

"Yo, why you pissed at me, dog? I'm just givin' you good 'vice."

Alvin didn't answer as he made his way. Jolie seemed unapproachable as she sat next to the girl, her face tight from her chin to her forehead. He swore he saw her nostrils flare slightly, and he thought her purse would scream if her fingers didn't ease up. As he neared, he heard the girl say, "I better say bye to my friends before Ty's ready to go." She leaned over and pecked Jolie's cheek. Then she sat back and looked at her strangely. "Are you mad about something?"

Jolie tore her eyes away from Alvin and looked at Robyn. "Oh, no, honey. I was just thinking about work."

"From the look on your face, it must have been a bad day. Oh yeah, my mom wants you to call her. She told me twice to give you that message. See ya." Robyn got up and slowly made her way down the steps. She whispered, "Excuse me," when Alvin moved in between the bleachers to let her pass.

He reached her far too quickly by Jolie's clock. Without speaking, he settled his 6'2" frame down beside her. She moved a little to her left to get away from him. What does he want? thundered through her mind. Why don't I just leave? But she didn't move. Some leftover link from the past kept her rooted to the spot.

"Go away." Her voice was clipped and controlled.

"No, we need to talk." He settled more firmly onto the bleachers.

"What makes you think so? Whatever we had to say to each other was said many years ago, and you said it quite clearly and succinctly."

He felt a pang in his heart and didn't respond. As she let him know exactly how she felt about the past, her words cut him deeply. At the time when he ended their relationship so many years ago, she hadn't said a thing, but instead had listened with bowed head as he went through the litany of reasons why they couldn't be together. With her head still down, she'd said, "Are you letting my hand go?" When he'd first asked her to be his girl, she'd grabbed his hand and intertwined their fingers before saying, "Yes, baby, I'll go with you and hold your hand for the rest of my life."

The simply asked question had stunned him, and he didn't respond. She'd lifted her head and looked him in the eyes. Then her hand reached out, palm up, and she'd asked the question again. "Are you letting my hand go, Alvie?"

His hands had stayed in his pockets and he'd sheepishly nodded.

She'd walked to the front door of her house, opened it, and he'd left. He'd seen her twice since then. He'd always known he'd hurt her. Hell, he'd hurt himself, but back then he'd thought nothing was as important as the ball. Inside Alvin winced as he sat beside her on the hard bench. He remembered thinking he'd done the respectable thing in driving back from college to officially end their relationship. He'd been going to school in California, and Jolie had received a scholarship to WAM so she'd stayed in Seattle. He was proud of the fact that he'd never cheated, ignored, or treated her badly while they were together. He could tell that the cold woman sitting beside him didn't give a damn about what he thought back then. But why was she so angry after fifteen years? She'd never struck him as vindictive. He had to remind himself that the Jolie he'd known was a teenager, an adolescent. There had been plenty of time for her to grow into another person.

Jolie's chest moved up and down with a silent sigh, as if

she'd come to terms with something. She filled the silence between them. "I know the only reason you're here is because of Ty."

Initially that was true, but right now he wanted her a hell of a lot more than he wanted to coach the kid. "I thought your brother's name was Randy."

"It is, Tyrese Randal Smith. We stopped calling him Randy years ago about the time that my mother passed."

"I was real sorry to hear about your mom. I didn't get a chance to tell you that at the funeral. She was a great person."

Jolie looked into his eyes and saw sincerity. She remembered seeing him at the back of the church and the burial site five years ago. He'd created quite a stir, an NBA player in their midst. Jolie had ignored his presence and hadn't spoken to him. She wondered then and now why he'd attended.

Again, Jolie interrupted the silence. "Don't worry. I'm not going to poison him against you. Basketball is a commodity, a business. You want to use him." She looked at Alvin. "No, don't interrupt." He closed his mouth. "There's nothing wrong with being used as long as you know it. That's what I tell Ty. See, that was the problem with you and me. I didn't know I was being used."

He had to interrupt this time. "I never used you. I loved you too much for that."

She shifted to meet him face to face. "If that was love, I would hate to see what you do to your enemies. But I don't want to delve into that mess."

No, you just want to hit me with pot shots, Alvin thought.

She continued, "As I was saying, being used isn't bad as long as you understand and get what you're entitled too. My brother is good. I'm not into sports, but even I can tell he's exceptional." Alvin nodded. "He's entitled to a good education that ends in a degree, and a school with enough clout that he has a legitimate shot at the NBA."

"Washington can give Ty both of those things."

"Can it? Aren't you two on the bubble?"

The question showed him that she was at least following the news reports about the program and, indirectly, him. "The media always makes it seem worse than it is."

"So, it's not true that you and your buddy, Rock, will be out if you don't have a winning season?"

He didn't want to get into the politics of the University in a high school gym that was semi-full with people. "Can I take you to dinner later in the week? We can discuss all of this among other things."

She looked at him long and hard before saying, "Me? What about Ty?"

"I would love to meet with Ty, but the National College Athletic Association or NCAA wouldn't like it. I can't have personal contact with him until April. Technically, I'm not supposed to contact you about him, but we have other things we can discuss."

"I don't want to discuss anything but Ty with you, so

we'll wait four months."

Jolie stood, and as Alvin rose, he automatically put a hand to her bare elbow to help her down the stairs. A jolt passed through them, reminiscent of a carpet shock. Alvin held firm while Jolie pulled away. With a deep breath to settle her nerves, she said, "Thanks, but I don't need your help." She rushed down the bleachers faster than her brother had.

Chapter 2

Jolie was putting her key in the lock when she heard a creak coming from next door. She turned to the left and saw a little gray head peeking around the door.

A hand lifted before Jolie heard, "Hold on a minute, dear, I have something for you."

Jolie finished unlocking the latch, but waited for Ethel Schwartz, her neighbor, to appear. When she saw the sliver of a woman, no more than five feet tall, carrying a heavy platter, she rushed to help her. Ethel's blue gray hair was assembled into an immaculate knot at the back of her small head. Her white skin was lined and wrinkled, and it surrounded eyes that still sparkled with the joy of life. She carried a plate of cookies almost as wide as she, precariously balanced on one arm. The other hand grasped a cane. Jolie relieved her of the heavy dish.

"Oh, thank you, dear. I know it's a big day for Ty, so I thought he might like some oatmeal raisin cookies. I know they're his favorite."

"That's really nice of you, Ethel." The older lady followed her into the kitchen where Jolie set the plate down. "Ty did great. He had a wonderful game."

"Good. Good." Ethel sat at the small dinette table,

obviously intending to stay for a while. "The boy talks to me, you know?"

Jolie nodded. She knew that Ty did odd jobs for Ethel like grocery shopping, walking her dog, and taking the trash out. She assumed that involved some conversation.

"No, he really talks to me," Ethel said, tapping her cane for emphasis.

Jolie took a seat across from Ethel, sensing that what she was about to say was going to be important, if not disturbing.

"He told me all about that bad stuff in California, and then I showed him this." With a gnarled hand, Ethel pulled up her sleeve. Jolie saw greenish, faded marks on the furrowed skin. Ethel pulled on her arm, smoothing it out a tad, and Jolie could make out numbers. It looked like 534. "Auschwitz, '43 to '44, I was there. Only one of my family to survive. Told the boy, I know pain and I had an idea of what he feels like. Then he broke down in my arms, cried like a baby, he did."

Jolie didn't know what to say. Ethel covered up the mark. "Like I said, we talk. You can't tell now, but I was a ballerina. Principal dancer for companies here and aboard until I was almost forty. Oy vey, in the ballet world, that's ancient, I tell you." Her laugh came out more as a cackle that was full of age and wisdom. "I did this despite what those animals in that camp did to me. I told your brother so. I said, don't let what those gangsters did interfere with your God-given talent. I told him to play basketball and to play it well!" Again, the cane banged the floor.

Jolie was taken aback, surprised that Ethel was a death camp survivor, and even more surprised that Tyrese had confided in their elderly neighbor. She blinked several times and said, "When did this conversation happen?"

Ethel placed her cane in her lap and rubbed it softly as she looked up in the air. "Oh, about a month ago. We've talked several times since, about that, and the fact that he's going to be a poppa soon."

Not knowing what to say or do, and feeling like a tremendous failure, Jolie said, "Gee, where are my manners? Would you like a cup of coffee or tea?" Jolie stood up and walked to the stove, reaching for the teakettle.

"No, dear. Me, I don't want anything. Sit!" She tapped her cane. "I'm not done having my say!"

"Yes, ma'am." Jolie sat down.

Ethel grabbed her hand and ran a blue-veined thumb along the back of it. "I know you worked hard for the boy. Such a pity your mom died so young and your brother was involved in a shooting, but these things happen. Now, look at me." Jolie looked into the bright brown eyes centered in the weathered face. "You've done a remarkable job, and you remind me of me, except I would of had a man by my side. Outlived five husbands in my time, I did, but that's another story. Tyrese is gonna be fine. He told me about counseling and that was a good thing. I should think the worst is behind the boy now."

Jolie squeezed the old widow's hand and said, "Thank

you."

Jolie walked Ethel to her house and as she was coming back, she murmured, "I guess it does take a village to raise a child." The old African proverb helped ease her guilt that she alone wasn't enough for her brother. Both sets of their grandparents were deceased, and maybe Tyrese just needed another ear to share things with.

When she stepped into the house, the phone rang. She was surprised to hear her father's voice. Interacting with his children had never been high on her dad's list of priorities.

"Hi, Jolie. Ty called yesterday and said he had his first game today. How'd it go?"

"It went great. He had a huge game."

"Good. How are you? Do you need extra money for anything?"

"I'm doing fine, Dad, and no, I don't need anything."

"Okay, that's good. I was cleaning out the storage shed and I found a box of your mother's things. I thought you might like to have them, so I shipped them to you. You should get them in a few days."

Jolie was disgusted. Her father didn't have the guts to deal with what was in the box. She'd had to arrange the funeral and handle all of her mother's personal effects. She tried not to be resentful about this latest responsibility.

"All right, tell Ty I said congratulations."

She'd hung up the phone before she realized that the man hadn't even asked to talk to her brother. Jolie intentionally remembered her mother's explanation of her father to halt the building frustration. "Jackson Smith thinks his obligations end once he gets home from work. He believes that running the family is my job." Twenty-six-year-old Jolie hadn't been satisfied with the answer. Twelve-year-old Tyrese also grumbled that he was going to do more with his kids. Jolie's mother made a noise somewhere between a grunt and a snort, a clear sign of anger. Both of her children fell silent as she wrapped a hand on the shoulder of each and made eye contact. "I'm not saying it's right or wrong, but look at it from his perspective. He grew up in the South in the late thirties. He didn't have the luxury of a father because your grandfather was lynched when your daddy was just a boy. Know why he was hanged?"

They both shook their heads.

"Some white man didn't like it that your granddaddy had red hair like him. Story goes that somebody teased the man and said that he and your granddaddy must be related. The crazy man got so angry, he led the mob and hung your grandfather that night.

"Feeling guilty because your grandmother had so many mouths to feed, your daddy left home at thirteen. He thinks he's a great success because he can work and provide for his family. So don't just judge him, Jolie and Randy. Just continue the cycle and do more for your children when you're blessed with them."

Jolie tried to follow her mother's advice, but her father's non-involvement was hard to take. That's why she knew she had to go get Tyrese when the incident happened about a year after her mother's death. Her father didn't have the temperament to deal with it.

Shaking off the irritation and the past, Jolie headed to the bathroom in her room to shower and get ready for bed. Finishing that task, Jolie was all set to sink in between the sheets, but first she had to face the mirror. She stood there not out of vanity, but to perform her monthly ritual. Both arms raised, she studied her chest from all angles to see if there were any oddities. Next, she put her arms down and turned this way and that as she observed the shape, size, and symmetry of the globes. Jolie thought of her mother as she went through the motions. Leena Smith had died of breast cancer, and Jolie's monthly ritual was a tribute to her. The phone rang. Jolie ran and grabbed the cordless from the kitchen before returning to the mirror.

"Hey, lady. What are you doing?" Robyn's mother Joan asked.

Jolie looked at her naked chest. "I'm spending quality time inspecting myself in the mirror."

"Oh, you're doing that monthly fondling thing, huh? See, that's one of the benefits of having a husband. He can do that for you."

"Fondle or the examination?" Jolie held the phone with her ear and bent forward. There were no bumps, lumps, or scaly skin.

"Is there a difference?" the chuckling voice asked.

Jolie was laughing too hard to continue the exam. Turning away from the mirror, she said, "Girl, you're so crazy. I guess there's only a difference if you find something, like a lump. It kind of changes the whole mood, you know?" Jolie didn't wait for an answer. "Is my brother still over there?"

"Yeah. He and Robyn are doing their homework. He ate enough to food to feed the Klump family. I guess having a great game makes you hungry. Robyn said he was terrific."

"He was. I thought he'd be a little freaked out because this is his first organized game since the shooting, but it didn't seem to affect him at all."

Joan worked in a woman's shelter where she constantly dealt with traumatized kids. Speaking from experience, she remarked, "It is truly remarkable how resilient children can be."

"Yes." After reflecting a moment, Jolie said, "But they're not really kids any more, are they? Robyn's in her first year of college, Ty's going to graduate, and they're about to be parents."

"Well, even if they have grown-up responsibilities, I tend to think of them as kids."

Jolie sat on her bed. "I worry about them." Even though she said "them," she meant Ty. The parallels between him and Alvin were uncanny, as if God were playing a cruel joke on her. She would hate for Robyn to feel the heartbreak she once felt. She'd kill Ty herself if he left her.

"Shoot, I'm not worried. It's better to be pregnant than to have an incurable disease. Things could always be worse.

Robyn's always been book smart. With our help, she'll graduate with a degree in something, and if things should go sour
between her and Ty, she can always support herself. It's not
the end of the world."

"You trying to convince me or your husband?"

Joan laughed. "My husband, girl. He's still having a
hard time with this. Robyn's his only child and he's not used
to the idea of her dating, much less being in a family way."

"Yeah, some days I'm okay with it and others...well,
let's just say I'm like your husband."

"Robyn tells me you're kinda rough on Ty at times. You
know, it takes two to tango."

Jolie knew this. Still there were times she wanted to
scream at Robyn, "How could you be so stupid?" But she
realized she really wanted to scream the words at herself.

"You're right, Joan." Both women were quiet for a
moment, until Jolie said, "You know, it's kind of funny that
you're defending Ty to me. In fact, it's kind of weird that
we're friends at all."

"Hey, it's too hard to find good people in this world.
You have to hang on when you do." There was a clicking
noise on the phone. "Oh shoot, that's my other line. Can
you hold a minute?"

Jolie went back to her exam while she waited for Joan.
She lay on the bed and trapped the phone to her ear with a
raised shoulder. With the other hand, she moved her fingertips in small circular motions, feeling for bumps. As her fingers worked, she reflected on her strange friendship with

Joan. Jolie had a circle of friends that she did things with, but none were as close as Joan. She'd never suspected that the mother of her brother's pregnant girlfriend would turn out to be her confidant. It was too weird to be predictable. But that's exactly what had happened a year ago when the two were first introduced. Tyrese and Robyn were so enthralled with each other, they kept insisting that the families meet. Jolie went over to Robyn's house for dinner and found that she immediately clicked with Joan. Their quick but deep friendship had been tested by Robyn's pregnancy and had survived.

However, Jolie wasn't as sure about Robert, Joan's husband. Around her, he was quiet, not exactly sullen, just extremely reserved. At first, he would smile when he saw Jolie and nod his head in greeting; however, since the pregnancy, he simply nodded. He didn't quite frown, yet he didn't smile either. Joan always said, "Oh, that's just Rob. He thinks words are like hundred-year-old Scotch; they should be indulged in sparingly. But watch out, every once in a while, he becomes a motor mouth." Jolie found that hard to believe.

Joan returned to the line. "Hey, girl, sorry about that. So, who was the hunk that sat by you at the end of the game?"

Jolie sat up in her bed and leaned back on the headboard. "Robyn's been talking, huh?"

"Yes, her exact words were, 'handsome, but old.'"

Jolie laughed. "He's a guy I went to high school with.

He's now a coach at WAM, and he's trying to recruit Ty."

"Is that all? Robyn also said you didn't seem too excited to see him."

Jeez, am I an open book or what? "I don't want to get into it. Let's just say our past isn't pleasant."

"Okay, girl, I won't press you. You keep your secrets. The real reason I'm calling is to remind you about Rob's birthday party at the Royal Esquire."

"That's not coming up any time soon, is it?"

"No, it's weeks away. But I know you, girl. Put it on your calendar now, so you won't forget, or schedule something else."

Jolie didn't really want to go to the Seattle icon. She thought Robert could care less if she didn't make it. Nonetheless, she knew that it mattered to her friend. "I'll put it down as soon as we hang up."

"Okay, then I'll let you go now, so you won't forget. Six weeks, Saturday night, all right?"

"Bye, Joan. I'll talk to you later. Send my brother home soon."

§§§

Later that night, Alvin sat in a small club chair watching the people around him. The Jazz Spot was packed. He found himself wondering about all the well-dressed patrons. Were they in committed relationships? Did they have a home where a loving family waited? His longest relationship had been with Jolie; a year and a half over fifteen years ago. He'd had a string of women since then. He'd even managed to live with a couple, but none of those liaisons amounted to much. He knew what the real thing was like because he'd had it with Jolie, and he wouldn't settle for less.

Glancing around the room, Alvin was amazed at the atmosphere. He'd been there once during the daytime to pick up Sophia after a rehearsal and concluded that the place was a dump. Pipes and vents stuck out under the glare of house lights. Uneven walls and crooked cement floors made it clear that absolute necessity was the only requirement for repairs. The Jazz Spot looked like what it was—a rundown warehouse that someone had tried to rig up to look like something better.

The shocking thing was that when the lights were turned down low and the music began to play, the dump metamorphosed into the hot spot, the place to be. That's when Sophia would come out and sing over the band's sweet, syncopated melodies. She sang songs that spoke to a person's heart. Songs about life, heartbreak, loss, and the never-ending search for a good man.

The emcee at the microphone drew Alvin's attention. "Ladies and gentlemen, it's my pleasure to introduce Ready Made, featuring Sophia Mack!"

All eyes were on Sophia as she came out wearing a form-fitting red dress that hit her mid-thigh. The outfit pushed her breasts up into teasing mounds that jiggled slightly with each movement. Sophia wore her long hair straight with just a little curl at the end, and as she approached the mike, the fingers of her right hand smoothed the long tresses behind an ear. "Good evening, ladies and gents," she cooed into the mike. "Are you ready for some wonderful music?"

The audience responded with, "Uh hum, yeah, and that's right, sister!"

"Good, because we're about to give you some..." Sophia leaned away smiling slightly, and then she tilted back and said, "Music that is."

Everything about Sophia oozed sensuality. From her word choice to the way she sang. Alvin sipped his mineral water and enjoyed the show. The cool drink and the music soothed him after the scene with Jolie.

Forty-five minutes later, the set ended. Sophia gracefully descended the steps to the side of the stage and immediately began working the room. Alvin watched as she walked around tables, whispering a word here, touching a shoulder there. A middle-aged man grabbed her hand, and she bent to speak with him. Her long hair slipped from behind her ear and flowed artfully around her cheek. The man grabbed a few strands and kissed them. Then he said something that made Sophia chuckle. Her daring neckline gaped, treating the man and the others seated at the table to a view of what lay inside. From experience, Alvin knew they saw a lacey black bra worn as a small token to convention.

He felt no hint of jealousy or possessiveness. He supposed that part of his attitude came from how they'd met last June at the downtown Nordstrom. Alvin was there searching for essentials: socks and underwear. Sophia was there, buying the same for her male friend, and they met when they each grabbed for the same pair of boxers. Looking at each other over a package of Hanes, they acknowledged the attraction that sparked between them. The encounter should have ended there as they left Nordstrom, each with bags of underwear. Instead, they spent the day and night together. Alvin's status as an ex-NBA player and now a coach seemed to be a turn-on for her; and Sophia's flirtatiousness, beauty, and insatiability had definitely excited him.

However, sometimes Alvin wondered what he was doing. As he watched Sophia flirt and laugh as she walked around the room, he wondered why he felt impatient rather than irritated. When Sophia reached his table, she trailed her fingernails down the side of his face and across his shoulder. From behind him, she leaned over and whispered in his ear, "Follow me, lover. I have a game plan I want to discuss with you." She walked off to a closed door on Alvin's right. With her hand on the handle, she looked back to see if he was complying. He rose slowly and went through the door with her. She pulled him into a small dressing room that was decorated only with a mirror, vanity, clothes rack, and a stool.

"Welcome to my house, Vin," she said. "I have home court advantage, and I intend to exercise it to the fullest."

Alvin laughed. "What if I hit you with a devastating full court press?" He trapped her between his hips and the vanity.

Sophia ground against him. "I just might have to call foul and complain to the coach. See if I can get you benched."

"But I'm the coach."

Sophia didn't respond. She grabbed his face and gave him a hot, quick kiss. "Where have you been?"

"I went to a high school game to see a kid I want to recruit. It turns out that I went to school with his sister, Jolie."

"Oh yeah? Interesting name. I bet that'll make it easier to get to the kid!"

He was about to contradict her when she said, "We have to hurry." She turned to look back at the alarm clock that sat on the vanity amongst bottles of unknown things that Alvin was sure were vital to her beauty. "This pressure-packed game has to end in five minutes. I'm due on stage in seven." Reaching into a vanity drawer, she pulled out a condom and handed it to him. While he prepared himself, she hiked up her dress and began kissing him again. Somehow, it didn't surprise him when she just moved her thong to the side, instead of taking it off.

Alvin went with the flow, literally. Sex between sets was a first for him, but she seemed very determined. He felt the pressure gathering quickly. Makeup was pushed to the side to make room for Sophia's bottom as he pumped himself into her. She sang encouragement into his ear. The woman had multiple uses for her extraordinary voice. A high-pitched yelp told Alvin that Sophia had reached the high score. He moaned when his explosion quickly followed, the high draining from his body much too rapidly. He wasn't satisfied. The image of another woman still plagued him. He felt an odd emptiness, hollowness.

He'd barely stepped back before Sophia was pushing down her dress and repairing her make-up. "Oh, that was great, lover," she said into the mirror. "Goodness, what a terrific set. I got so worked up." She smiled at him over her shoulder. "Thank goodness you were here for a quick game of one-on-one. There's nothing like that to relieve things when my adrenaline's going wacko." She winked at him and then turned back to the mirror and her lipstick. Done, she was about to whiz out the door when she asked, "You staying for the next set?"

He shrugged his shoulders.

"You coming by tonight?"

"Probably not. I have an early practice tomorrow?"

"Oh, well." She didn't seem too disappointed. Neither was Alvin. He understood Sophia because one day she'd got talkative as she gargled her throat after a particularly long set. In between retching sounds, she'd explained her philosophy to him.

"I like you, Vin," she'd said. "You understand that I don't want what my mother had, a noose around her neck. That poor woman cooked, cleaned, and ironed my daddy's funky clothes, and for what? The privilege to get old and wrinkled up with his crusty butt! No, I could identify with my old man's mistress much better. She got the presents and some of his money, and all she had to do was lie down for a moment or two. That woman wasn't a maid to anybody. I compared how those women lived, Vin, and I immediately decided I wasn't going to be anything like my mother."

Listening to her, Alvin couldn't help but wonder what kind of nut would let his child know about the other woman. He didn't care enough to ask Sophia.

Shaking his head at the memory, Alvin took a moment adjusting his clothing and looked at himself in the mirror. He told the reflection, "This isn't cutting it, buddy. This isn't what you want." Jolie's face flashed before him.

As he stepped away from the mirror, his father's words came to him. He'd been in the eighth grade, and he'd just finished his best game ever. His father and mother had done a rare thing when they left work early to see him play ball. He'd played his heart out, but his team still lost. As they walked out the gym, his father had put his arm over Alvin's shoulders. "Son, there's one thing I want you to remember. It's not always whether you win or lose, it's how you went for it. Can you look at yourself in the mirror and say you gave it your all. If you can answer yes, then you should always be a winner in your own eyes. So hold your head up, boy. I'm pleased with how you played tonight. I'm very pleased with you, son." He hadn't appreciated the words then, but the message had sunk in. It had become part of his creed. Looking at himself in the mirror, he knew he had to do the same with Jolie. If she shot him down, well hell, at least he could move on without wondering what if.

Alvin didn't stay for Sophia's second set.

Chapter 3

The gym was cold the next morning. Alvin knew he was the first to arrive when he had to use his key to gain access to the foyer and then the gym. It was raining outside and his tennis shoes squished loudly as he made his way across the wooden floor. Once the vestibule door closed, the gym was smothered in darkness. "Where the hell is Crump?" he muttered to himself as he made his way to the light panel and flipped the switches by feel. The student manager was supposed to get there a half hour before practice to make sure everything was set up. The lights crackled and popped as the huge fluorescent beams struggled to come to life. Alvin jumped in place and rubbed his arms as Rock Softli strolled into the gym. He was dressed almost like Alvin: black and gold sweats with the WAM panther emblem. Alvin's mascot was on his shirt and Rock's was on his pant leg.

"Hey, Rockhead. How's it going, cuz?"

Rock squinted through the twilight at him. "All right, doggie dog."

Soon after the two met in college, they had discarded formal names. Rock became cuz, and Alvin became dog.

Rock walked over to Alvin. He was about 5'10", which

was short in the basketball world, and every movement Rock made with his stocky frame seemed to have a specific purpose. His name was Ruben until the sitcom Rock aired in 1991. Ruben and the actor Charles Dutton, who played the garbage collector, had the same bald head and stout body. Also, when Rock got really happy or mad, he'd kick his leg out and cross his arms just like the actor. Rock's last name was appropriate as well: Softli. He had a smooth, consistent jumper and it helped to get him a scholarship at UCLA, despite his size.

"You get to the heat yet? It's freezing in here."

"No, cuz," Alvin answered. "Where's Crump?"

"I gave him the day off to study for a big test. I knew you'd get here early enough to set the gym up, dog."

"Uh huh, that's why you came in five minutes behind me."

Rock laughed and then said, "I'll get the heat on my way to the office. Why don't you get the balls." Rock went to the opposite wall where the heat control was mounted. Alvin turned to a side door to get the balls. He wheeled out a rack, then went to get another. By the time he rolled the second rack out, the main lights were just about awake.

As Alvin held a ball between his long, thin fingers, he glanced around the gym. Then it hit him. He'd known something was different for a while now, but he couldn't quite describe it. Now he had the words. "The vibe is gone," he whispered. The old excitement or crackle that used to light up his bones when he held a ball or walked into a gym wasn't there. Alvin didn't know when it had left; he just knew he didn't feel it.

He rolled the orange sphere around and reflected on what he'd gained and given up because of the game. As a kid, basketball had become his life when his first coach told him, "You've got some skills, Al. Keep up the hard work and I bet you'll make the pros." He'd remembered those words every time he wanted to slack off. He didn't have a hoop at home, but he did have a driveway. He spent hours practicing his ball-handling skills on that short stretch of concrete. When it rained, he harassed his parents until one of them moved the car out of the garage, and he'd practice in there. He was so into it that his parents had used it as a form of punishment. If he didn't do his chores or, heaven forbid, his grades slipped, they'd take the ball away. It had worked better than any lecture or spanking.

Alvin took a couple of dribbles and then rolled the ball around in his hands. Yes, he'd loved the sport and he always would even if he didn't tingle at the mere thought anymore. It took a lot of hard work to achieve what he'd done. He wasn't a natural like Tyrese. The good thing was he'd always know that. He was about thirteen when he complained to his father about his lack of height and size. "Dad, you're only six foot, and Mom's short. Your height works against chances."

Although Alvin senior worked hard, drank hard, he wasn't a sloppy or mean drunk. He got home from his job at the plant by five, and he'd have his first drink shortly thereafter.

By eight, he'd be in his easy chair in front of the television and out for the rest of the evening. Somewhere between eleven and one, Alvin or his mother would get him in bed. The weekends worked much the same way. "A functional alcoholic" his mother called him. The experience made Alvin avoid any drink stronger than a pop. But despite his weaknesses, Alvin's father was the wisest man Alvin had ever met. You just had to talk to him before the bottle and the chair claimed him.

Now Alvin remembered his father's answer, to his complaint about size. "Boy, stop whining. Stop focusing on what you don't have because you can't control that. Instead, concentrate on what the good Lord did give you: quickness, speed, and a good mind. Make those as sharp as you can. If you learn that simple thing, Alvin, you'll be a step ahead of others."

He'd never forgot his father's advice. Alvin's height topped out at 6'2", which was far from giant status by NBA standards. When the Boston Celtics drafted him, his college coach paid him the highest compliment he'd ever bestowed on a player. The man told him he was the best-conditioned athlete he'd ever had the pleasure to coach, and the one with the most heart. Music to Alvin's ears. He'd relayed the praise to his dad, and they'd shared a congratulatory drink together. A beer for his dad and a diet cola for Alvin.

Alvin smiled at the memory, dribbled over to the three-point line and took a shot. The ball hit the backboard and dropped through the net. Once again, he grabbed the ball and stared at it. With the rewards had also come sacrifice. Jolie was a prime example. He'd been drawn to her because of her beauty, but what had captured him were her other attributes. As his father would say, "She had a noodle." She was smart, witty, fun, and full of surprises.

She was also a distraction at a time when he could ill afford it. He remembered the words of his UCLA coach. The man had pulled him aside after practice and stared into his eyes. "You could have what it takes, Alvin, but are you willing to work and sacrifice? That means no drinking or partying to excess, and no letting women get in your way. You have to stay the course if you want to flourish here and beyond." Alvin remembered how scared he'd been. He was the new kid who'd been highly recruited and now it was time to prove himself. It wasn't like high school where he stood out. This was college at UCLA where everyone was a superstar.

Giving Jolie up had been the hardest thing he'd done in his life; however, fear had been a strong motivator. He hadn't believed in his ability to be that passionate about two things at the same time. Even though he'd changed his mind quickly and tried to get her back, it had been too late.

Looking at the ball in his hands, he heaved it against the wall, caught it when it bounced back to him, and then heaved it again. In a matter of minutes, he was no longer cold, and a little less frustrated.

Alvin stood at half court, breathing heavily, when the other coaches began to arrive along with the players. He shouted greetings and passed out balls. Rock came and joined him and the two other coaches at half court.

"Dog, what did you do? Run a few laps to warm up? You're already sweating."

"Gotta stay in shape, cuz," was Alvin's only reply.

"Oh, yeah? Just don't blow that knee out again."

Rock then turned to the players and practice began. Two and a half hours later, the exhausted players slowly left the gym, Alvin said to Rock, "I saw No Neck's kid last night." They each pushed a rack full of balls back into the closet.

"So, what's the verdict? Is this kid the second coming of Jordan, or is Torso Man's mind turning green from all that fake jewelry he wears?"

Alvin chuckled. They both found it hard to believe that there could be a senior as good as Mac had described and they'd be unaware of him. Scouts scoured local areas for talent like prospectors sifting for gold. It was inconceivable that someone had escaped their notice.

Alvin said, "Cuz, I looked real close and I couldn't find anything between his head and shoulders, but I think Big Mac's jewelry is real, and so is Tyrese. Both are certifiable. Shoot, I'd draw up the papers and stamp them myself. This kid has a clean jumper that hits the net like Charmin. His cuts to the basket are so sharp it makes my knees hurt just thinking about it, and the poor defenders are left confused while this kid is sinking it for two."

"Yeah?"

"Yeah!" Alvin's head nodded.

"Okay, do your thing, Mr. Top Recruiter in the Northwest."

"Cuz, I've only brought in one recruiting class."

"Yeah, but you brought in four guys off the top ten list for our region. One of them was off the national list, dog. You're a head coach's dream, and now you're helping me mold these young bucks so we can get to the playoffs this year."

"Okay, since you put it that way, I guess I am pretty great. But there's a catch."

Rock stopped walking towards his office and turned back to look at him. Before either could speak, the other two coaches said goodbye to both of them and left the gym.

"He's Jolie's brother." Alvin knew no other words were necessary. He and Rock had known each other since college and his friend was fully aware of the situation.

Rock shook his head. "I guess I don't need to ask if you're talking about the Jolie, the woman who's kept you single all these years?" Without giving Alvin a chance to rebut the 'single' comment, he continued, "My grandma always used to say that truth is stranger than fiction. Well, she ain't never lied!" He shook his head again. "So, is she doing some blocking?"

Alvin shrugged and leaned against the gym wall. "I'm not sure yet. She hit me with tons of attitude and anger, then she said she wants to do what's right for her brother."

"Humph, if this kid's as good as you say, the right thing

for him is to be in our program."

Alvin agreed. In Rock's tenure, ninety percent of the players had graduated with degrees. "I'm working on it. She not only has a problem with me, she's been following our wonderful press coverage."

Rock whispered an oath and then said, "Okay, we knew we'd have to deal with that, so be as honest as you can without spreading our dirty political laundry."

"I hear you, cuz, but this is Jolie. I need to be completely upfront. She and I have too much history."

"Are you still trying to get with this girl?" Rock crossed his arms, leaned towards Alvin, and looked into his eyes.

Alvin avoided the stare by pushing away from the wall; then he began walking back and forth. "Shoot, I'd need a jackhammer to get through the fortress she's built around herself. Sister doesn't want a thing to do with me. But that's not the point. Point is, if I'm not upfront and your truth is stranger than fiction stuff happens and it somehow gets back to her, it wouldn't be good. Tyrese's got game, and I don't want his big sis, who happens to be taking care of him, to have a legitimate reason for being pissed at us."

"What's with the living arrangements?

Alvin quickly explained the tragedy that kept Tyrese away from organized basketball until the middle of the season in his senior year.

Rock threw up his hands. "Okay, dog, if this kid's the second coming of Jordan, I'll trust your judgment."

Alvin laughed. "Hey now, I didn't say the boy was

Michael Jordan, cuz. He just may be a Kobe Byrant, or an Allen Iverson."

"Yeah, well, with either a Kobe or an Iverson, we'd dominate the Pac Ten next year. So get on it!"

℮℮℮

Jolie walked through the door of her house feeling pretty good. She was returning from mass at Our Lady Queen of Heaven Catholic Church, where Father Ignacio had been on fire. The Filipino priest had been so animated that Jolie had flashbacked to the Baptist church she'd experimented with during her college days. She hadn't strayed long. The word of God was just as powerful no matter who the messenger; however, Jolie missed the customs associated with Catholicism. She'd been born and raised Catholic and making the sign of the cross when someone said, "Let us pray," was second nature to her. She felt comfortable with the kneeling, standing, and automatic crowd responses, which were the same whether you were in a Catholic church in Seattle or Istanbul. Plain and simple, she'd missed her Catholic family. It was a rare Sunday when Jolie didn't spend her hour in the Lord's House. And she had especially enjoyed those sixty minutes today.

The small priest had delivered the homily with waving arms and thought-provoking examples. He'd asked the question, "Do you think the Lord gives you more than you can handle?" Jolie was surprised that Alvin had popped into her mind. She thought Tyrese and Robyn's situation deserved top billing on her worry list. She pushed Alvin to the side and focused on Father Ignacio as he flitted across the altar. In a heavy accent, he told several stories, demonstrating that even in the worst of times, the Lord is present.

Father's right, Jolie realized during communion. When she went back to her pew and knelt to pray, a surge of power and self-confidence passed through her, making her feel blessed enough to handle whatever challenges were destined to be in her path.

Jolie was still feeling empowered when she returned home and hung her coat in the hall closet. She whispered a small prayer. "Lord, I will rely on you and find peace in your strength."

"What'd ya say?" her brother asked as he came from the kitchen with a mouthful of cookie.

"I was saying you should come to church with me sometimes." She responded to her brother's short hug and followed him into the kitchen. "Father Ignacio gave quite a sermon today."

"I would have, but I was pooped. I think the Lord wanted me to sleep."

"Uh huh, and the Lord wanted you to eat Ethel's cookies for breakfast too."

"How'd you guess? You been calling the psychic network again?" Tyrese lifted the plate and offered her a cookie. Jolie took one and went to the refrigerator to get some milk.

"Umm. These are good," she said as she sat at the small table across from Tyrese and placed a glass of milk in front of him. He was dressed in dark brown pants and a loose tan shirt. "Where's your name tag?"

"In my pocket. I don't like to put it on until I get to the hospital. It bugs me when people say, 'Hi Tyrese,' and I'm wondering how they know my name."

Jolie nodded. "How do you like being a dietary aide?"

"I like it, sis. It's pretty easy. I cart the food up to the floors, the nurses deliver the trays to the room, then I go and cart the dirty trays back. Thankfully, someone else washes them. I study while the people eat."

"A lot better than MacDonald's?"

"Oh, yeah. I worked my tail off there. This gig is plush and I get paid more."

Jolie reached across the table and grabbed his hand. "I'm so proud of the way you played. Dad called and I told him so."

Tyrese took a big gulp of milk and answered her through a thin milk mustache. "During warm-ups, I was kinda freaked out. I started thinking about Compton and that gym was so crowded with us." Tyrese pointed to himself with his thumbs. "I felt a little shaky, ya know? But I looked up and there was Robyn, smiling at me." A look of such puppy love covered her brother's face. It didn't go with the milk mustache. Jolie handed him a napkin, but he only rubbed it between his hands.

"No, your lip, Ty."

"Oh," he wiped his lip with his shirtsleeve. It was on the tip of Jolie's tongue to complain, but he was already dabbing at his wet cuff with the napkin. He saw her expression and smiled sheepishly. "Hey, at least my lip's clean. Anyway, I thought about Ethel and what a tough old bird she is."

"Ty! That's not nice!"

"Come on, sis. Ethel knows I love her, but she's survived some rough stuff. Did you know she was in Auschwitz?"

"Not until yesterday when she delivered the cookies."

"How tall is Ethel? About 5'2"?"

"Maybe in high heels."

"Well, I decided if that little lady was tough enough to survive what she did, then I was certainly man enough to play basketball for a team. My stuff was over like that." He snapped his fingers. "Ethel lived in that camp for over a year. Thinking about her made me get beyond the Compton thing and focus on playing."

Tyrese always referred to the tragedy as Compton, or the California thing. He avoided words like gun or shooting.

"And, sis, it was fun!" Her brother's brown eyes sparkled.

"I could tell. You were smiling a mile wide when you waved to me at halftime."

"Oh, sis, it's hard to explain. The buzzer goes off, stuff is pumping inside of me, and I don't even think. It's like I don't have to because I know my body will take over and make the right moves, deliver the right passes, block the right shots. I'm just having fun. Letting my body do its thing." Tyrese came back to the table and looked at her. His chest hollowed as he drew in his shoulders in embarrassment. "I know it sounds corny."

"No, Ty. It doesn't sound corny at all. It sounds like you have a gift. Basketball comes to you like loving animals comes to me. I'm just happy that what you're good at is also what you love." Jolie said the words to her brother and she meant them. However, his enthusiasm provoked thoughts of Alvin. No wonder he'd dumped her for basketball. She could never compete with the euphoria her brother described. Could any woman? What would Tyrese do if basketball conflicted with Robyn? Probably the same thing Alvin had done—dump her. She watched her brother shovel the last of the cookies in his mouth. The milk moustache was back. "Ty, what about Robyn?"

She sensed his defensiveness. Jolie understood because she'd been less than kind when she first heard the news. She remembered how he had screamed at her. "Don't you say it, sis! Don't you dare ask me that question!"

Exasperated, she'd found herself shouting back. "What the hell are you talking about?"

Tyrese's young eyes bore into hers. "Don't ask me if it's mine!"

Dammit, she recalled thinking, if only she were another ten inches taller she would shake some sense into him. "Boy, the thought never crossed my mind. You two are so nauseatingly in love, it never occurred to me that you would be anything but the father! But..." There had been an awkward pause as she'd stopped before yelling, how could you be so dumb! Berating him wouldn't help the situation. Instead, she'd taken a deep breath and said, "How could you have unprotected sex? Have you heard of syphilis, gonorrhea, AIDS?"

"Yeah, yeah," he waved a hand at her. She'd had to clasp her hands together to stop her palm from striking his impudent cheek.

Then he said, "She was a virgin, sis. I don't have to worry about that."

"What about her!" she'd yelled at him. "A condom protects two people!"

The smirk left his face. "I don't have that stuff." Tyrese took a step back and looked her up and down.

"How do you know? Were you a virgin, too? Or did you take a test?" She knew the last suggestion was far-fetched, but she was having a hard time believing that this sexually irresponsible human being was her brother.

Then she felt that pang for the first time. A pang she felt so often nowadays that it had become a part of her. The way a person with bad knees gets used to walking with an aching limp. She was used to the soreness of guilt right in the middle of her chest. How could she condemn her brother when she'd done the exact same thing fifteen years ago? He'd been three at the time and had had no idea she'd been pregnant. Only she, her deceased mother, her distant father, and the doctor knew. She remembered how the weight of being two–faced had made her plop down in the chair. Here she was in the same situation only the enemy was in her family, in her house, her responsibility!

During the confrontation, Tyrese had flounced down in the armchair across from her. She recalled glancing at him and wondering at this late date if she herself should get counseling. Talking to the doctor had helped Ty a little. Her mother had been opposed to counseling for Jolie. "Black women are strong and we don't need to go see head shrinks. No one offered us a psychiatrist when they were devastating our families during slavery or lynching, and raping us during Jim Crow. No, we had to face our problems on our own and solve them," her mother had said. Jolie often reminded herself of her mother's words when times got tough. Maybe that was the reason why sisters had such a reputation for being hard. Figuring all this stuff out for yourself made you resilient, but resentful. Maybe a shrink could tell her how to deal with this mess and maintain her tenderness.

"So, what're you going to do?" she remembered asking.

"I'm gonna start playing ball again, make it to the NBA, and support my shorty and my baby."

She still chuckled when she thought of his answer. It was so easy and simple to him. Like he could twinkle his nose or click his heels three times and all that wonderful stuff would happen. Her mirth then as now was short lived because her brother's situation was too close to what her own had been. Concern for Robyn, made her frequently ask the question she'd just asked.

She stated it again. "Ty, what about Robyn?"

"What about her?"

Jolie tried to halt the wall she felt going up between them. "I'm not going to say 'if' because I know it's going to happen. You're good, and the recognition is going to come. I don't want Robyn or the baby getting lost in the shuffle."

"What exactly are you saying, sis?" Tyrese moved around in his chair. "You think I'm worse than Dad, don't you? That I won't provide for my family emotionally and financially."

The "Dad" comment threw her. She was measuring him against Alvin, not her father.

"You think I'm some punk who's going to dump his woman and his kid just because his name's in the paper?"

Jolie didn't answer.

"God, I don't believe this bull sh…!"

"Don't you talk to me that way, Tyrese Randal Smith!" She only used his full name when angry, a habit she'd picked up from their mother. She forgot all about walls and the kinder, gentler approach.

"Listen to how you're talking to me! I'm not a mack, a pimp, or a player. What makes you think success is going to turn me into a jerk?"

The sound of Tyrese's metal chair leg scraping against the vinyl floor made Jolie flinch. With short jerky motions, he scooped his crumbs into a napkin.

Jolie sat back in her chair and crossed her arms. She took a deep breath. "Ty." He glanced at her, then stood holding the napkin in his cupped hand. "I understand that you are eighteen and upset, and you think those two things entitle you to speak your mind; but let me explain something to you. As long as you are living under my roof, you will treat me with respect. You will not cuss at me, and I will not cuss at you. Please sit down."

They were at a crossroads. They stared at each other across the table. Her brother's fury was clear in the way he crushed the napkin in his fist. She remembered Father Ignacio's message, the Lord doesn't give you more than you can bear. She released a deep sigh and said a silent prayer of thanks when Tyrese sat down. She could tell he still had an attitude brewing because he presented a stone face with upturned eyes. She knew his eyes were positioned so to prevent them from rolling. Both she and he knew that, in this situation, all hell would break loose if those eyes moved around in a circle.

"Look, Ty, I'm sorry. I'm like Mom. I'm a worry wart, okay?" Tyrese's head was now slightly down, and Jolie lowered her head, but kept her eyes lifted, trying to force eye contact. He looked at her and she saw the hurt.

Jolie's voice softened. "Hey, I know you love Robyn."

"I'm crazy about her, Jolie. I want to get married and do like Mom said, take care of my family, do better for them, but she said no."

This was news to Jolie. *How's he going to support her when I support him?*

Tyrese continued, "She wants to wait until she finishes college. She's like you sometimes and accuses me of stup…," he looked at Jolie and smiled slightly. "No mean things. She thinks I only want to marry her because of the baby, which is true, but I love her, too. We'd just be getting married a few years before I'd planned."

Oh, Ty, you're so young. The words almost slipped past Jolie's lips.

"Robyn says we're both changing too much right now, and the trick is to change together, then get married. She thinks it's too early. But I know who I am and who I love now. That's going to be the same today and twenty years from today." Tyrese's tight lips and bright eyes dared her to differ.

If her mother were alive, she knew she would have some pearl of wisdom perfect for this situation. A sentence or a phrase that would help Tyrese put things in perspective. She consoled herself with the fact that at least Joan was getting through to Robyn. She could hear Robyn's mother speaking through Robyn's words.

Jolie decided that now was a good time to change the subject. "Hey, did I tell you there was a recruiter at the game?"

"No you didn't tell me. How did you know he was there?"

"I knew him in high school. Now he's a coach at WAM."

"Oh, this is great!" Tyrese bounced around in his chair a bit. "That's the school I want to go to. It's the only major university in Seattle. My playing can get national coverage, and I can still be with Robyn!"

Jolie sat back in her chair and crossed her arms before saying, "But Ty, the program has problems."

He gave her a strange look. "How do you know? You've never been interested in basketball?"

The words struck her as funny. If you only knew, Ty. When she fell in love with Alvin, she went to the library and borrowed books and instructional videos about basketball. She studied them as well as Alvin's statistics in the paper. If the rules hadn't changed, she probably knew them just as well, or better than her brother. However, she couldn't tell Tyrese that. It would raise too many questions she didn't want to answer. She also couldn't share that she knew about WAM's basketball program because she'd been reading the sports section for over a year now. Ever since Alvin had come back to Seattle.

Instead of talking about the past, she said, "I catch the sports on the news. I know what's happening over there."

"So, did he talk about me? What did he say?

"No, we talked about the weather. Of course he talked about you. He was sitting by Big Mac, who probably had told him about you."

"Wow, this is great!" Tyrese looked at his watch. "Oh, man, I have to go, sis, or I'll be late for work. I'll probably stop by Robyn's after, so I'll be back sometime tonight."

"Okay, but remember tomorrow's a school day, so don't stay out too long."

"All right." Tyrese grabbed his backpack, came over and pecked her forehead. Jolie was surprised. "Sis, don't worry so much. Everything's going to be fine and I love you." Jolie shook her head and nibbled her cookie, amazed at the optimism of youth.

Chapter 4

Several weeks later, Jolie found herself asking, Why does my usually punctual brother have to be late today? She had just sat down at the table in Philadelphia Fevre when her cell phone rang. Tyrese was full of legitimate excuses, so she really couldn't be mad at him. Basketball practice ran a little late, he had to pick up his check at the hospital, his gas guzzling Chevy Impala needed fuel, and traffic along Twenty-Third Street was still horrible at 7:10 p.m. The restaurant closed at eight. Jolie had intentionally set the meeting with Alvin at 7:15, so she'd only have to be in his presence for forty-five minutes.

Setting the meeting had been a difficult thing. At first, Alvin had refused to meet with Ty, once again voicing his concerns about violating the NCCA rules. But Ty had already received the scholarship letter from WAM, and he was ready to verbally commit. No way was Jolie going to allow him to do that before they spoke with Alvin, together. Finally, Alvin agreed after she promised that if this leaked out, she would swear that it had been a chance meeting between two old friends, and her brother had just happened to be there. She told Alvin she and her brother would tell the world that the word basketball wasn't even mentioned.

However, her well-laid plans were going awry because her dear brother was late. Jolie felt panicked because she needed him as a buffer. Now she'd have to face Alvin alone unless, of course, he was late, too. She glanced at her watch for the thousandth time. Well, in about three minutes, her question would be answered. She hoped and prayed that he'd be less than prompt.

Trying to ease her anxious mind, Jolie glanced around the restaurant that was full of Philly memorabilia. She saw the Phillies winning the World Series, the 76ers winning the NBA championship, and Patty Labelle with her mouth wrapped around a cheese steak. The picture of Patty always made Jolie laugh because Patty's mouth was almost as wide as her hair. Jolie didn't blame her for trying to get the whole thing in. She also loved the hoagie sandwich filled with thinly sliced grilled steak, peppers, onions, and melted cheese.

Jolie sat in the small dining area that was three steps up from the counter. She normally sat at the counter portion of the shop, so she could watch the food being made, and chat with Tom and Crystal, the couple who ran the place. If asked, Jolie thought she could pick Tom's backside out of a police lineup because that's what she usually spoke to. He did most of the cooking and was in the habit of talking to the customers over his shoulder while he chopped and sliced the meat with two spatulas. Both Tom and Crystal enjoyed people and they naturally made everyone feel welcome. They shouted greetings, remembered names, faces, and little tidbits about everyone who had the good fortune to wander into the shop.

Sitting at a table near the large windows, Jolie had a clear view of Madison street and even a little of the cross street, East John. The building that housed the restaurant had a unique triangle shape, and the steak shop resided right in the tip. The fact that it was built on a hillside only added to its character.

Jolie signaled to Crystal and ordered a tea called Calm Spirits. She'd been sort of keyed up ever since she told Tyrese about Alvin. That had been four weeks and numerous basketball games ago. Washington State was quickly becoming aware something special was going on at Rainier Beach High School. Tyrese's name was everywhere in the sports section, and a reporter had left a message last night that she wanted to do a full page, feature story. That same night, Tyrese's coach had called to say that four colleges had contacted him asking if the rumors were true. All of this had Tyrese in an uproar, but that wasn't what made Jolie jumpy. It was the fact that she had to contact Alvin.

Despite the attention from other schools, her brother was adamant about going to WAM. She had to do some fast talking to get him to wait until she could set up a meeting. Her brother was ready to commit yesterday.

Her heart had beat fast when she picked up the phone, despite the fact that she was only dialing information. By the time she got Alvin's direct line, her palms were sweating. She knew exactly what she was going to say. "Ty wants to commit to you, and I want a meeting first. When and where do you want to do this?" Her strategy was to keep it short and sweet. She was a good twenty seconds into her spiel when she realized she was talking to a recording. It surprised her so that there was another awkward pause after the beep before she timidly left a message. Of course, she had been completely unprepared when he called her back. She froze at the sound of his voice just as she had when she'd hung up on him. She forced herself not to stammer and stutter like a fool, and then her nervousness was forgotten when he refused to meet.

Jolie took a small sip of Calm Spirits. It burned her tongue. She sprinkled in a generous amount of sugar and waited for the hot brew to cool.

Sensing someone standing by her, she looked up into a pair of gentle brown eyes. Crystal was looking down on her with concern. "Hey, what's wrong?"

God, am I that easy to read? "Nothing, it's just been a long day."

"Yeah, I've had a few of those lately." Crystal rubbed her very pregnant belly. Then a slightly off-center smile formed on her face and she said, "Remember, sunshine follows rain, like light follows the darkest of nights. At least that's what my granny used to say and she lived to be a hundred and two."

"Oh, yeah. I guess your grandmother didn't live in Alaska, did she?"

Crystal chuckled, lighting up her eyes, "Even there,

night ends eventually."

Jolie nodded her head. "I can't argue with that..." Then her breath caught and died in her throat.

"Are you all right?" Crystal's brown hand patted her back.

Jolie sipped some more tea. "I'm fine, thank you. Something just caught in my throat." More like my eyes, Jolie thought as she watched Alvin step out of a black Mercedes parked across the street. Her heart leapt the same way it had when she saw him in the gym. Then she attributed it to the fact that she hadn't seen him in person in years. But today she was fully prepared, and her heart still jumped in her chest. It annoyed her and set her more on edge.

"Be careful," Crystal said. "Do you want to order now?"

"No, thanks. I'm waiting for my brother."

"Okay, holler when you're ready." Crystal made her way to the counter.

Jolie watched as Alvin negotiated the traffic to cross the busy street. Irritated or not, she had to acknowledge that Alvin looked good. He wore tan chinos, black sweater, and what looked like black ankle boots. He was coatless in defiance of the cold, damp weather. Jolie lifted her arm to see her watch. "He has no issues with time," she mumbled.

Alvin's hungry eyes absorbed every detail as he climbed the short stairs into the dining area. The first thing he noticed was her attire. She wore a patchwork denim skirt that left her shapely calves bare. Determined not to stare, he forced his eyes up to the white, V-neck tunic she wore over the skirt. The effect was kind of funky and so Jolie.

Feeling his eyes on her, Jolie knew he must have seen her sitting by the window because he came right to her. She played with the water glass, moving the beads of sweat around, hoping that some of the coolness would travel through her fingertip to calm her boiling blood. "Hello," Jolie said as Alvin settled his muscular frame into the small wooden chair.

"Hi, yourself." He gave her a slow smile. She talked to cover her nervousness, explaining that Tyrese was running late, repeating each one of his legitimate excuses almost verbatim.

So you still babble when your uncomfortable, he thought, so I make you nervous, Jolie. It was a pleasant surprise to Alvin. At least she wasn't indifferent. He hid his smile and listened patiently while nodding.

"Let me call to see how far away Ty is."

He watched as she retrieved her phone from her purse. A few tendrils of hair had escaped the ponytail and swung delightfully as she reached into her bag. He admired her long, thin, ringless fingers that held the phone and pushed in the numbers. He was captivated by the slight wrist that was covered by smooth copper skin.

"Darn, I can't get him. He must be driving through a bad air patch."

Alvin nodded, and then asked, "So how have you been, Jolie?"

The softly asked question threw her. She almost said that things were going pretty good until he showed up. Instead, she said, "Some days are rough. I feel like I'm made of sandpaper and all Ty and I do is rub each other wrong. But on the whole, it isn't bad. And you?" Surprisingly, she was really interested in his answer.

"I can't complain."

"I see you reached your goals?" It was meant to be a statement; however, it came out as more of a question. It was said without rancor.

"Yes, professionally, I've reached them."

Professionally. Jolie paused at his use of the word. What was he implying?

Alvin answered the question he saw in her wide eyes. "I'm failing miserably in my private life."

Why is he saying this to me? Jolie wanted to know. Is he trying to rub salt into the wound? He's the one who let go of my hand. Out loud Jolie said, "Why the hell are you telling me that? Do you think I care?"

He'd hoped she would. He quickly backtracked. "I wasn't trying to start an argument, Jolie. I was just making conversation. So, how about you? Do you have someone special?" The glare from the game was back full force.

"Let's not get personal, okay? And maybe we can both get through this. We're meeting to discuss your university and my bother."

"Hey, sis. What's up?" Jolie tensed when Tyrese squeezed her shoulder "Sorry, I'm late, man." Tyrese offered Alvin his hand. Alvin accepted it, and the two exchanged a firm shake.

"That's okay, man. My name's Alvin Guillory."

"I'm Tyrese, and hey, Jolie explained the situation to me. I just want you to know that there's no way I'd bust you. If anyone asks me, I'll swear up and down that I just listened to you two reminisce the whole time we ate."

Alvin nodded. "Your sister and I have already been doing some catching up. I guess she told you that we went to high school together?"

"Yeah, she mentioned that." Tyrese looked at Jolie, and then looked again, wondering why his sister looked pissed. He misunderstood, assuming she was mad at him because he was late. Damn, why won't she ease up, he thought, I didn't mean to be late and I called her twice! He sat between the two and positioned himself so that most of his back was towards his sister. "I'm excited to meet you, man."

Tyrese's enthusiasm surprised Alvin. The kid was practically beaming. "You're not nearly as excited as I. You're a great player!"

"Excuse me." Crystal said. "I hate to interrupt, but the grill closes in ten minutes. Jolie, do you want the usual?"

Jolie nodded.

"I'll take a Jolie." Tyrese said as if Jolie's special sandwich was on the menu.

"You have your own sandwich?" Alvin asked, eyebrows raised.

Jolie shrugged. "I come in here a lot."

Crystal elaborated. "The sandwich has chicken instead of beef with hot and sweet peppers, mushrooms, and extra cheese."

"Sounds like something worth investigating. I'll take Jolie, too."

Jolie looked at him sideways. He flashed a smile at her.

Tyrese missed the exchange because he was too busy asking Crystal for cheese fries. He turned to Alvin. "You ought to try them, man. They're good."

"You got it. I'll take the fries, also."

Crystal said, "I hope you're hungry." Then, she looked him up and down. "But you're a big boy. You can probably handle it."

Is she flirting with him? Jolie didn't like the idea, even if she was full of another man's child, and that man was downstairs cooking. Jolie felt silly before Crystal had the time to walk downstairs. Why did she care? Her feelings for Alvin had died the day she lost the life in her belly. Inwardly she groaned, Now why did you have to bring that into it, Jolie? Remembering past pain won't help this be a productive meeting.

She forced herself to focus on Tyrese and Alvin. From the sound of the conversation, it seemed as if her brother had already committed to WAM. Jolie cleared her throat, preparing to speak. Tyrese's back still faced her, and he kept right on talking, but Alvin looked at her.

"Excuse me, Ty. I think your sister has something to say." Tyrese shifted and scooted back a little. Now she faced his profile.

"Ty, I think we're getting ahead of ourselves, don't you?" She rushed on before he could contradict her. "We have a few questions about what's going on up there."

Tyrese looked hard at Jolie, then turned to Alvin. "Yeah, I do have a few questions. How much playing time will I get?"

This wasn't what Jolie wanted to ask and Tyrese knew it. Alvin began speaking, and rather than interrupt, Jolie sat back, crossed her arms, and decided to wait out the love fest.

Alvin was looking Tyrese in the eyes. "I promise to push you and work your butt off, so you'll be ready to go every game. Now, you have a part to play in this equation. You have to meet me more than half way. If you sign on with me, and give me your best, I'm sure you'll play lots of minutes."

Tyrese was nodding his head. "Okay. Okay. I can get with that. What about my number? Can I have number 15?"

Alvin did a quick mental check, and Jolie wondered what in the world was so important about number 15?

Alvin said, "I don't think that'll be a problem."

Tyrese visibly relaxed, the air whooshing from him. "That's good, man, because that number's really important to me."

"Why?" Jolie joined the conversation. She'd been so quiet, she suspected that they both had forgot she was there. She was focused on Ty, so she missed the look in Alvin's eyes when he swung to her. If she had caught it, she would have known she hadn't been overlooked.

Tyrese stilled and curved in a little as he answered his sister. "Two reasons. When I was a kid, I was pissed because I couldn't get 32, Magic's number. Mom said, 'Why do you want someone else's number anyway? You should pick your own and make it great.'" Tyrese smiled at Jolie.

"That was Mom, full of good advice," she said.

"Uh huh. The other reason is because of Pookie. He wore 15 that day. We were tight and you know," Tyrese shrugged, "it's my way of honoring him."

"All right, if you come to WAM, I'll make sure 15 is waiting for you."

"Thanks, man."

The food arrived, brought by both Tom and Crystal. Tyrese and Jolie stared. Tom's usual chef hat was gone, revealing three long, blond dredlocks that sat in the middle of a buzz cut. "Hey, it's after eight," Tom said. "We're officially closed, and I get to take off the hat. Not that you have to hurry," he quickly added. "It takes us about an hour to clean up."

Crystal laughed. "I make him wear the hat during the day because I don't know if the customers will understand, but I think it's sexy." She pulled on a long dred. Light chuckling rose from the group. "Bon appetite," Crystal said as the two drifted back downstairs. Tyrese, Jolie, and Alvin dug into their food.

At first, Alvin picked up his fork until he saw the other

two grab the large sandwiches and take a bite. He followed suit and was soon smacking his lips. "My goodness, this is delicious!"

"You ain't never lied, coach. I love these things. But be ready to be thirsty for hours. All these peppers make you want water."

Jolie looked at her brother, who wasn't paying her any attention. He spoke to Alvin as if he were a part of the family. Why was he calling him coach?

Tyrese's head popped up. "Hey, what about TV? How often are the games televised?"

"This year we will be on TV thirteen times?"

"Oh, yeah." Tyrese's eyes lit up. Jolie knew he was off somewhere in TV land, and it was up to her to ask the tough questions.

"How many games are there in a season?"

She had Alvin's complete attention. "'Bout thirty. This year we have thirty-two."

She disregarded the warm look in his eyes as he sat there looking relaxed, wiping his hands with a napkin. "So when you look at the total, not many games are on television."

"I wouldn't say that. More than a third of our games are televised."

"Are you on ESPN?"

The question amazed Alvin. He'd never thought a sports channel would interest Jolie. "We will be on ESPN 2 once this season."

Ah ha, Jolie thought. "So, that's the only time you'll

have a national audience?" Her eyes were centered on Alvin, but she caught Tyrese in her peripheral vision. His slouch and pursed lips told her he didn't like her line of questioning. She wanted to take her hand and push it between his shoulder blades and tell him to sit up straight before he ruined his back. Instead, she listened to Alvin's answer.

"No, we have a guaranteed national audience three times this season. We're on CBS twice. Also, the rest of our games will be on Fox Sports Northwest, which can be picked up by satellite. So, all thirteen games have a potential national audience."

"All right, man!" Tyrese interrupted.

Jolie continued her examination as if her brother hadn't spoken. "What about you and your boss's stability? Aren't you two about to be fired? Will you be there for the tip off of Tyrese's first game?"

Tyrese believed his sister could ask the questions, but he was shocked at how rudely she put them, and how hard her voice was. "What's wrong with you, Jolie? Are you trying to ruin this for me?"

Uh oh. Jolie looked at her brother winding up. She glanced around, thankful that they were the only customers. But still, the last thing she wanted was a scene with Alvin present. She felt the hot redness start over her chest, stretch to her neck, and creep into her face. "No, Ty. I'm just trying to do what's best for you." Her voice was a bit too high.

"Best for me!" It wasn't a shout, but it was loud enough to make Tom glance up the stairs. Ty saw him, too, and he managed to lower his voice a little. "You've had an attitude since I got here. So what! I was late. I called you twice to let you know why."

Jolie's heart beat fast. "Ty, I'm not mad because you were late." She tried to ease the mood with a stiff smile, but it was futile. The harm was done. She remembered the old adage that had been drilled into her head by elders: We don't talk about our mothers in public. She wondered if Tyrese realized that the saying applied to sisters who were acting as mothers also.

"Then what's the problem? Why are you acting like the Gestapo?"

"Ty," Alvin began, "your sister's asking good questions. Anyone who is following us in the media would be thinking the same thing."

"Well, I'm not thinking that." He turned to face Jolie. "Ever since Robyn got pregnant, you've been on my case. Nothing I do or want is right." Suddenly Tyrese stopped talking as if he were embarrassed by his outburst. He looked at Alvin with wide, confused eyes, rimming with moisture. "I gotta go." In a blur of teenage angst, he was gone.

Jolie couldn't meet Alvin's eyes. "I'm sorry," she whispered, apologizing to Alvin, to Tyrese, and to herself. "He's usually not this emotional. This situation has been difficult for all of us." She looked up at him. "Was my tone that harsh?" She hastily lowered her head again when she realized whom she was asking. Tom and Crystal were both at the bottom of the stairs now. Jolie saw them and wanted to sink into the floor. She reached for her purse and began pulling money out.

"Jolie." She wouldn't look at him. He reached across the small table and grabbed her hands to still them. It was another violation for Alvin to pay the bill, but in this situation, he didn't give a damn. He hated to see Jolie so upset. "I've got it. Just relax a minute while I take care of it, and then we can talk." He got up and went downstairs.

She wanted to flee, but it seemed like such a childish thing to do. Oh hell, I'm a child then. She got up and slipped out the side door.

Chapter 5

About a week later on Friday evening, Jolie sat on her living room couch concluding that there was one thing her mother was wrong about. That wise woman had always claimed, "Ain't nothing like a bone drilling, exhausting day of work to wear out one's problems." She professed that nothing seemed that bad when all one's body wanted to do was lie down and die! Jolie had tried the 'you can rest when you're dead' philosophy all week, and she could attest to the fact that, for her, it didn't work. Her problems refused to be banished.

Jolie's aching hands were a testament to how hard she'd labored. They were chafed and white at the webbing. She got up to lotion them and groaned as her thighs reminded her why she never wanted to walk again. Mentally apologizing to her sore legs, she sat back down and decided a little bit of ash wouldn't kill her. All the pain made her remember why she was so happy to now be the educational zoo keeper. For the last two years, her main function had been to organize, promote, and represent the zoo at community events. She'd spent time training certain animals so they could interact with the public, but she hadn't had to do the hard physical labor that went hand in hand with providing a clean habitat. Her memory had dulled, and maybe even glorified, about how tough the job could be. She had quickly responded yes when she received a phone call from her boss late Sunday evening, asking her to cover for a coworker who had a family emergency. "This will be good for me," she'd told herself, remembering her mother's advice.

On the third day, she'd stared at another big pile of feces and pondered her sanity when she'd agreed to this madness. She loved all animals and the big hoofed ones were some of her favorites, but between them, per day, the animals left about a hundred piles of pancake size dung for Jolie to pick up. The smell wasn't the problem. After all these years, she was immune to it. It was the constant bending and lifting that had her ready to cry. By the fourth day, she was using profanity to let the hundred and fifty pound bail of hay she was bucking know how she felt. She called it a plethora of names as she sorted through it to make sure there was no mold or bailing wire hidden inside. Mold caused toxic shock in the animals and could kill them within a half-hour. The wire could do all kinds of nasty damage to the animal's insides.

Jolie moaned softly as she massaged her thighs. Tyrese breezed through the house with barely a nod in her direction. He was gone within ten minutes. They were engaged in a cold war. The scene, as Jolie began to think of it, had yet to be mentioned. Her brother pretty much used their small house as a place to lay his head. Every minute beyond work and basketball he spent at Robyn's house. In fact,

Joan had left a message that morning asking why she had to kick Tyrese out of her house every night.

That wasn't the only call back Jolie needed to make. Alvin had phoned several times. Jolie cursed the fact that her phone number was listed. In the last couple of days, she had developed an addiction to Caller ID. The four times she'd read Washington Agricultural or Alvin Guillory in the display, her blood pressure had risen. She'd paced around the phone nervously, knowing she should pick it up, but not doing so. Jolie got the shakes listening to his deep, smooth voice. It was a strange feeling of embarrassment left over from the scene, or something else she refused to put a name to. But if she were in a guessing mood, yearning would probably be the best label she could come up with. A dangerous and preposterous idea, considering their history, and exactly why Jolie avoided self-analysis on this particular issue.

She did examine what had happened at Philadelphia Fevre, and in no way did she hold herself completely accountable for the ugliness that occurred. Despite what Tyrese believed, he was still an adolescent and she was the adult. In Jolie's mind, that meant it was up to her to fix the situation, or at least get everyone on the road to recovery. If her brother really wanted to go to WAM, she wouldn't allow herself to be in the way. She'd have to put her feelings aside and stop being confrontational with Alvin. Not an easy thing when she'd spent the last fifteen years hating his guts. There's a thin line between love and hate. The old saying popped unbidden into her head. "Well, I'll just have to get out my marker and make the line thicker," she uttered. "Maybe build a barb wire or electric fence." Jolie picked up the phone, looked the number up on her Caller ID display, and made the dreaded call.

She held the phone between her ear and shoulder, so she could wipe her hands on her pants. It rang three times, giving her hope that she could leave a message and prolong that horrible first contact. Her prayers went unanswered when Alvin picked up.

Jolie paused. He said "Hello" again.

"Uh, hi. It's me, Jolie. Did I call at a bad time?" She heard the creak of what sounded like an office chair. She imagined his large form sitting up straight.

"No, no. You could never call at a bad time. I'm just happy to hear from you."

She wrapped the phone cord around her finger and sat back on the couch. "Sorry about how the other evening turned out."

"Look, Jolie. Don't mention it. I don't have any kids." She gasped because his innocently said words hurt. Apparently, he didn't hear her because he kept right on talking. "But we get the boys when they're seventeen or eighteen up here, and I know it can be difficult at times." Pain didn't stop her from hearing the sincerity in his voice. "Why don't we meet privately, and you can get all of your questions out of the way."

"All right."

"Why don't I come over when Ty has a game, and I'm in town? Let me grab my calendar."

"No, that won't work." She'd almost shouted no way, but she remembered her promise to be more courteous. Jolie felt as if she could protect some part of herself by not allowing him into her space. "Besides, won't that cause problems for you?"

"No, I talked it over with Rock, he's the head coach. We both agree that all we have to do is claim that we're dating if the NCAA starts snooping." The gasp was much louder this time. Alvin must have heard it, but he kept right on talking. "However, it's very unlikely that they'll even notice this. Heck, I'm not flying out of town because we live in the same city; we really are old friends, and we used to mean something to each other. It's very believable that we're just rekindling an old flame."

Jolie was silent. She didn't like it, but she couldn't find fault with his reasoning.

"Would you like to come to my office, or maybe my house?" His deep voice was even deeper.

Yeah, right. "No, let's meet at a neutral place. Not Philadelphia Fevre. I'd be too ashamed to go back there."

"Do you like Creole food?"

"I loved the stuff your mother used to make, but I haven't had it since."

"Good, that means you're in for a treat."

"What? Are you taking me to your parents' for dinner?"

Alvin laughed. "I would, but they retired, and moved

back to Lafayette, Louisiana."

Jolie had always enjoyed Alvin's parents. When his dad wasn't asleep, he always shouted a greeting, and his mom was forever ready to tempt her with some delicious meal she'd just whipped up. "How are they doing?"

"Great! Cost of living is cheaper down there, so their retirement checks go a long way. Plus, they've reunited with old friends. I'll tell them you asked next time we talk. But back to my surprise, I'm taking you to MudBugs."

"Mudbugs?" Jolie features went towards her nose.

"I can hear you squenching up your face."

Jolie put her mouth and lips back were they belonged.

"It's crawfish, and the dirt tends to be gone by the time they serve them."

Jolie laughed softly.

"God, that's nice!" Alvin said with conviction.

"What?" Her head turned in the direction of the receiver as if she would see him standing there.

"Just the sound of you laughing."

His words set off a pang somewhere deep in her chest. "Look, Alvin, I can't do this if you say things like that. In fact, it makes me angry. Don't try to butter me up to get to Ty."

She heard the office chair squeaking. "Now, you know that's not true! Have I ever been dishonest?"

No, she acknowledged silently, you've always been harshly candid. "Maybe you've become devious. Fifteen years is a long time."

"Okay, get ready because I'm about to be brutally upfront now. It's the other way around. I'm using your brother to get to you!"

Her stomach, or maybe it was something down lower, jumped into her vocal cords, preventing speech. Finally, she managed to croak, "I'm not available."

"Why? Do you have someone?"

Jolie slumped into the couch. The whole conversation was draining. "I'm not going to answer that."

"Okay, Okay. I can tell by your voice that you're ready to get off the phone. Here's the address and I'll see you Sunday at four.

Chapter 6

Sunday at three-fifteen, Jolie was just about to leave when her phone rang. In a rush, she answered without looking at the display. His voice caught her by surprise and she clutched the receiver.

"Hi, Jolie. I have a bit of an emergency. My car died right as I pulled into my place. I don't live far from Mudbugs. Would you mind picking me up on the way? It would save me the cost of a taxi."

Jolie's mouth said "Yes" before her mind actually consented.

"Great! Here's the address."

She grabbed a pencil to write it down.

Twenty minutes later, she pulled up in front of his condo downtown. "Thank goodness it's Sunday," Jolie whispered as she maneuvered into a space right in front of his building. Parking downtown would have been a nightmare on a weekday. A doorman let her in, and a concierge greeted her as soon as she stepped inside. Jolie felt like an intruder in some exclusive hotel. She expected the suited man sitting behind the desk to stop her, but after asking her name, he went back to what looked like paperwork. She rode the elevator to the third floor and peered at numbers until she found the right one. Her hand had lifted to knock when the door opened of its own accord to reveal a visually striking woman. She wore a crimson silk suit with rhinestone buttons that matched her earrings and her necklace. Her long hair was fluffed around the skin of her very smooth face. Both women stared. Jolie was too shocked to flee as her nose was assaulted by the sensual and musky perfume that radiated from the woman.

"Well, come in," the woman said in a throaty voice. Jolie did so after she moved away from the entrance. The woman put down the brown bag she held in her right hand. In her left, she carried a fancy gold dress. She opened a door and put the dress inside. Then she crossed her arms and stared at Jolie once more. Since she knew she'd be dashing in and out, Jolie had left her coat in the car. Somehow, she felt inadequate in her comfortable, water print floral dress as the woman continued to eyeball her. After a long awkward moment, the woman picked up the bag and said, "I suppose three's a crowd." Then she yelled over her shoulder, "Vin, your date's here," as she sauntered out the door.

Jolie winced. She wasn't sure if she was reacting to the familiarly in the woman's tone when she said, "Vin," or because she'd referred to her as a date.

"Sophia, did you say something?" Alvin appeared in what Jolie assumed was the bedroom doorway. She put a hand to her chin to stop her mouth from dropping open. However, the move made her look as if she were appraising what was before her. Alvin stood there with a small green towel attached to his waist while he used another to vigorous rub his head. Anger, or at least irritation, should have been the dominant emotion, since it seemed as if he'd invited her over when his lover was there. But his appearance had her gaping. Alvin saw her and stopped. He recognized the slightly dazed look, and an answer flickered through his eyes as he admired the lines of her long dress. "You look great in bright pink and yellow flowers."

"Thanks." Unable to stand the look in his eyes, Jolie made the mistake of glancing down. His body was long with lean, sculpted muscles and gleaming, dark brown skin. The tall, wiry youth she'd been intimate with had disappeared into this...hunk. Jolie was close enough to see tiny drops of water quivering on the exposed flesh. She was mesmerized by the drops on his upper chest that broke away, slid down between his nipples, crossed his stomach, and disappeared into a thatch of hair that sprouted out from the low hanging towel. Jolie licked her lips just in case she was drooling. Realizing how the action must look, she lifted her eyes quickly back to his face. She sucked in air as the temperature between them rose to unbearable degrees. Alvin was moving towards her to answer the look in her eyes, the invitation in her tongue as it swept across her lips, when she whispered, "No."

He stopped and Jolie lowered her eyes to see the towel that was inches away from falling from his waist. She strangled a gasp and took a deep, hopefully calming, breath. Then she looked up with a different sort of fire in her eyes.

"Isn't one a day enough? Please get dressed, so we can go to the restaurant." Her chin hollowed, making her dimple prominent as her emotions shifted.

Never one to follow orders unless it suited him, he grabbed the towel at his waist, insuring it wouldn't leave his body. "Oh, you're referring to Sophia. What we had was really over before it started. She was just here picking up the last of her things." Alvin had frowned when she'd shown up right after he'd called Jolie. He hadn't had time to wait while she gathered her stuff. As he had rushed to the shower, he wondered why she'd chosen now to appear. He had called her days ago to let her know that whatever they had together was over, and she needed to come get her stuff. Her timing couldn't have been worse.

He remembered that after he'd told her it was over, there'd been a long pause before she'd said, "Okay, lover. That'll do me fine because you really are too slow for me."

Alvin had laughed and said, "I thought it was the other way around."

"What do you mean?"

"Well, Sophia. I thought you were too fast for me." The phone being slammed down was all he'd heard. That's why he was surprised when she let herself into his condo after he'd hung up with Jolie. Rather than argue, he'd asked her to hurry and leave his key on the coffee table when she left. He looked at the empty table and inwardly sighed.

Shifting his focus back to Jolie, he said, "You look...warm, Jolie." He moved a step closer. "Would you like a cold drink?"

Her eyes widened and her nose quivered. She could smell him. It was a clean, fresh, appealing scent. "No, I ...." She knew she could speak coherently if he would just back up. She backed up. "If this time doesn't work for you, we can reschedule."

He smiled at her and swiped at his chest with the towel. The sparse, damp hair laid flat. Jolie eyelids briefly lowered and raised again when he spoke. "I wouldn't think of it." He stood gazing at her a moment longer. Jolie noticed that his curly chest hairs were springing back up. Alvin smiled slightly and said, "Give me five." He turned and walked away. Jolie couldn't help watching the gliding muscles in his backside and calves as he moved. Right before he disappeared into the room, he snatched away the towel, revealing a toned cheek.

"Just breathe," she told herself. She closed her eyes and tried to remember how Sensei, her instructor, had said to do it. She'd decided to take karate a few years earlier when she was the nighttime zoo keeper, and vandals were breaking into the zoo on an average of once a month. She'd soon discovered that she liked karobics more than karate. Karobics was an hour-long torture session where Jolie got to shadow-box, lift weights, and punch a bag. At the end of the workout, Sensei would make them do a breathing exercise to lower their heart rate before directing them into the warm down stretches. Now Jolie put down her purse and exhaled while stretching out her arms. Then she slowly pulled her arms in and inhaled. She did this four times before she felt her emotions leveling out. My God, it should be a crime to look that good in terry cloth, Jolie thought as she turned to study her surroundings.

She stood in a sunken living room that featured ceiling-to-floor windows, which provided a wonderful view of the waters of Puget Sound. Jolie ran her fingers along the back of the dark green velvet couch and admired the polished dark wood of the end and coffee tables. Glancing at the walls, she noticed they were covered with some kind of material. Jolie went to get a closer look.

"Do you like it?"

The question made her jump. Without really looking at him, she covered up her nervousness with a question. "What is this? I love the color."

"It's a linen cloth wall covering. The designer called the color saturn."

"It goes well with the couch." Jolie shifted her attention to the floor. She pointed to it and said, "I like this. It brings brightness and keeps this place from being too dark. What is it? Some sort of tan matte?"

"Yes. It's called a Rattan carpet. I chose it because I liked the texture. It's rugged and a nice contrast to the softness of the couch and the polish of the tables."

Jolie nodded and looked at him for the first time since he'd returned. He looked good in olive green pants and a shirt. The black belt and shoes rounded out his ensemble perfectly. Determined not to be caught staring, Jolie turned and headed for the door. "We'd better get going." Alvin grabbed his coat from the closet and followed.

§§§

Is this a restaurant or someone's house? Jolie looked at the door she'd just passed through. The outside looked like several storefront businesses housed in a small, one story building smack dab in the middle of a residential neighborhood. But once Jolie stepped through the door, she'd been transported to another time zone, another era. She'd been jettisoned back to a parlor in the early 1900s. Peach and sage walls treated to look old wrapped Jolie in comfort. Lace tablecloths covering what looked like antique tables pleased her eyes. A well-used couch resting at one end of the room invited her sit down. A pristine old-fashioned refrigerator combined with the extraordinary aromas made her hungry.

Alvin excused himself and disappeared through a lace curtain. Excited female voices drifted from the back of the restaurant.

"Herah, honey, taste a l'il of dis." Jolie looked up to see an attractive, light-skinned woman with shoulder length hair coming through the curtain. She wore a 1930s style dress that had buttons all the way down the front. It fit her thin frame perfectly. As the woman moved swiftly towards her, the dress swung around her calves.

Taking a leap of faith, Jolie ate the food on the outstretched spoon. Seasonings sank deep into her tongue. Spices came alive, making her mouth vibrate with joy. The small sample was gone too soon. Before Jolie could decipher the delicious things thrilling her palate, it was moving past her throat and gone.

"Will that do fer ya, yeah? Now, that there was gumbo. I just made it dis mornin'." The woman nodded her head sharply as if she were answering her own question.

Wow, Jolie thought, of course it will do! In fact, I could do a whole bowl. Out loud she said, "The closest I've come to gumbo is Campbell's. That was heavenly!"

"Hush yo mouth, gurl!" The woman waved her spoon playfully. "That soup company done did blasphemy tryin' to pass that stuff off as gumbo."

Alvin's laughing voice alerted Jolie to his return. She looked up to see him strolling through the curtain. He smiled at the two of them. Without thinking, Jolie asked, "Why didn't your mother ever cook gumbo?"

Alvin chuckled, "My mom made gumbo all the time. I guess you just didn't come to eat on those days." He nodded at the woman with the spoon. "I see Cathy's already made you a part of the family, and you've been taste testing."

"Yes, indeed. Ya see, honey, when you come to eat heah, you a part of my people for the night. Commo ca va, cher?" Alvin and Cathy exchanged a hug. Jolie could tell that Alvin cared deeply because of how firmly he held her. She wondered about their relationship.

"I'm doing fine. Et toi, how are you?"

"I'm great, sugar. I'm just so happy ya brought us a new friend to meet."

Alvin looked at Jolie's face and decided that he liked the slight frown. Jealousy could only help his cause. He formally introduced the two women, and then he found himself watching Jolie as Cathy showed them to one of the two tables in the restaurant. He stared at her longingly as he followed her gently swaying dress.

As darkness dominated the winter evening, Cathy went around lighting the lamps in the one–room dining area. Then she drifted towards the back, running her hand over Alvin's shoulder and the antique French armoire angled across the corner of the room near the curtain.

"She's quite attractive, just as the woman was at your condo," Jolie said.

"Yes." Alvin had a big smile on his face.

Jolie lowered her head to hide her reaction.

Alvin wasn't fooled. "Jolie, Sophia means absolutely nothing to me. She just picked a bad time to come and get her stuff. There's nothing between us any more."

Jolie looked at him, not quite sure if she was satisfied with his answer. The woman's attitude had been challenging and possessive. Then she caught herself. Why should I care? How the man looks, whom he sees, and whom he doesn't see is none of my concern.

"And as for Cathy, she's just a good friend," Alvin continued. "She's married to a wonderful guy named Anthony

LaBeau. They just celebrated their tenth year together. Believe it or not, I met both of them in church. Immaculate Heart on Capital Hill. There're a lot of blacks from Louisiana that go there."

She looked up quickly. The fact that they'd both grown up Catholic had been important to her when they were teenagers, but Alvin had always pooh-poohed it off, saying he hated going because it was boring. He went only out of respect for his mother.

"Yes, I go to church now. I stopped when I went to college, but I picked it up again about eight years ago. I go every Sunday that I'm in town."

"Why?"

Alvin shrugged. "I was playing pro ball and I wasn't happy. I wouldn't say depressed, I just knew something was missing. I just wasn't satisfied. I told Rock and he said I was out of balance. Told me that I need to come up spiritually." Alvin wasn't telling the whole story. Rock told him he had only one line of the triangle. He needed religion and a good woman to be complete. Going back to church was the easy part. He was having a hard time with the good woman sitting right in front of him. He'd sent her a card around the same time he'd returned to God's house. Two weeks later, he'd literally jumped for joy when he saw her writing on an envelope addressed to him. He'd sunk to the floor in despair when he ripped the seal to find his own letter, unopened. There was a sticky attached that read, "Don't contact me again."

"So, did it work? Are you whole now?"

"Almost. There're still a few things I'm working on."

Something about his eyes warned her that she didn't want to ask him what those few things were. The restaurant's environment was too romantic, and if Jolie wasn't careful, she could do something she might regret.

"This place is wonderful. I'm shocked it isn't full."

Alvin lowered his head and looked up at her, and she knew she wouldn't like what he was going to say. "There was a zoning law snafu and Bug's compromise with the city is that they will be open only for catering purposes and private dinner parties. We're the only party tonight."

Jolie took a deep breath. Alvin couldn't help noticing how the movement affected her dress.

"Look, I'm about to tell you some very confidential stuff tonight. I didn't want to worry about looking over my shoulder to see who might be listening."

Jolie couldn't think of a valid argument, so she nodded and tried to let it go. She picked up the menu and began studying it, reminding herself that she had to keep her emotions under control for Tyrese's sake. The curtain parted again to reveal an older woman this time. Alvin whispered, "That's Cathy's aunt, Mona." The woman wore the same style dress as her niece, and it swirled around her calves hypnotically as she made her way to their table. She greeted them both warmly, and then placed a fresh catfish appetizer before them. Then she hugged Alvin from behind and asked if they were ready to order. Jolie ordered gumbo, and

Alvin ordered his usual.

"What's that?" Jolie asked.

"You'll see," Alvin answered.

"Perrier, Alvin?" Mona asked.

He nodded.

When asked, Jolie requested a merlot.

Alvin looked at Jolie's lips. They reminded him of the dark red wine.

"Sure, hon." Mona walked back through the opening.

"I love these things." Alvin said as he picked up a piece of fish. "They start frying it the minute I hit the door. They're nice and crispy without being greasy." He didn't have to ask Jolie twice to try some.

"Uh, mum. It is good." Jolie wiped her hands on the cloth napkin. It was time to get down to business and ask the hard questions. Without preamble, she said, "So tell me, how stable is your job? If Ty goes to WAM, are you going to be around next year for the start of his college career?"

Alvin coughed into his napkin. The fish he was eating caught in his throat. "I don't have to worry about cavities with you, do I? You don't sugarcoat a thing."

Jolie just looked at him.

Alvin put his napkin on the table, crossed his arms and legs, and sat back as comfortably as he could in the small, antique chairs. "It's never easy to follow a legend. Marv Wood coached at the University for fifteen years. Ten of those years he won national championships. That's phenomenal. But you know what? Rock Softli is living up to that challenge. Consider this: Rock is in his fifth season as head coach. No other coach in WAM's ninety-three year history has won more games, or taken more teams to post season play in his first four years."

"If he's so good, why are the papers critical?"

"Three reasons. One, I've already explained. It's no fun to be compared to a legend, even when that legend is a strong supporter of yours. Rock worked with Wood two years before he retired. He actually recommended Rock for the job."

Jolie didn't say the words, but she gave her slightly lowered head and raised palms a little shake. He knew she was asking, well, what's the problem then?

He waited until their delicious food was served before answering. He took a big bite of succulent seafood floating in a light brown gravy on top of rice.

Jolie studied his dish. "Crawfish etouffe, right?"

"Wow, you remember!"

"I recognized the smell. Is that," Jolie pointed, "as good as your mom's?"

Alvin nodded his head. "Don't tell, but this is a little better. Here try it." He scooped some up with his fork and reached out to her.

The gesture, taking food from a utensil that had touched his mouth, was intimate in such a romantic environment. She looked at his lips and felt her own quivering softly. She remembered high school and his sensuous bite of her cookie. She slowly leaned forward and took the food while avoiding his eyes. She sat back and looked at his face. He was smiling. Instinctively, she knew she'd allowed some invisible line to be crossed. She frowned, mentally telling herself that she'd jumped right back over the divider to the other side. He'd hurt her terribly once, and she'd be damned if she would allow him to do it twice.

Alvin found her change of expression puzzling. Here, he thought they were getting somewhere, and then she was suddenly scowling at him. "Would you like some more? I can put it in this saucer." He held up the delicate blue and white china.

"No, thank you. Let's get back to what we were discussing. What's the problem if everybody likes your friend, and he's a good coach?"

"Now, I didn't say that everyone likes him." Alvin put his fork down. "The second reason involves privileged information, so I would appreciate it if you kept it to yourself."

Jolie nodded. "I would never repeat something you told me in confidence. That hasn't changed about me."

Knowing that she spoke the truth, Alvin continued. "The AD or Athletic Director is a good 'ole boy from the South, and he doesn't think a young, spunky black man should be leading a major university's basketball team. He likes to leak little tips to the press that imply Rock's on the way out."

Jolie stopped eating. "Geez, this is the new century and there are so many blacks in sports. Are we really still facing those problems?"

"Oh, yes. Racism is alive and well. It's out of fashion to be blatant with it though. Jimmy the Greek learned that when he said blacks were good athletes because we were bred like horses during slavery. So now the racist ones smile in your face and slither around in the grass like a snake trying to bite you when you least expect it."

"Hey, I like snakes. They don't deserve to be compared with the likes of your athletic director and the Greek guy!"

Alvin laughed. "I forgot I'm speaking to a zoo keeper." Her wide eyes told him that she was surprised he knew her occupation. "The first time I saw you, you were wearing your work shirt. You look good in khakis and hiking boots."

The mischievous look was back. The slight smile and soft eyes that affected her every time. She frowned again. "Let's get back to what we were discussing."

He didn't argue, but the smile remained. "We were warned by a reporter at *The Seattle Times*, so we knew what was up. Right now, we're leading the Pac Ten, or the Pacific Ten Division, but the season started out rough. We were one and four after our first five games. The AD actually tried to manipulate Rock. The man came into his office and told him to take the high road and quit. He really thought Rock was some dumb nigger that would just turn tail and run. However, Rock's far from stupid."

Alvin leaned in and continued the story. He noticed that Jolie bent slightly forward to listen. So caught up was she, that he doubted she even knew how close they were becoming. "Now, what I'm about to tell you involves the third reason Rock isn't going anywhere. Two years ago, he signed a guaranteed five-year contract. Unless he quits, he gets $600,000 for the next three years. The university can't afford to fire Rock and hire another quality coach."

About five inches separated their face. "Anyway, after the conversation with the AD, Rock went straight to President Kendal. He assured Rock that he had no intention of letting him go before his contract was up. Apparently, the AD was acting alone. Rock thought it wise not to mention his conversation with the AD, but now he knows in which office his enemy sits. So, to make a long story short, Rock and I aren't going anywhere for the next three years, at least. We've won eight out of twelve this year, and we're undefeated in conference play. If we keep winning, there won't be much the AD can do. He'll have to learn to live with the black folks down the hall."

Jolie's eyes blinked rapidly when she realized how close their faces were. She sat back and said, "Wow, sounds stressful."

Her response surprised him and he laughed.

The sound was infectious and Jolie grinned when she asked, "What's so funny, Alvin?"

His name on her lips sounded superb, a sound he hadn't heard in fifteen years. Alvin pulled himself together and intentionally crossed the line. "Nothing, I just think you're wonderful." He saw the smile melt off her face. "I'm sorry. I know you don't want to hear that."

"Alvin, this is hard enough for me without you making it

personal."

"Why? Why is it so difficult? I know I ended it before, but I was a stupid and scared kid. That first year of college was terrifying. Everybody was somebody all-city, all-county, all-state, hell, all-world. The point is I wasn't the only good player. I came there with a lot to live up to because I was so heavily recruited. I had to prove to myself, and to them, that I deserved the starting position and the acclaim."

Alvin paused and looked into her eyes. Her blank look revealed nothing, one of the rare times when he was unable to read her. "I faltered at first. Nerves got to me and I missed shots, made bad passes, generally made an ass of myself. I lost my spot in the lineup up and panicked. That's why I did what I did. Can you understand that?"

She failed to answer and again her face didn't reveal a thing.

"Can you forgive that?"

Before Jolie could even begin to formulate an answer, they heard the soft rustle of the curtain being moved. "Hey now. Isn't the food good? Y'all aren't eatin.' " Cathy's question reminded them of their meals.

"Oh, it's delicious," Alvin answered. "We've just been talking so much we forgot to eat." Both of them lifted their forks.

"Y'all eat now. It's not as good when it's cold."

The situation was awkward as they both concentrated on the food. His question hung in the air, pressuring Jolie for an answer. His explanation didn't make the past any easier to deal with, and Jolie was irritated that he constantly brought it up. She was here for Tyrese, not to re-hash their unpleasant history. Anger and self-pity had kept her from considering the question before, but now it forced its way to the forefront of her mind. The question vibrated in her temples and tried to force its way to her lips. I was pregnant and miscarried, how do you feel about that? You still want to reconcile with the woman who was almost your baby's momma, but couldn't carry it to term?

She looked at Alvin putting food in his mouth and considered his question. Can I forgive that? A part of her admitted that she had no right answering the somewhat innocently asked question without telling him the whole truth. Shaking her head slightly, she knew she wasn't ready to do that.

Alvin saw the head movement. This time he had more clues to try to interpret her. Emotions showed on her face and through her body language. He could tell she was having some intense conversation in her mind. He knew the issue was them, but he could only guess at the content. His instincts told him that the little headshake didn't bode well for what he wanted.

They finished the scrumptious food, and Cathy brought out a tray of desserts. Jolie's full stomach insisted that she resist until she spied the sweet potato pie. Alvin watched her ogle it. "Go ahead," he encouraged. "Cathy gets the pies from the Pie Man whose real name is Alvin Arnold. You know a guy with my first name must make incredible pies."

"Doesn't that recommendation do it fer ya?" Cathy asked, practically placing the plate under her nose.

"No, I'm really stuffed," she said, although her eyes never left the pie.

"Come on. We can share a piece." He turned to Cathy who had stepped back with the heavy tray. "One slice, two forks please."

"Comin' right up, cher."

"Wait a minute!" Jolie almost shouted, reaching an arm towards Cathy. "Can you cut it into two piece with two forks?"

Cathy's eyes shifted between the two of them. Then she said, "Sure sugah. I'll do that."

§§§

She and Alvin were in the car driving back to his condo when she said, "I'm satisfied with your answers. I guess it's no secret that Ty is dying to go to WAM. His girlfriend is a freshman at South Seattle Community College, and he wants to stay near her. At any rate, I'm not going to stand in his way. I'll do whatever I can to help." She pulled up to his building and held out her gloved hand. The soft fur inside the black leather rubbed her flesh as he moved his large fingers over the back of the glove. "I expect you to watch out for my brother," she said as she pulled away from the warm massage.

Alvin made no move to get out of the car. He kept his

long body angled towards hers in the Volkswagen Jetta. "This is a lot roomier than the bug." He patted his legs.

Jolie laughed, remembering Alvin's knees tucked under his chin. He joined her. When the chuckling eased, Alvin said, "Jolie, I will do everything in my power that I can for Ty, but he has to meet us more than halfway. I won't baby him. It's a tough world out there, and me coddling Ty won't help him grow."

Jolie slowly nodded. "He does have a bit of that to do."

Changing the subject, Alvin asked, "How about a night-cap?"

"No, Alvin."

"So this is it? Sure you're ready for this evening to end?"

Jolie was too tired to take offense. Maybe it was the wine at dinner that was responsible for the relaxed feeling. She glanced at her watch. "It's getting late, and I have work tomorrow. Good night, Alvin."

Clearly he was being dismissed. He chuckled and looked at his own watch. Rather than make a point out of the fact that it was barely six o'clock, he held out his hand. Hesitantly, she met his for a handshake. He flipped his palm up and kissed the back of her gloved hand. "Goodnight, Jolie." He was gone before she recovered. Leather and wool didn't stop the warmth from reaching her skin, making her tingle.

§§§

She'd expected to walk into an empty house, but three pairs of eyes greeted her when she stepped into the living room. As the eyes focused on her longer than necessary, she felt like saying, what?

Tyrese sat on the floor between Robyn's legs. Robyn sat on the couch, and her outstretched hands continue to move in Tyrese's hair as she focused on Jolie. She finished the last braid and then broke the silence by saying, "I'll see you later, honey." She pecked Tyrese's head, rose, and gave Jolie a hug on the way out.

"I'll go, too," Ethel announced. Tyrese got up and helped her out of the armchair and handed her the cane. "I can do it, Ty," she said, yet she left his arm on her elbow as he escorted her out the door to her house.

Jolie yanked off her boots and sank into the couch. Tyrese came back and plopped into the armchair next to her. He broke the silence by saying, "Those two have been fussing at me. They say I need to talk to you and get things straight."

Jolie sighed. "Listen, Ty, I'll make this easy for both of us. I just had dinner with Alvin and I'm satisfied that WAM would be an excellent university for you to attend."

The grin spreading across her brother's face was infectious. It disappeared as suddenly as it appeared. "He probably thinks I'm a punk kid 'cause of how I behaved."

"Ty, I'm not going to lie. You embarrassed everyone with how you acted. Part of being an adult is controlling your temper."

"I know, but why were you so pissed? I was being responsible. I called and told you why I was late."

"I wasn't mad at you, Ty. I appreciated your updates." Jolie was at a loss for words. How could she tell him her anxiety was caused by Alvin, not his lateness? "I was just keyed up because I knew how important this was for you." She stood and pulled him to his feet. "I worry about you, bro. You're the only little brother I have."

He returned her hug. "Don't worry so much, sis. I'm not a stupid kid. In fact, I was never a stupid kid and I'm going to handle my biz."

Geez, I hope that's true. Jolie didn't voice her thoughts.

"Guess what?" Her brother was back to bubbly. Before she could guess, he continued, "I got four scholarship offers in the mail today. Michigan State, Duke, North Carolina, and UCLA all want moi." Thumbs pointed backwards, Ty shouted, "I'm the man, sis!"

Laughing at his antics, Jolie grabbed his arms for another hug. "I'm so happy for you, even if you are turning into a big head. I read the article in the paper today. How does it feel being on the front page of the sports section?"

Ty didn't answer. He was too busy strutting around their small living room taking imaginary jump shots.

"Boy, if you knock something over, I'm going to get you!" Jolie collapsed into a chair and watched his graceful movements.

Ty began singing. "I'm the man and I'm gonna take

care of my family. I'm the man and I'm gonna take care of my family."

Breathing hard, Ty finally spread out on the couch. His stocking feet hung over the edge and he stuck one hand behind his head, causing his elbow to stick out. "I feel good, sis. It's all going to work out."

Jolie nodded. "I know it, Ty. One way or another, I know it will." Then she whispered a silent prayer, asking the Lord that Ty not be like Alvin.

Chapter 7

Six days later, Jolie sat at a nightclub table in the Royal Esquire Club with Joan. Joan raised her wine glass and said, "This is to our young people. I'm so happy Ty committed to WAM."

Jolie's glass lightly tapped hers. "I'm pleased, too. Next year, they'll both be college students. That's an accomplishment!"

"And you'll have an entire house to yourself," Joan's grin was mischievous.

"Girl, if you don't stop. The animals at the zoo get more action than me."

"Only 'cause that's how you want it. Most of the men here tonight have been ogling you."

"Joan, most of these men are old enough to be my granddaddy, it doesn't count!"

Joan hooted and then tapped Jolie's arm, "Look at my husband, girl. He's as happy as pig in slop surrounded by all these old geezers."

Jolie cracked up as she watched Robert, Joan's husband, circulate through the men and women with canes and walkers.

Joan continued fussing. "I told him, let's have dinner

catered and have a nice house party with all our friends for his birthday, but no, he wanted to spend the evening with all these old cronies, his new best friends."

"How in the world did he get a real membership? He's not even retirement age." For a fee, the club offered associate cards, allowing holders to come and dance on weekend nights only. However, the real memberships that gave one voting power were jealously guarded.

"He's fifty-five, the youngest. The club lost seven percent of its real members due to death last year; it decided to let in one new guy, my husband. Rob's late father was a member, so he had an edge. "

"That's a trip. This is a great, safe place to dance. It would be a shame if it disappeared because the people running it died out."

Joan nodded her head. "Did you know the Esquire has been in Seattle since '48? It's fifty-two years old."

"Wow! Has it been a dance place for that long?"

"I think so. It started because black folks didn't have a good place to relax, drink, and socialize back then. So some brothers got together and formed the club in somebody's house. They've only been in this building since '85 though."

Jolie nodded, taking in the environment. Most of the people sat at tables or in booths with vinyl benches. Others leaned against the wooden bar sipping drinks. A few sat around a circular table playing poker. Jolie didn't understand why the big screen in the corner was playing a Kelly Price video. It held as much interest as lint in this crowd.

"Look, Jolie. Here comes Robert to introduce me to another one." They both watched Joan's husband make his way to their table. His hand was at the elbow of an old man using a walker. He appeared to be missing a leg. "Honey," he said when he reached the table, "I want you and Jolie to meet this gentleman, James Grayson. He's one of the founding members of the club." Introductions were made all around, and with Robert's assistance, the man sat at their table. Robert left to get them all drinks.

The man looked at them with a gleam in his eye. "I told your husband to help me get to the beautiful women." The man had to be eighty plus and he was looking them up and down as if he were still full of teenage testosterone. "Well, now. You two sure brighten this place up. How y'all doing this evenin'?"

"We're doing great." Joan answered. "You look pretty dapper yourself in your tux."

"Why thank you young lady. It's nice to get dressed and come out to the club for a special occasion. All the members made it, except two. We used to do this sort of thing all the time, but age has slowed us to a crawl. We no longer meet once month to handle club business. Now we do it once a quarter." James looked at his watch. "Whew, it's already nine o' clock. We only have another hour or so before those youngsters start coming."

"You're not going to stay and shake a leg with me?" Joan flirted.

"Oh, no. You young folk scare me! Shaking all that

stuff, it's a wonder something doesn't fall off."

Jolie and Joan rolled with laughter.

"But we do like the money you young folk are willing to pay two nights out the week!"

After she stopped laughing, Jolie asked, "This is a non-profit club, right? What do you do with the profit?"

"Providing scholarships is the main thing. We also have an Easter egg hunt every year in a Southeast Seattle housing project, and we started the baseball league in the Central District."

Jolie was impressed and it showed in her raised brows.

"See, I bet you thought we old geezers weren't up to much, huh? We've been getting stuff done for fifty-two years, girl!"

Robert returned with a tray of drinks. "Ahem," he said as he handed the glasses around. James got a gin and tonic, while Jolie and Joan enjoyed red wine.

Just then, a bartender walked up holding a cake with two burning candles shaped like number fives. The tops of the fives were beginning to melt by the time all the people manage to gather. "Do we have to sing the song?" James asked. Looking at Jolie, he explained, "None of us can sing. We sound like a bunch of boys in the middle of the voice change!" Everyone chuckled and ignoring James' protest, they started a lively rendition of the birthday song. Jolie resisted the urge to cover her ears as James' prediction came to life.

"That man ain't never lied. These folks should be

banned from singing," Joan whispered. Jolie was in full agreement. However, the quality of the singing had no effect on Robert. He stood up straight and smiled so broadly that his cheeks were pushed into his eyes. She'd never seen the usually quiet man so animated.

☙☙☙

By ten-thirty, the party had pretty much broken up and most of real members had fled before the associate card holders flooded the club. James had left an hour ago and a married couple named Connie and Jim now sat with them. Sitting between the two established couples, Jolie felt like a large third wheel.

The club was coming alive as throngs of people strode in, proud as peacocks, dressed in all their finery. Jolie felt anxious and was about to voice her intention to leave. The problem wasn't the club, per se. To the contrary, she enjoyed dancing to near exhaustion. The difficulty was Paul, her ex-boyfriend. He loved the Esquire because the security was tight. Lots of officers patrolled the interior and exterior constantly. Paul also liked the size of the club. It sported two dance floors. One played hip-hop and rap that drew a younger hipper crowd, and the other featured old school and classic soul, which attracted people thirty-five and up. That was the side where Jolie now sat.

Paul always said it was like partying with everyone in the family: The old folks in one section and the kids in the back. He got a kick out of how the club managed to cater to both. In order to keep the peace, a big elongated room that had a bar and an area to take pictures kept the divergent dance floors from each other. The strangely-shaped room attracted people in its own right. Well-dressed couples and singles would crowd around the popular picture area, waiting for their turn to sit in the wicker fan chair, which sat in front of a wall size mural of Tupac. At the top of Tupac was a large curtain to cover him for those who didn't want him glaring from behind in the photo.

"Joan, I'm about to go." She thought she was whispering, but when everyone except Robert said, "Oh no, you can't go, we're going to dance tonight," she knew how loudly she must have spoken.

Joan grabbed her hand and put it in Robert's. "Dance with Rob while I visit the little girl's room."

Robert kind of nodded and pulled her up. The other couple decided to join them on the floor. Trapped, Jolie let Robert lead her to the dance floor. Dancing with him did little to ease her tension. He kept staring at her, but there was nothing sexual in his scrutiny. To the contrary, it made her feel as if she were the unfortunate frog in a high school science lab being picked apart underneath a large microscope. The song ended and he led her back to the table, while Connie and Jim kept dancing. As they sat, Joan yelled and waved at them from across the room. She was sitting and talking to a couple of women. Jolie sat down, expecting a weird, awkward silence. She was about to excuse herself and go anywhere when Robert spoke. It startled her so much, she jumped a little.

"You know, I blamed you when this whole mess began."

Jolie sat back and looked at him. He studied his nails as if he hadn't just spoken to her directly for the first time in months.

Robert picked something from beneath a nail, and said, "It's my birthday, I've indulged in some of my favorite Scotch, and I guess I feel entitled to express myself since my wife is determined to maintain a friendship with you. My daughter has so much potential, and now it's ruined. I blame the boy and the moralless woman who is caring for him."

Funny how the brain picks silly things to focus on when one is under attack, Jolie thought. She wondered if moralless was a word. She felt like yelling, if you're going to say bad things about my brother and me, at least use proper English and don't speak about me in the third person.

Robert's fingers brushed against his lapel. "You've been quite a disruption in my household. It seems my women can accept that I don't like the boy; however, they feel I'm being unfair to you."

Although she was no longer a third person, he was making Jolie nervous and she began to wiggle in her chair.

"I just can't help thinking that if the boy had stayed with his father, this ugly mess would have been avoided. That's the problem with our youth today, you women are not equipped to raise men."

Jolie stopped fidgeting. How dare he! I wouldn't be handling this situation alone if a man, my father, was doing what he was supposed to be doing. Doesn't this fool know that most black women are strong because they have to be? We are constantly being put in situations where we have to step up! Jolie fired at Robert, "Robyn has a father, and a wonderful mother too, and she's managed to be a part of this situation, not mess. I guess having a father figure in her life didn't solve everything."

His head snapped up and he looked at her. "You need to stop looking for someone to blame, unless you want to look in the mirror, and aim some of that crap at yourself," Jolie added.

Robert's look was becoming a glare. Jolie could have cared less.

"What's happened has happened. We need to stop finding fault and focus on both of them moving forward with their lives." Jolie was fuming. She took a large gulp from Joan's water glass. She knew her friend wouldn't mind. When the water was gone, she munched on the ice. I need to just leave, she told herself. But she valued her friendship with Joan and wanted to avoid offending her. She knew leaving without saying goodbye would hurt her feelings.

"Would you like to dance?"

Jolie didn't even look towards the masculine voice. She just accepted the offer to get away from Robert. She hesitated when she stood and saw Paul. He looked as good as ever: tall, clean cut, and in a full suit. She followed him to the dance floor but pushed him away when he moved to take her in his arms.

"Jolie, lighten up. It's a slow song."

She allowed him to pull her into an embrace, mentally fussing the whole time for being too distracted and allowing herself to be put near this man, a place she'd sworn she'd never be again.

Jolie remained stiff and mute. Half the song was over before he spoke. "How's your brother?"

She answered, "Ty's doing great and so am I."

She knew where he was going with the question. They had lived together about six months before the Compton incident. He didn't like sharing her with Tyrese and had issued an ultimatum. Send her brother back to California or he'd leave. Tyrese had won hands down, and it was easy to tell Paul to take a hike. Every once in a while, he called to see how she was doing, or so he claimed. Jolie knew his real reason was to see if she was having second thoughts about her decision.

About three years ago, he'd caught her at a weak moment. She hadn't been with anyone since they'd ended their relationship a year prior. Jolie had looked into his handsome nut-brown face and found herself caught up in the sweet words flowing from his lips. She'd gone with the current and wound up in his apartment physically satisfied. Hesitant because she'd never spent the night away from Tyrese, she was debating whether to force her exhausted body to get up and go home or just call Tyrese and make some excuse.   When Paul opened his mouth and made the decision easy.

"So when does he leave, so we can get back together?"

Jolie was out of the bed almost before he finished the sentence.   She'd done her best to avoid him ever since. Their paths had crossed three times and each of those times, he was like a purring cat, trying to rub up against her leg.

"He's a senior now, isn't he?"   Paul asked.

Jolie was irritated.   "Paul, why do you ask?   It's been four years.   Haven't you found someone else?"

"Yeah, actually I have.   She's not here tonight."   He leaned away and looked down, "But you look good in your open toe heels and bare shoulders.   And that little front slit in your long skirt is treacherous.   I bet more than one brother tonight will go home with neck strain from trying to get a glimpse of your legs."

Oh God, he made her want to change clothes.

"Makes me have second thoughts."

"It's too late for that."

"Ahh, Jolie.   We were good together before you became a single parent.   Who knows, maybe we could be that way again."

"Not on your life," Jolie muttered.   "I've seen your true colors and I recognize them."   Paul had turned into a different person with just the thought of her brother coming to live with her.   He was way too self-centered for her taste.

Paul's breath whispering across her ear as he spoke made her want to slap him.   "Did you say something?"

Jolie leaned away slightly and said, "Look, Paul. If you want to finish this dance, let's not talk, okay?"

Jolie's eyes shifted up and sideways, and what she saw almost made her faint. Paul hugged her closer, assuming God knows what when she slumped against him after she momentarily lost her step. Alvin sat at their table. The way he was positioned in the middle, between Joan and Connie, gave him an excellent view of the dance floor and her. His eyes bore into hers. Jolie felt as if everyone else had been zapped away and there was only this laser beam connection between them. The intensity of it had her gasping. Tight arms squeezing had her struggling for a different reason. The steely, unwanted grip reminded her of where she was and whom she was with.

"Now that's what I'm talking about." Paul snuggled in even closer.

The song ending and Jolie pushing away happened simultaneously. The DJ mixed in another slow song, and Paul tried to hold on to her fingers. "Let's go for two, Jolie."

She didn't even look at him when she lifted her hand in the general direction of his face and said, "No." As she and Alvin's eyes did battle, she contemplated leaving without going to the table. She loved Joan like a sister, but she could explain later. Alvin must have read her mind because he slowly shook his head from side to side. He beckoned with a wiggling forefinger. The others didn't seem to notice as he reeled her in. She stiffly made her way among the patrons, tables, and chairs. Just as she arrived, Alvin stood, walked around the table, and moved the only empty seat back.

"Thank you." Jolie sat down.

She was sitting in between Robert and Jim, which was directly across from where Alvin sat. The placement couldn't have been better, according to Alvin.

No one seemed to notice the tension between them. Probably because Connie was talking non-stop. She paused a minute to acknowledge Jolie and then continued. "And I just couldn't believe it when Alvin actually called. Junior didn't believe me when I called him to come to the phone." Connie circled Alvin's arm with both hands and squeezed when he sat back down. He smiled at Connie.

The pang was automatic and unwanted. Jolie wanted to pinch herself for reacting when a woman two times Alvin's age grabbed his arm.

"Oh, Jolie, you missed the first part of the story." The large woman took a deep breath. "About six years ago, we were really worried about our grandson, Junior. We raised him, and he was starting to hang out with the wrong crowd, you know?"

Jolie nodded as if she knew. She'd never heard of the boy, much less met him.

"I was so worried and I didn't know what to do. Jim," she looked adoringly at her husband, "suggested we write to Alvin. Junior played basketball, and he idolized Alvin because Alvin had gone to his high school and he'd made it." Another deep breath. "Imagine our surprise when he called and asked to speak to Junior."

All eyes turned to Alvin. He shrugged. "The letter touched me."

"He spoke to Junior for an hour. Junior's eyes were so big. He couldn't believe an NBA player was talking to him on the phone. He almost fainted when Alvin sent him tickets when his team played the Sonics. He met Junior in person and introduced him to the other players. Let me tell you, we didn't have any more problems with Junior."

"What?" her husband interrupted.

Connie laughed. "I stand corrected. We didn't have problems with him running with the wrong crowd. We still had to fight the battle about school and girls for a few years."

"How is he?" Alvin asked. "The last letter I got from him was over two years ago."

"He's doing great. He lives in Arizona and works for a construction company out there. He spent a couple of years in the Army, and married a woman he met in Japan. That was an adjustment! You know, my husband and I didn't believe in that marrying outside the race, but we're trying to be open. Having grandkids helps."

"I'm glad he's doing well," Alvin said.

Jolie was more uncomfortable now that Connie's monologue had wound down. It was much easier to hate someone from afar. When you discovered some good in that person, it caused irritating second thoughts. Well, she didn't want to second-guess herself. Alvin had dumped her when she needed him most. That was the important thing, not how good he'd been to Connie's grandson. Jolie's thoughts only made her more anxious. To keep from fidgeting, she clasped her hands together in her lap. What I need is an exit plan, she thought. The problem was she was too frazzled to think of one.

Alvin took a sip of his mineral water and watched Jolie. Rock was on the other side of the club with his wife Latisha. He knew they were probably curious about where he was. Earlier in the evening, when he'd driven his recently repaired car to the Softli house to enjoy a home-cooked meal, Latisha had asked him to go to the club. Rock worked long, hard hours during basketball season, but he did his best to maintain the balance he always preached about. He told Alvin he was taking his wife dancing to remind her how special she was, and he wanted him to join them.

Once Alvin knew the purpose of the night out, he had no intention of going, but Latisha had had other ideas. It was strange, but he and his best friend's wife had always had this connection. She'd look at him with her soft, caring eyes and knew that something was bothering him. His mood hadn't been quite right since Jolie had reentered his life. Rather than pester him to open up, she teased him about being by himself too much and told him that his head was going to turn into a basketball if he didn't find other interests in life.

"Oh, he's coming out with us," Latisha told her husband with a nod. "He owes me a dance for all the steak he ate this afternoon."

Laughing, Alvin said, "That's all? The food was delicious, as usual. Shouldn't I have to pay for the cover and a few drinks as well?"

They all had laughed and no further discussion was needed. It was decided that he'd join them at the Royal Esquire.

So here he sat across from the object of his desire with a sour taste still resonating in his mouth from having to endure watching her being crushed to another man's chest. Logically, he knew he had no claim over Jolie. However, that didn't stop jealousy from vibrating through him. It burned so much that he couldn't take a deep breath. He breathed shallowly and managed to nod when appropriate as Connie raved about him.

Another slow song came on, interrupting Alvin's thoughts. He looked at Jolie and caught her eyes. He arched one dark eyebrow. He wanted what she'd given to the other man. He needed to feel her body pressed close to his. He craved to be only inches away from those exposed shoulders.

Jolie didn't need words to know what he was asking. She quickly shook her head and lowered her eyes. She felt relieved when Alvin stood, assuming he was finally leaving. Her heart sank to her feet when he rounded the table and stretched out his hand.

Joan reached across the table and patted her hand. "Go on, girl. The man's asking you to dance!"

It was on the tip of her tongue to say, "I don't slow dance," but she knew how idiotic that would sound after her dance with Paul. Sighing heavily, she avoided his hand and stood. For his ears alone, she said, "Only one, okay?"

He didn't acknowledge her question. He just led the way to the floor with a hand at her back and took her in his arms. She kept her body stiff and a little away from his. Out of respect, Alvin immediately loosened his hold until his hands only lightly cupped her hips. Jolie's fingers were barely brushing his upper arms.

He didn't waste time voicing what was on his mind. "All right, let's see. I know he wasn't your man or he would have returned to the table with you instead of staring longingly when you showed him the hand. But obviously he wants to mean something to you because he's standing at the edge of the dance floor glaring at us."

Jolie whipped her head around and saw Paul standing just off to the side with a drink in his hand.

"He just wants to have his cake and eat it too."

Alvin chuckled, thinking there were several ways he could respond to that. He chose to say, "If you're the cake in that metaphor, he's not the only one who wants to eat you." He didn't have to see her face to know she blushed. He felt it in the little hiss of breath and the momentary misstep.

Then she surprised both of them by laughing. "You're incorrigible, you know?"

"Incorrigible!" He leaned away from her and looked into her face. "Lucky for you I paid attention in college. I know what words like incorrigible and Svengali mean now."

She smiled at his reference to their earlier days.

"Or did you say adorable instead of incorrigible? Here I thought you were insulting me when you were really trying to sweettalk me!"

He was being silly and despite herself, Jolie loved it. The top of her head rested against his cheek as she found herself relaxing into the softness of his buttoned silk shirt, just enjoying the moment. She was very clear about that. The moment, not the dance. In fact, the annoying lemony smell of his aftershave tickled her nose and annoyed her. The body heat that drifted from his cheek to her forehead made her hot and sticky. No way was she finding the situation pleasurable. She just grinned and laughed at his silly comments and made herself endure it. At least that's how she justified allowing his arms to pull her even closer.

Oh, but her body was treacherous! It remembered how it felt to groove with Alvin, and it completely ignored her brain. The moment and her body were a lethal combination, and Jolie blamed them when she realized her arms were linked securely around Alvin's waist, and his were wrapped around her shoulders. The combination had her so distracted that she didn't notice when the slow song glided into another. The only thing that brought her back was his removing himself from her body. The spell was dissipating and her brain took over. "I have to go."

He looked at her funny. One minute she's laughing and holding me tight, and next she acts like an anxious rabbit? "Okay Cinderella, just let me say 'bye to my friends and I'll walk you to your car. Don't worry. We still have fifteen minutes until midnight, so you won't turn into a frog." He knew she would say no, so he whirled around and left before she could get the word out.

Jolie said quick goodbyes to the others and headed to the coat-check to retrieve her jacket. "Excuse me," Joan whispered to the table as she rushed after her. She caught up with her at the counter.

"Girl, if I didn't know better, I would happen to guess that you're rushing out to be with that hunk of a man. No self breast examination for you tonight!"

Jolie took the time to chuckle as she signaled the coat check woman to hurry up. "No way. I'm trying to get out of here before he comes back."

"I know I've been married a long time and things may have changed, but I don't get it. He's gorgeous, and he's wearing the hell out of that silk shirt and brown slacks. According to Connie, he's right up there with Gandhi when it comes to goodness. What in the world could be the problem?"

Jolie retrieved her coat and slipped it on. "I knew him before and it didn't work out. Like my mother used to say, 'I'm looking for a darker berry on a higher bush.' "

"Well shoot, Jolie. That brother is a beautiful, deep, polished brown. If he were any more chocolate, you wouldn't be able to see him at night unless he smiled! And if he were any taller, you could call the carnival or the Guinness Book of World records!"

"Very funny, Joan."

"Wait a minute!" Joan put her forefinger to her lip. "This guy is tall, dark, and handsome. I'm sure my daughter would think he's ancient. Is this the guy Robyn was talking about? The one she said she saw you with at the game?"

Jolie looked around furtively as she tried to get by Joan who practically had her pinned against the counter. "Yes." Jolie didn't elaborate. Joan stepped back and Jolie would have raced to the exit, but another obstacle presented itself before she could take ten steps.

"Hi, Jolie. You weren't going to leave without saying 'bye," Paul said.

She felt Joan come and stand beside her. Her presence prevented Jolie from being as rude as she wanted to be. "Paul, this is Joan. Joan, Paul." The two exchanged pleasantries. "Ah, Paul..." She couldn't get 'it was nice seeing you' past her throat, so she said, "Take care of yourself, Joan, I'll see you later."

"Wait!" Joan grabbed her arm. She waved at someone with her other hand and pointed at Jolie. When Jolie saw Alvin striding over confidently, her foot inched forward as she fought really hard against the urge to kick her.

"No, no, no," Joan wagged her finger. Then she leaned forward and whispered in Jolie's ear. "At least let the man escort you to your car. Any neighborhood is rough this time of night."

With a strangled groan, Jolie spun and headed to the door. Paul was forgotten as she rushed away. By the time she reached the exit, Alvin was at her side. She glanced sideways. "Where's your coat? It's freezing out here."

"Someone was in such a rush that I didn't have time to get it from the coat check."

Disregarding that comment, Jolie said, "It's rags and pumpkin, not a frog." They were crossing the street to her car. Alvin stopped her from opening it by placing his body against the door.

"What?"

Jolie patiently explained. "At midnight, Cinderella's beautiful gown became rags, and her carriage became a pumpkin. The frog is part of the Prince Charming fairy tale."

"Oh, now I get it." Alvin crossed his legs and appeared to be quite comfortable against her car door, despite the cold. "Sorry I got it wrong. What I meant to say is that I'm a prince masquerading as a frog. Why don't you kiss me and we can live happily ever after."

She rolled her eyes and put the hand with the key on her hip. The other clutched her hanging purse. "I tried that about fifteen years ago, remember? It didn't work. I kissed you many times and you went from a frog to a toad. You let go of my hand."

The comment cut him to the quick, but he kept up the teasing attitude. "I'm an older, wiser toad now. The process is a lot quicker. One flick of your tongue and I'll be a prince forever."

The barest of smiles breezed past her lips and eyes.

"I know, I know," he said as he straightened. He moved away from the door, deciding not to test his luck beyond her limits. "I'm adorable, right?"

"No. You're annoying," she said as she opened the car door and slipped inside. Once she was driving away, she whispered, "Annoying because I'm responding to you and that's the last thing I want."

Chapter 8

When she got home, she found Tyrese asleep on the couch. She pushed until he woke up and she told him to go to bed. As he shuffled down the hall, he said, "Oh yeah, Dad sent a box addressed to you. I put it on the kitchen table."

Jolie changed into nightclothes and then walked into the kitchen to look at the cardboard box. She lifted it to test the weight. Despite the late hour, she wasn't sleepy. The scene with Alvin had her feeling awake in too many places. Jolie gazed at the box. Going through her mother's things had been painful enough years ago. She wasn't looking forward to repeating the process. The box was about eight inches across and light, but awkward. Something loose inside banged as she shifted it. Her father had duct taped the box well, forcing Jolie to get a steak knife to slice it open. Once she'd sawed through, she tore the top flaps apart. A faint, musty smell drifted up, tickling her nose, and the slight, powdery dust made her sneeze. Jolie realized her assumption that her father had sealed the box was incorrect. Her mother had probably closed it many years ago.

Peering inside, Jolie could see a Converse shoebox resting on its side. She lifted it out, wiped it off with a napkin, and carried it into her bedroom. Jolie sat on her bed and lifted the cover. A Ziploc bag full of gray stuff immediately caught her attention. She turned the heavy bag over and saw a white label that read, "Mount Saint Helen. Erupted May 18. Bagged May 21, 1980." She recognized her own writing, and smiled, remembering the day the souvenir had been collected.

Her family had been in Spokane, Washington, visiting friends when the mountain lost its top early one Sunday morning, preventing them from going to church. One of many earthquakes had struck a mile below the surface, and the battered mountain gave in, releasing the largest landside in recorded history. As the north face slid away, trapped gasses popped out of the earth's crust as if from a well-shaken bottle of pop. A big ash cloud rushed from the mountain and was blown east. Spokane, at the very edge of eastern Washington, was showered with the yucky gray stuff that had turned the day into a purple- colored night. The city had received much more volcanic debris than Seattle, which was surprising because the Emerald City was much closer to the volcano.

Everyone speculated wildly about the effects of the ash on the human body, so the adults pow-wowed and decided to barricade everybody indoors. The family they were visiting didn't have children and Tyrese hadn't been born yet. Jolie recalled being bored to mischievousness, the adults' patience running thin with her and each other, and the depleting food supply. Jolie had shouted for joy and danced a jig when her mother finally announced it was safe to venture out after about three days of cabin fever.

Despite Jolie's protest, her mother had still made her wear long sleeves, pants, gloves, and a handkerchief worn gangster style, covering her lower face with the knot tied at the back of her head. The dull gray stuff piled everywhere had drawn Jolie's attention as if she were a wiggly puppy sniffing around a beehive. She couldn't resist sneaking off the yellow dishwater gloves to touch the strange stuff that was causing such a fuss. She rubbed it between her thumb and forefinger and watched it gum into dirt. Lifting it to her nose, she sniffed. It smelled like dirt. She was about to give it the final test with the tip of her tongue when her mother yelled at her to put the glove back on. Now, Jolie turned the bag over in her hands, smirking at the memory.

She put the baggy back and flinched a little when the edges of two pieces of typing paper folded together grazed her skin. Tears came to her eyes after she unfolded the sheets. On one piece she read her mother's long, spindly writing, "Jolie 1st grade." It was a picture of a flower composed of one large circle surrounded by smaller circles and a scribbled stem. Underneath the flower, she'd written, "I luv u." The other picture also had her mother's writing in the corner, "Tyrese 1st grade." Her brother had drawn some kind of futuristic monster that had a body like a cucumber and a million legs. In the monster's body was scrawled, "four momy lov you."

Jolie rushed down the hall, wiping tears from her eyes.

She burst into Tyrese's room to find him sprawled out and asleep. She wrestled with the desire to wake him and share her precious find. Deciding against it, she clutched the pictures in her hand and went back to her room.

Jolie sat back on the bed and pulled the other items out of the box. There were two stacks of letters. The rubber band holding one of the stacks snapped from brittleness. She opened a letter from that stack first, and recognized her father's handwriting. If it weren't so brief, she might have mistaken it for a love letter. All it said was, "I'm doing fine. Work is okay. I love you." All the letters were equally short. Her parents had had a six-month long distance romance before they were married. Obviously, her mother had treasured each and every correspondence.

The other stack of letters was not from her father. Jolie was totally taken aback when she saw Alvin's handwriting. Alarm rushed up and down her nervous system, making her hands jerk as she handled one of the letters. Although the faded postmark was difficult to read, Jolie was able to determine that the letter had been mailed sometime in the eighties. "What the hell?" she whispered. There was a small note taped to the backside of the envelope. Again, she recognized her mother's writing. It read, "I know you'll find these one day. I couldn't throw them away. Hopefully, by the time you see these, you will have kids of your own, and understand why I hid them and didn't allow any contact." It was signed, "I love you, Mom." A weird numbness filled Jolie as she ripped open the envelope and read the one page note.

Baby, I'm so sorry. I was temporarily insane. I love you and I need you.

It's hard for me to explain how it is up here, but it's hard, baby. I didn't expect this and I panicked, and I dropped the most precious thing in my life.

Can you understand and forgive me, baby? I lie in my dorm at night and stare at the ceiling and all I see is your beautiful face. I hear your wonderful laugh, and I smile. Then I ache because I know we aren't together. Please let me come back and hold your hand. I'm cold and alone without you.

$$\text{\$\$\$}$$

Jolie quickly ripped open all the letters, discovering similar content. After she read the last one, she said, "Oh shit!" Then she lay back and cried harder than she'd cried at her mother's funeral. She hadn't sobbed so hard since she'd lost her child. "How in the hell am I supposed to take this?" she asked the empty room. "Why did you hide this from me, Momma?" Jolie asked the question, but she already knew the answer. She'd been ripped down by the pregnancy and the aftereffects.

When she'd first realized her condition after using the home pregnancy kit she'd bought at the drug store, she'd slipped to the floor and cried for it not to be true. Her mother had always told her to be careful what she wished for. She should have heeded that wise woman's advice because when she lost the child, she'd felt such gut-wrenching guilt she'd wanted to die.

She couldn't lie; at first she'd felt relief. The only persons who knew were her parents. Even though she had been in her fifth month, she was barely showing, so her reputation and life could continue on as before. But then the gravity of what had taken place had begun to settle upon her. She hadn't dodged a bullet; she'd lost a life that was a part of her. Guilt convinced her that bad thoughts had made her lose the baby. What right did she have to reject a gift from God? She started crying every time she saw a baby in a magazine, on TV, in a mother's arms. She became so morose that even her father became concerned. She'd overheard her mother telling him, "She just needs time. She'll be fine in a couple of months."

Her mother had constantly tried to help by telling her that thoughts don't cause miscarriages or else there wouldn't be any teenage pregnancy, and that certainly wasn't true. She'd told Jolie that maybe something was wrong and this was nature's way of solving it. At times, her mother's words sank in, and she'd stop focusing on herself and shift to Alvin. This always caused cold fury. She had read somewhere that stress could cause miscarriages. Maybe if she hadn't been dealing with the pain of being dumped, she'd have kept her baby.

Jolie remembered that all this stuff floating around in her head had made her an emotional wreck, and she knew that's why her mother had kept Alvin away. She'd loved him with all her heart and soul, and she knew he'd felt the same way. For weeks after he left, she'd waited for him to make contact. Waited to tell him about her condition. The weeks had become months, and the months, years. Then he'd sent a letter to her. Now she knew that hadn't been the first, but by that time, her yearning had disappeared. Anger was the only thing left. She hadn't wanted a thing to do with him, so she'd sent the letter back unopened. She'd ignored him when he popped up at her mother's funeral, and she'd hung up when he'd called. Jolie lowered her head and wondered how it would have been if her mother hadn't gone into guard dog mode. Would she and Alvin be together right now?

The phone rang, interrupting her thoughts. She reached to her nightstand and managed to croak out a hello.

"Hi." Alvin's warm voice reached in and touched her soul. "I was just calling to make sure you made it home okay."

Jolie was speechless, fighting desperately to keep the torrent of tears from starting again.

"Hey, Jolie? Are you there?"

She didn't know what to say or do. He'd called when she was too raw. Her emotions were too close to the surface for friendly conversation.

"Jolie, are you all right?" No answer. "Jolie, if you don't talk to me, I'm coming over right now."

The click came before she managed to yell, "No!" The sound of her heart pounding made it difficult to think. She lay back on the bed and prayed to God for serenity and wisdom.

$$\text{\cite{}}\cite{}\cite{}$$

She's being kidnapped; no, she's being held prisoner, or maybe she's sick and close to death. No, more than likely, it's her brother. They've fought and he's done something crazy. Or maybe it's her brother's girl, complications with the pregnancy. All sorts of thoughts went through Alvin's head as he rushed to his car to drive to Jolie's. Tomorrow was the start of a four-day road trip. The team was traveling to Oregon to play the three major Universities there. If he didn't see Jolie now, he wouldn't be able to for several days.

His imagination caused him much agony before he finally pulled up to her modest house on Beacon Hill. The homes that formed the street were indistinguishable except for color. He hopped out and ran up the two steps to the front door. It opened just as he was about to beat his knuckles against the varnished wood. Alvin wanted to grab her and hold her in his arms. He needed her body heat to soothe his worried soul. Instead, he said, "Are you okay?"

She nodded. He looked closer and noticed the red eyes, the tear tracks, the disheveled dark red hair. He hadn't seen it that mussed since they'd last made love. A pang thumped through him. Her clothing didn't help the situation. She wore a skimpy orange tank top over loose fitting but drapey light blue pants. The outfit left little to the imagination, and Alvin found himself shifting his feet for reasons other than the cold.

Jolie stepped out on the landing and closed the door behind her. It was clear to him that she had no intention of letting him inside. She rubbed her hands together nervously. Why aren't you chattering, Jolie? That's what you usually do when something is wrong. He was determined to discover what had caused her present state.

"May I come in?"

She shook her head.

He smiled and leaned forward a little. "Jolie, it's cold out here, and I'm not leaving until I'm sure you're all right." She looked in his eyes and quickly glanced away. Then she backed up, opening the door as she moved. He took it as an invitation and followed her inside.

Jolie glanced at him looking around. Her father had helped her with the down payment after Tyrese came to live with her. Guilt money, but she'd taken it. A house wasn't in her near future on a zoo keeper's salary, so when her father offered, she'd gladly accepted. They stood in the living room, and through an open doorway to the right, a small kitchen could be seen. A dark hallway led to the bathroom and two bedrooms. Jolie sat down on one of the armchairs that flanked the couch. She imagined how he saw her small, tidy house as tight as a ship's quarters.

Alvin continued standing, and then he finally said, "Wow!" The smallness and inexpensive furniture were lost on him because he so was enchanted by the other decorations. They gave the place flair and pizzazz. "You have so many different things in here and yet, it all seems to fit."

Jolie laughed. "I prefer to think of it as eclectic. I helped to lead expeditions to Africa three times. On the way back, I always stopped in Europe for a week or two. These items reflect my travels."

Alvin nodded. He liked the sparkle in her eye as she looked at her living room with him. "What's from where?"

Jolie pointed as she spoke. "The batiks and masks are from Kenya and South Africa. The statue of the naked, white guy is David about to throw a stone at Goliath. I got that in Italy, and that's where I got the Pieta, as well. That's the statue of Mary holding the dead Jesus in her arms. The multicolored vases are Venetian glass from Venice, and the money set in stone is a lucky coin from Ireland."

Alvin sat on the side of the couch nearest Jolie's chair. "I like it, Jolie. It's so you."

Jolie whispered, "Thanks." She was distracted. His stretched-out legs were very close to her crossed ones. She resisted the urge to move nearer to him. She was so used to hating him. Now that she'd read the letter, it seemed as if her body were ready to give in and say, Have your way with me. Her mind vehemently rejected the notion. He still had too much power to hurt her. She angled her legs away. The small movement wasn't lost on Alvin.

"How'd you know where I live?"

"I followed you when you took off like a bat out of hell

that day from Philadelphia Fevre."

Jolie stared at him wide eyed. The fact that he'd followed her was a shocker, but she was even more astonished that she hadn't had a clue.

"I was right behind you the whole time, and I watched you go into the house. I just wanted to make sure you were safe." After he'd seen her disappear inside, he'd parked, intending to knock on the door and tell her it was okay. He'd taken the keys out of the ignition and had a finger on the handle when he thought better of it. He knew she was safe and she probably needed some space.

She sighed and looked him in the eyes. "Alvin, what is it? Why do you still care? I'm not the same person I was fifteen years ago."

He leaned forward and crossed his large hands between his knees. Jolie looked at the long, slim fingers. If he straightened one out, both of them knew he could stroke her leg, and perhaps more.

"We all change, Jolie. I'm not an insecure boy anymore. I can look at you," his smoldering eyes jump-started her heart and a few other organs, "and tell you're still a good person."

"What? Do you have x-ray vision?" Oh God, why did she say that? His eyes became more focused as they traveled her body.

"I wish I did have the power to see all, but more importantly, I wish you could read my mind. Then you could see my sincerity."

Jolie closed her eyes, then opened and slowly rolled them.

He was happy to see the fire back. That meant that whatever was bugging her couldn't be that awful. He continued to try to convince her. "If you want me to give you an example, I have plenty. Your goodness shows in how you care for Ty, and your wit and intelligence shine, a little too much, in how you're always dissing me. Your independence is there in what you've accomplished, achieving your dreams and working with animals. You ask why I still care, and my response is, isn't it obvious?" Alvin waved his outstretched hand. "And besides all that, I adore your…quirkiness, for lack of a better word. Look at this place, Jolie. You take all this stuff that doesn't fit and turn it into art! It takes a special woman to do that. A woman I want to spend time with."

Jolie took a deep breath. She'd made a decision. Maybe if she'd had more time to reflect upon her mother's actions, her decision would've been different. But as she sat there looking at him, trying not to respond to the puppy love she saw in his eyes, she knew she couldn't take it anymore. Jolie was a nanosecond away from throwing hesitation out the window and letting this man back into her life on an intimate basis. But if she let that happen, he had to know the complete truth.

"Stay here. I'll be right back."

Alvin watched her disappear down the hall. She came back and tossed an old, small pad in his lap. "Go ahead.

Look at it. I haven't been able to sketch since I did these."

Alvin leafed through the yellowing pages completely confused. "What are these? Sketches of Tyrese when he was a baby?" Then he came to the last one where there was a picture of what looked like an explosion. "I don't get it, Jolie."

She had returned to her chair where she'd grabbed a leopard print pillow that she held against her chest. "It was hard to imagine what our child would look like. I tried to take features from each of us and mix and match them. I still wonder if any of those," she pointed at the pad, "were close."

Alvin dropped the pad on his legs. "Pregnant! Are you trying to tell me that you had a baby?" Alvin wanted to rewind this whole conversation. Did he hear her correctly? He was a father!"

"Lower your voice. Tyrese is sleeping back there. This is none of his business."

Alvin sat back, hands on knees. "Jolie, did you or did you not have my baby?"

"I was pregnant. I didn't have the baby."

He wanted to scream, yell, and shake the heck out of her. "You…you aborted my, my child with…without telling me?" His voice was very low, and his fingertips were a weird combination of red and white because of the death grip he had on his knees.

The accusation pissed her off. "What the hell do you care? I was going to tell you when you came home that last time, but you couldn't wait to break up with me. Couldn't wait to let go of my hand. I wasn't going to tell you after you'd dumped me." She got up and went to the door. "This conversation is over. Get out."

"What! You drop a bombshell like that and...and expect me to just leave!"

"Ssshhhhhh!" She hissed at him with finger to lip. Tyrese was a hard sleeper, however, she didn't want to take any chances. She broke out in a cold sweat just thinking of trying to explain this mess to him.

Alvin stood also. He put his hands on his hips, angled his head upwards, and closed his eyes. Taking deep breaths, he drew lots of air in to fill up his lungs. Then he slowly exhaled. He repeated the process about five times before he looked at Jolie standing by the open door. "This conversation isn't over. We can take a half-time break, but no way is it over." He walked past her and out the door.

"Alvin."

He stopped on the porch and stood looking down on her while she leaned against the doorjamb.

"I miscarried. I would never have an abortion."

She shut the door before he completely understood. He felt like putting his hand up and calling time-out. All this was happening too fast for him, as if his head were spinning around in a dryer and there wasn't an off button. Questions were forming and only Jolie knew the answers, but there was already a closed door between them, shutting him out. He turned and put his right hand on the rail. Suddenly, his knee ached. He slowly made his way down the steps.

Jolie watched him from the curtains covering the living room window. Sadness filled her as she saw him stagger to his car. He sat in it awhile before driving off.

"That went well," she whispered. Tired of crying and completely drained, she picked up the pad from the floor and went to her room. As she prepared for bed on automatic, another thought crossed her mind. Out loud, she said, "I will kill him if he lets this situation affect Ty." The idea of it, along with everything else, made sleep very difficult.

Chapter 9

Unsettled didn't even begin to explain how Alvin felt during his three-game road trip. He left the morning after the scene with Jolie, and he functioned in a fog that refused to lift even though the team was winning. He fought hard against the mist and managed to stay focused enough to do and say the right things. However, every once in a while, he'd be hit by a disjointed thought: Jolie pregnant, abortion, my child lost, miscarriage. The words or phrases would come out of nowhere and almost floor him. The random thoughts were like sharp pinches in his heart, head, and stomach. Just like someone had taken his flesh in between their finger and thumb and twisted viciously. The experiences were usually brief, but extremely unsettling.

The most recent had occurred while the squad was having dinner before the third and final game on the road trip. Alvin had just come back from being disoriented to find Rock looking at him strangely. As he asked Rock if he'd said something, it occurred to him what was happening. Flashbacks! The term seemed appropriate, considering that Jolie had dropped a hell of a bomb on him. At least now, the fifteen-year cold shoulder made sense. Somehow, he preferred the confusion. The truth was much more horrible.

"I asked if you were okay, dog." Rock pointed at his plate. "You haven't touched your food."

Alvin looked down. They were having the same dinner as the team. A specially prepared meal to fuel the well-tuned, athletic bodies. Glancing at Rock's plate, Alvin realized it was empty. His was still filled with a grilled chicken breast, pasta, and broccoli. He pushed it away. "I just don't have an appetite, cuz."

Rock made a show of looking at his watch, turning over his wrist and raising his arm. "Yeah, right, dog. The ham and eggs we ate for breakfast were only about five hours ago. Strange thing is, you didn't eat then either."

"Maybe I should start calling you Mamma Rock."

"No, Pappa will do. Do I have to act like yours to get you to eat, dog?"

The other two coaches sitting at the table chuckled.

Smiling himself, Alvin said, "Cuz, stop worrying about my eating habits and let's focus on the game coming up. We've already taken care of Portland State and The University of Oregon. I want to go home with Oregon State, too."

Rock continued the piercing look and then sighed. "Okay, you can switch the subject, but you better not fall out on me during the game, dog. It's cool if you don't want to discuss whatever has you fasting, but I need you with enough energy to coach, so we can end this road trip undefeated."

§§§

Several hours later, Rock, Alvin, and Rock's wife, Latisha, all sat in the hotel bar reliving the game. Latisha made the men laugh with her descriptions of the roller coaster ride she endured in the stands as she watched the action. Todd, one of their star players, had let the trash talking of the other team affect his play until Alvin sat down with the boy and had words with him.

"What in the world did you say, Alvin?" Latisha asked.

Alvin shrugged. "We talked about the movie *Silence of the Lambs*. It's Todd's favorite. I told him he was like that guy, Miggs, that Hannibal made swallow his tongue just by talking to him. I told him to stop choking."

Rock shook his head. "See that's why I have you around, cuz. After you were done with Todd, he was playing off the page! That's the only reason we won!"

Rock's enthusiasm made everyone laugh. Once the chuckling had died down, Alvin took a sip of his mineral water and asked Latisha how the manuscript was coming. An infectious grin spread across her face.

"I finished the final draft this afternoon, about two hours before my flight out here. I dropped it off at my illustrator's on the way to the airport." She leaned forward and spoke as if she were revealing a great secret. "This is going to be my best children's book yet." Rock put his arm around her and squeezed. "That's why I'm here. I'm rewarding myself by hooking up with you guys on this trip."

Alvin congratulated her, and then they all slipped into a comfortable silence. After a time, Alvin found himself glancing around at his surroundings and his thoughts drifted back to Jolie and what had been.

"What in the world are you thinking about?"

Latisha's sharply-asked question made him blink and come back to the reality of the bar. "Hmm. Did you say something, Tish?

"Did you have a nice trip? Because you certainly weren't here with me at this table!"

Alvin lifted the mineral water to his lips and drained the glass before answering. Latisha was looking at him closely. He saw concern marring her dark brown eyes.

He stalled. "Where's Rock?"

"See!" She pointed a bent forefinger at him. "You were so out of it, you didn't notice him leaving. He's been gone for five minutes at least." Latisha tossed her head to the side and Alvin spotted Rock talking to a group of three men: two white and one black. "He's over there talking to some very excited, drunk supporters. You were so lost in La La Land, or maybe it was nightmare, land that you didn't even notice. You were scowling something awful."

"Oh."

Latisha put down her margarita and leaned forward. "You want to talk about it?"

He gazed into the warm glow of her eyes. He'd always considered his best friend's wife to be a beautiful woman, and kindness radiated from her petite, square face and full

154

lips. Alvin assumed that Rock's high stress and hectic schedule had to put some sort of strain on their relationship, but Latisha always seemed happy and very content. He felt her patience as she studied him, not saying anything else as she waited to see if he'd confide in her. Latisha had a way of capturing folks with her eyes. Not quite demanding an answer, but creating a vibe which encouraged talk. Alvin found that he was always honest with Latisha, cutting to the heart of the issue, and waiting for her wholesome advice.

The first time Alvin had chosen to bear his soul with her had been when she and Rock were only dating. Alvin's friend understood the healing power of his wife. He'd just silently sat back and let her work her magic, as a devastated Alvin told her that it had finally sunk into his head that Jolie didn't want him. After inviting him to speak, Latisha hadn't said much. She'd just listened until he was done. Then in a low, quiet voice she'd told him about the loss of her twin brother. It wasn't like his loss, she explained, where the person was still living, but inaccessible. However, pain was pain, she claimed, and the look on his face was telling her that he was experiencing a similar hurt.

They'd both grieved that night before Latisha sniffed and said, "I know this will get easier when you let go. From how you describe it, she's as gone to you as my dead twin is to me; and, frankly, I haven't let go as much as I should. Let's make a pact to move on together."

Alvin had tried, but he'd never fully gotten over Jolie. Maybe because he felt there wasn't closure. Sure, he'd ended the relationship, but he'd been unable to speak to her when he'd tried to grab her hand back and hold tight. Perhaps if her mother hadn't blocked access and he'd been able to talk to her, face to face, and then she'd rejected him—he'd be able to move on and find another woman.

Alvin looked at Latisha now, remembering their shared sorrow. It struck him as ironic that it was the same woman who had brought him to this low point again. "You remember Jolie?" Her eyes didn't widen, narrow, or react in the slightest. Her response let him know that Rock had mentioned the situation.

"Yes, I remember. Rock told me her brother is joining the program. Are you still trying to get Jolie to sign up on a more personal level?"

Alvin lowered his head and chuckled a bit before meeting her eyes again. "Am I that transparent?"

"Call it women's intuition. But I have to ask, is this wise? This woman has refused contact with you for so long."

Alvin was too shook up by the knowledge that Jolie had lost his child to even try to examine whether or not his feelings were sensible. All he knew was that they were there, and they were constantly pulling him towards Jolie.

He answered Latisha's question with a simple, "I don't know. But I now have a clue about why she wouldn't speak to me."

"Yes?" Latisha prodded softly when Alvin went silent.

"She was pregnant."

Now Latisha's lids shot to the ceiling. She just stared. Then she sat back in her chair and said, "Wow!" She took a sip of margarita. "That threw me, so I can imagine how it must have thrown you."

Alvin nodded. "You're right, and I'm not sure I've landed. Stray thoughts keep hitting me, slamming me back into the air." Alvin tossed ice into his mouth. The coolness gliding down his throat felt good. He stared at the remaining chunks as he continued. "When I first saw her again, she came with all kinds of anger. I didn't get it. I knew that I'd broken up with her, but hell, I was calling and sending letters a week later trying to get back together. I didn't get the attitude. Now I get it."

The waiter came by and Alvin ordered another mineral water. Latisha declined, lifting her half-full cocktail glass. "Now I'll just faint if you tell me the kid you're recruiting is really your son."

Her tone was light,but Alvin could tell it was a serious question. "No, the ages don't match up and I remember Jolie having a little brother."

"Okay. So what happened to the baby?"

"Well, I screwed that discussion up. I jumped to conclusions and assumed she'd had an abortion. Jolie got really pissed and kicked me out of the house. Right before she slammed the door in my face, she told me she'd miscarried."

"And you didn't know any of this?"

Alvin shook his head. The waiter delivered his water and he took a drink.

"So, I guess the real question is, why didn't you know any of this?"

"I don't know. I don't know why the hell she told me now, but it's really messing with my head." Alvin rubbed his neck.

"You have to talk to her."

"Yeah, I know. But that's easier said than done. She was very angry. I have so many questions. God, it's like finding out your daddy isn't really your daddy, or something awful like that."

"What's that about your daddy, dog? Did he call and tell you to start eating?" Rock clapped Alvin on the back with his blacksmith hands. Then with the grace of a boxer, he pivoted to his chair and sat down. His sudden entrance into the conversation surprised Alvin and made Latisha jump. After he settled, he noticed the seriousness of the mood. "Oh, you've been working your mojo, honey, and getting him to talk."

"Yes, but you just scared the mess out of us and probably shocked him back into silence."

"I doubt it. He's pretty good at clamming up on his own regardless of what I do. So what's the problem?"

Alvin sighed, "Jolie."

"Jolie?" Rock's gaze shifted between the two of them. "There's no problem there. The kid verbally committed to us. I know he can't do it in writing until April, but heck, he even told *The Seattle Times* that he's going to WAM."

"Honey, that's not the concern." Latisha placed a hand

over his.

Rock sat back. "Oh, I get it, dog. You're trying to relight the flame and sista's throwing water on you."

Alvin laughed and Latisha shook her head. "That's my baby. He has his own way with words."

Alvin took a sip of water and began twirling the straw, pushing the lime around. "It's deeper than that, cuz. She was prego all those years ago, and I just found out."

"Prego?" Head to the side, Rock stared at Alvin with a crinkled brow. "I assume you don't mean she was a spaghetti sauce freak."

"Nope, I don't even think she likes the stuff."

"Damn, don't tell me this is some Jerry Springer mess and that Ty is really your son!" Still holding his wife's hand, he sat up straight.

The angst in his voice and face was too much for Alvin. He was half-tempted to let him believe that he'd just recruited his own son. But the situation was too new for him to play practical jokes. However, that didn't stop the humor in his voice when he answered Rock. "No he's really her brother. If he were my son, he'd be about three years younger, cuz."

Rock sagged back into his chair. "That's a relief. Not that I was worried anyway, dog. You know, there's lots of situation where pops coach their sons in college. There was Danny Manning and his pop up in Kansas State. I was more worried about how the boy would take it if you were the daddy he didn't know about!"

"Ahh. See there, you weren't even worried about me, cuz. You're protecting the recruit!"

Rock knew Alvin was teasing, and he responded accordingly. "Damn right, coaches that can calm a self-destructing player are a dime a dozen. I don't even need ya, dog."

The three laughed uncontrollably, which drew the attention of the boosters. They decided to join their table. The conversation switched to lighter topics, and good times rolled for about another hour. The hotel bar closed and everyone shared an elevator as they were all staying in the hotel. The coaches and all the players were on the same floor, and so Rock, Alvin, and Latisha left the car together leaving behind shouts of drunken glee.

"Geez, I don't see how they get up in the morning after being that drunk."

"They don't, Tish," Alvin answered. "Those guys are so rich, they can sleep a week if they want. That's why they follow our team around. It gives them something to do."

"I heard that." Rock took the card key his wife handed him. "But I don't care as long as they keep up the sponsorship." Then Rock said, "Hey, dog."

Alvin and his wife turned to him.

"I was joking earlier. I really am sorry about your situation. You know our friendship is more important than any recruit or basketball."

"I know, cuz." The two shared a hard, brief hug that ended in a sliding handshake and a finger snap.

"You been pinning over this woman since forever.

Maybe it's time to just go for the gold, you know? Figure out what's up with the pregnancy thing, and then convince her like you do the recruits."

"I hear you, Rockhead." As Alvin entered his room, he thought, old cuz may just be right. Sure the miscarriage thing had thrown him for a loop, but it really didn't change anything. He still wanted Jolie.

Chapter 10

Jolie wanted rest. Her days were exhausting, but they weren't wearing her out. It was the nights that were filled with everything except sleep. She rolled, fretted, punched her pillow, cried. Nothing eased the anxiety that chased sleep. She almost thanked her boss, Tim Elliot, when her phone rang at five o'clock Saturday morning. He gave her the perfect excuse to get up, and gave her something to do on a Saturday that loomed ahead like an appointment for a root canal.

"Jolie, Tina's sick, and if you don't go in, I'll have to go myself and I've got my daughter today." Tim was recently divorced, and he cherished the one weekend a month that he had his child.

"I know you just covered for Zack while he was on vacation, but could you pleeeeaaase go in and take care of the feline house? You'd only have to do it for today 'cause Susan said she could do it tomorrow. Only you, Susan, and I are qualified to handle the big cats."

Jolie yawned and stretched before answering. She didn't want to seem too eager. She hadn't worked with the cats since 1996, but she'd enjoyed the dangerous, graceful animals. The thought was a lot more appealing than sitting around moping about Alvin.

"Hey, Jolie, are you there?"

"I'm here. I'll do it. Kiss Alice for me and enjoy your day."

The breath Tim let loose hit Jolie's ear as a loud whoosh. She slightly moved the phone. "Thanks. I owe you one. You know I can't give you overtime, but you can have two comp days. Oh yeah, watch that jaguar we got last year; he's a mean one, okay?"

"Aren't they all?" Jaguars were like school administrators; they had a zero tolerance policy. If a lion or tiger had an opportunity to attack and it wasn't hungry, it might ignore you, or play with you before it killed you. Not so with a jaguar. They were solitary animals from South America, and it was in their nature to strike at whatever was in their space.

"Yeah, but this one has a particularly bad attitude."

"Okay, I'll be careful." She hung up the phone, then prepared herself for the day.

હહહ

Jolie reached the feline house at eight o'clock sharp with a Starbucks double tall latte in hand. After gulping down the last of the coffee, she tossed the cup in the trash and opened the three locks on the heavy, solid wood door.

The smell was the first thing that hit her. Most would find the hearty, musky scent that was slightly underlined with waste and disinfectant offensive, yet Jolie loved it. She took a deep whiff of the odor of healthy, strong animals and smiled. It was a comfort to Jolie, reminding her that she was doing what she loved: working with animals. There was a little nip in the air, so Jolie just unzipped her jacket instead of taking it off. Automatically she placed her hiking boots in a large pan containing a big watery sponge full of disinfectant. The inner confines of all exotic animal habitats had several such pots in various places to prevent the valuable animals from catching a disease that was alien to their system.

Jolie cooed and said nonsense things to the big cats as she walked up and down the long corridor doing her visual check. The morning was the best time to look for illness or injury in all animals. Survival of the fittest dictated that the crafty creatures hide their weakness so they wouldn't be perceived as easy prey. The hardest time for an animal to hide its problems was the time it first woke up, so that was the optimum time to observe.

All the big cats were stretching and moving about, except the jaguar. He was laid out with his eyes closed, and Jolie thought he was still asleep until he opened his eyes, saw her, and quickly shut them again.

"Okay, big boy. You can pretend to sleep. I don't mind. You just chill." Jolie stood just outside the bars. She didn't dare put her hands on the actual rods. A bored or threatened cat could easily take a finger off. Jolie zipped up her coat to go outside and stepped around the traveling cage that rested in the middle of the aisle. She let her fingers run along the bars and thought about what a wonderful invention the cage was. It opened on both ends and it was attached to two big pulleys, so it could be rolled along the corridor where the animals were housed. That way, if an animal needed to be moved for any reason, the cage could be brought to the particular chamber and the animal could be shooed inside. Once in the cage, both doors could be locked, and the animal could be transported to almost anywhere in the feline house safely.

Jolie reached the door at the back of the house and went outside. She began cleaning the exterior exhibit area, the portion of habitat that the public could see. She picked up feces, hosed down, and disinfected areas where muck had gathered. A light rain kept her company the whole time she worked out in the open. After she finished and went back inside, she was ready to take off her coat. She did so, but she kept it tucked under her arm because she knew she'd soon be returning to the elements.

Jolie had come inside to prepare the morning enrichment exercise for the animals. The name had always struck her as funny and a little pretentious. The goal of the activity was to give the animals something to do besides pace back and forth in their outside enclosures. For the big cats, it involved a treasure hunt of scents. Cinnamon, nutmeg, catnip, and pine cones were placed throughout the exterior habitat, and the animals would hunt these things out and enjoy them thoroughly before moving on to find the next aroma. True, the activity gave the animals something to do and gave the public something to watch, but it was nothing compared to what the animal would experience in its natural environment. The term enrichment seemed too grand and too self-serving to Jolie.

Although it had been a while since Jolie had worked in the feline house, her body soon fell into the familiar routine. As she gathered the bouquet of odors into containers to carry outside, her mind wandered to her least favorite subject. She reasoned that she really shouldn't be so upset about Alvin's reaction to her pregnancy. Heck, it took her months to get used to the idea, and then her body had taken care of the situation. At least now the information was out there. She'd always harbored some guilt for not telling him.

The inner confines of the feline house were shaped like a capital T. The stem of the T was short and the line across was long. The spices were housed in the stem of the T and Jolie couldn't actually see any of the animals as she gathered the materials. Grumbling, roaring, and the tick tick of claws scraping metal were normal sounds that didn't really register in Jolie's mind. But the long scraping noise that interrupted her thoughts was unusual. It sounded like metal being dragged across metal. With the large jar of cinnamon still in her hand and her coat tucked under her armpit, Jolie walked forward and peered around the corner.

Her heart leapt into her throat and stopped beating. She saw a flash of sleek black before a loud clang stopped her short. She stared for a weird, eerie second before her mind could accept what she was seeing. Her body reacted much faster, but Jolie didn't even feel the warm urine that ran down her legs.

The jaguar was out. It stood down the hall about thirty feet away. The animal reared back a little when it noticed Jolie. Apparently it was just as surprised to see her or she'd already be dead. Pepper spray. The thought raced through her mind, but she knew the big cat would be on her before she could drop the cinnamon and grab the bottle that was attached to her hip. Going on pure instinct, Jolie threw the cinnamon at the jaguar and raced for the traveling cage. The jaguar avoided the jar and came straight for her. As she ran, Jolie threw her coat behind her. Somebody from above was smiling down because the coat landed on the jaguar's head and he tripped over the disinfectant dish. This gave Jolie the precious few seconds she needed to hop in the traveling cage and almost slam the door down before he reached her. One paw made it in and the animal let out a horrific roar when the cold, dense metal of the cage door struck his right front leg. The loud noise startled Jolie, and she let up a little. The jaguar slipped his injured leg out the cage, and the door slammed completely to, creating a patchwork barrier between Jolie and death.

The cage swung violently on the pulleys and Jolie hung on to the top of the door. She felt nauseous and faint, but she gripped it for all she was worth. From her position, she couldn't insert the pin that would lock the door, so her only option was to hold it closed. Otherwise, the jaguar could bang on the door to create an opening, and then slip a paw under to lift it up. The very thought had Jolie frozen in place. No way was she going to risk going for the pepper spray.

The jaguar continued his attack with his left front leg. Unlike the lion, his paw was small enough to slip through the bars when he turned it sideways. Holding on to the top, Jolie anticipated when he would strike and she used the bottom of her heavy hiking boots to kick violently at his paw. She knew her challenge would have been near impossible if the vicious cat hadn't been injured because he'd have been much too fast for her to avoid. Even so, Jolie felt the claws digging into the rubber of her boot and at times getting stuck. When this happened, she tried to slam her foot down to do as much damage as she could. After a particularly successful stomp, the jaguar roared and sat back. He seemed to be resting. His left leg was planted firmly on the ground, and his right was lifted slightly; so his injured paw dangled.

Again, Jolie thought about the pepper spray. She looked at the jaguar. He had a fix on her. Nothing on earth was like having a wild animal put a fix on you. The jaguar's ears lay flat against his head, his nose flared, and he pulled up his lip to show off his long, pointed incisors that Jolie knew were ready to rip into her flesh. She looked in the yellow eyes that concentrated on her with fierce hatred. On a primal level, Jolie understood the message: When I get my paws on you, I'm going to tear you to shreds.

For the first time, Jolie heard the other animals as well.

They were all restless, pacing, and roaring as if in celebration that one of their patriots had gotten out, or maybe they were just surprised to see one of their own in an area where none had been seen before. Jolie didn't know. She did know that the lion roaring its head off was almost as threatening as the jaguar staring at her. The king of the jungle couldn't yell once and be done with it. It took the animal about five minutes to complete its roaring sequence. He started out with an odd series of little grunts and moans as he gathered his power for the mighty roar. Once he was ready, he'd let out a full-fledged bellow that vibrated the walls of the building. With brief seconds to gasp for air, the lion could howl at full strength for two or three minutes. Then, it would go back to the grunting and look as if it were hyperventilating.

Jolie, herself, was afraid she might lose her air. She concentrated on breathing and trying not to cry. Tears would distort her vision and she knew in a blink of an eye, the jaguar could decide to attack again. The problem was not only the jaguar's paws, but also her fingers. They were exposed as they lay on top of the cage holding the gate down. If the jaguar noticed and went for her hands, she'd have to let go. Then the animal could pound the door with his paws or body until it shifted enough for him to get a paw underneath the door. Then it could push it open and slide into the cage. Jolie had enough trouble fighting off the paw with her boot. If he went for her fingers, she'd have to let go, and if he pounded the door, she'd have to grab the top again. She'd stay alive until she ran out of fingers and palms. The thought had her shaking uncontrollably.

After a time, which seemed like five hours to Jolie, the jaguar's ears lifted back up and he looked towards his enclosure. The movement was puzzling to Jolie until she remembered the cinnamon. The jar had spilled and the scent fought mightily with the other smells. The jaguar kept shifting from her to the brown mess on the floor. Throwing one last menacing look her way, the animal turned and, with a slight limp, made his way to the cinnamon.

With her eyes still on him, Jolie sank against the bars of the door. She kept her eyes on the big cat and reached for her cell phone that was in the pocket of her pants. The cat walked to the spilled spice and started doing the Flehman Response. The jaguar squenched up his face and put his tongue halfway out, looking as if he was snarling, except there was no noise. During the Flehman Response, it was assumed that the animal was opening all of its nasal passages and taste buds to enjoy whatever scent it was experiencing.

While the jaguar was distracted, Jolie dialed the emergency number she'd memorized. Her fingers trembled and the still swaying cage didn't make matters easier. She didn't bother with hello when the phone was answered; instead she frantically whispered, "I'm in the feline building. Jaguar is out."

The calm, professional voice said, "Out in the building or out with the public?"

"Inside."

"Are you safe?"

"Yes, but I'm in the unpinned traveling cage and he can slip paws through."

"Hold your position. Help is on the way."

Later, Jolie reasoned she must have blinked when she heard she was going to be saved. She didn't even see the big cat. All she knew was that her feet left the floor, and she was hurtled against the side rails. She screamed and the phone went flying. Pain vibrated through her hip when she hit the cage floor, reminding her of the pepper spray on her side. She yanked it off her waist and sprayed in the direction of the jaguar. He let out a horrific howl and clawed at the faint mist hovering over his face. Spitting and roaring, the animal reared back as if he didn't understand the nature of this enemy.

Jolie was on fire. Some of the vapors had filtered back and settled on her face. One thing kept her focused. From her position, she could see a gap between the door and the floor. Struggling to stand up in the rocking cage, she dove for the gate and slammed it down. The noise seemed to give the animal direction, and it made a blind attack at the cage. Jolie held on, angled her body, and stomped the vicious claws when they slipped through the bars.

Men's voices from up above sounded like angel trumpets to Jolie. She threw her head back and saw two forms on the catwalk that ran the length of the animals' cages. Just as she saw one lift a gun, she felt a searing pain in the space between thumb and forefinger. She leaned forward instinctively wanting to get at the source of the pain, but common sense prevailed. The jaguar possessed the second strongest jaws in the animal kingdom. No way was she going to put her face near that killing power. Instead, she leaned back and grabbed the paw with her free hand and pulled up.

The pain left and she fainted.

§§§

As Jolie felt the first stirrings of consciousness, she heard several male voices coming from above her.

"Look at her shoes." She felt her foot being moved slightly. "They're ripped to shreds on the bottom and there isn't one scratch on her legs."

"Yeah, but she'll need stitches for that hand."

"Oh, maybe one or two. The claw just went in and out. This is truly amazing!"

A female voice closer to her said, "Shush, I think she's coming out of it. Jolie, Jolie, can you hear me?"

She moaned and opened her eyes. What she saw made her yell and attempt to scramble to her feet and run like hell. Strong hands braced by even stronger arms held her down. "Relax, Jolie, relax." The woman said. "The jag's unconscious. He can't get you now." Jolie stopped fighting but trembled uncontrollably. She didn't know the woman speaking to her, but she recognized the paramedic's uniform. "Okay, Jolie. We're going to put you on a stretcher now."

Jolie felt herself being lifted onto the cot. She looked down at the big cat who had tried to take her life. Fear coursed through her even though the animal was no longer a threat. He lay on his side with his tongue slightly extended from his mouth. The peaceful face she now saw was so different from the angry snarl the jaguar wore when he attacked her.

She looked up and saw Tim, her supervisor. He reached down and hugged her. Jolie's face must have shown her confusion.

"I was paged the minute you called the operator. Good thing I was at home and my ex and I both live near the zoo. My daughter's with her mother."

Jolie nodded and spoke. Her voice sounded odd to her as if she were talking from a distance. "You darted him, right?" She didn't see a pool of blood, so she knew the animal wasn't dead. Tim's nod let her know she was correct. On some intellectual level, Jolie felt relief. The animal was doing what the Creator had meant him to do, it wasn't his fault he was being held in captivity. "It looks like we both came out of this alive," she said with a voice that still sounded like an echo to her.

As they wheeled her into the ambulance, Jolie shouted, "Hey, I'm sorry this ruined your time with Alice."

Tim said, "Please, Jolie. I'm just happy you're all right."

Jolie looked at the paramedic. "If I'm okay, why am I on this stretcher?"

"You've had quite a shock. We just want to check you

out for a while to make sure you're doing fine."

Chapter 11

That same Saturday, Alvin called Jolie's house and got Tyrese. He didn't know what Jolie had told her brother about them, so he decided to assume that he knew nothing. Without identifying himself, he asked for Jolie. Tyrese told him she was at work and wouldn't be back until five. At six o'clock, Alvin parked across the street from her house. He planned to call using his cell phone just in case her brother was there. An unexpected visit from him might lead to questions from Tyrese that he was sure neither he or Jolie wanted to answer. Voicemail picked up. Alvin hung up without leaving a message. He settled back into his car seat, prepared to wait as long as necessary.

An hour later, Jolie's car pulled into the uncovered driveway, closely followed by a battered red truck. Alvin was surprised to see Jolie get out of the passenger side of her car and a brown-haired white man exit from the driver's side. His eyebrows rose even further when a middle-aged white man got out of the truck and joined Jolie and the brown-haired guy near the car door. Alvin was about to get out and join the huddle when the two men turned and began walking away. He and Jolie watched as they got into the truck and drove off. Alvin got out of his car and quickly crossed the street. It was dark, but visibility was still good thanks to a street lamp and Jolie's porch light. Alvin didn't want to startle her. She was at the front door and he was at the edge of the small lawn when he said her name in a normal voice. She turned to look at him, and he could see her face clearly. It was flat: no shock, no alarm, no anything. Am I so unimportant that I don't even provoke anger now? he thought with a wholly male feeling of annoyance.

Then he took another look. Something was definitely wrong. He saw it in her face. She looked stiff or stern, as if she was holding on to the expression with all she had. When she turned and opened the door to lead him inside, her movements were jerky and fast. The way she walked was different, also. It wasn't an easy pace, but a quick motion executed with stiff, bunched shoulders. Alvin couldn't tell if she was furious or afraid; however, one thing was clear: she was struggling to hold herself together. He followed her inside, mildly surprised she hadn't demanded he leave. In fact, she hadn't said anything to him. He began to worry. What had her in such state?

"Jolie?"

She looked at him with blank eyes and didn't answer. Then she turned and walked away. He followed her into the kitchen. With her coat still on and her purse hanging from her shoulder, she opened the freezer and pulled out a bottle of Absolut Mandarin vodka, her father's favorite drink. He liked it cold, so Jolie kept it in the freezer. That way, it would be ready if he decided to visit his two children. The bottle had been there at least a year, and it was unopened. She chuckled and shook her head.

Alvin stared in disbelief as she went back into the living room, opened the bottle, and took a swig straight from the neck. She took a deep breath and her eyes watered, making her blink furiously, but she didn't gasp. She took another swig before setting the bottle aside. The drink went down cold and rough. Her hand traced from her breastbone to her stomach as if it were moving with the alcohol. In her belly, the vodka settled in, heated quickly, and radiated comforting warmth. "What are you doing here?" Her tone was dull almost detached.

He took off his jacket and laid it across the couch. "We need to talk." His voice was harder than he meant it to be.

Jolie threw her purse on the chair, then removed her jacket, and flung it on top of the purse. She was wearing an old T-shirt and overalls. They'd allowed her to take a shower at the hospital, and Tim had brought her extra clothes from her zoo locker. Next she slammed her hands on the back of a living room chair. Her grip was so hard that the skin of her dark tan fingers turned white. She tossed her head, exposing her throat, making her long, auburn ponytail bounce. Breathing deeply and evenly, she struck quite a pose as she attempted to gain control. Alvin was truly becoming concerned. He was reaching out to place a soothing hand on her back when she turned and looked at him. The utter misery in her eyes stopped him short.

She whispered his name. The pet name that only she

called him. The name he hadn't heard in fifteen years. "Alvie, I …." She was going to say that she'd almost died today, but the rest of the sentence got stuck in her chest.

Alvin stepped back initially because he was so startled by what he saw in her eyes. Then he was moving forward, wrapping her in his arms. He didn't have a clue what was really going on, yet the look on her face sent every protective instinct in his body into overdrive. Next thing he knew, hands began searching his face, gently but quickly rubbing over his forehead, across his cheekbones, grazing his mouth, brushing his mustache. He noticed the bandage on her hand, but before he could ask, she lifted her head from his shoulder and their lips found each other. Passion exploded between them, hot and wild.

Jolie had heard that people who experience near death episodes go out and satisfy some basic instinct to the fullest. They ate, drank, or had sex in excess to reaffirm that they were indeed alive. Well, when Alvin reached out with his hand, some primal part of her decided which necessity she wanted to indulge in. She gripped his face and deepened the kiss.

The taste, the smell, the texture of her, so long denied him, was more than an aphrodisiac. It drove him wild and he wanted to consume her. Still he held back, confusion making him a little hesitant.

Jolie was too lost in emotion to sense Alvin's uncertainty. She pulled at his clothes, managing to haul his T-shirt over his head and yank his sweat pants down. Alvin took care of the rest. He put toes to heels and pushed his tennis shoes off. Then he used his feet to free himself of the dangling fabric. Jolie gorged herself on heated, hard male flesh. Her hands traced and her lips followed, over cheeks, down his corded neck, dallying in the hollow at the base of his throat.

The telephone rang. Without missing a beat, Jolie lifted the receiver of the cordless handset and switched it to off. Then she tossed the intrusion in some unknown direction. It was probably some zoo mucky-muck who wanted to ask more questions. Answering questions was the last thing on her mind right now. She was beginning to work her way down Alvin's chest when he gripped her face between his hands and seared her with his kiss. He looked at her, trying to fathom what was going on. All he saw in her half-closed eyes was need, and wild, intense desire. The look drove him over the edge and into her soft neck. He nibbled and kissed along the long, slim column of her throat until she began to whimper. He removed his lips only to help her undress. Overalls were unclasped and slipped to the floor. Her shirt was raised and added to the pile at her feet. When she lifted her arms behind her to unfasten the bra that clasped in the back, he swiftly twirled her so he could do the honors.

Jolie didn't remember traveling to the wall, but she found her front pressed against one as he showered her back with kisses. He removed her hair band and flung it behind him. Inhaling deeply, he buried his face in the long tresses. Cinnamon, her hair smelled like hot cinnamon. The zesty scent was intoxicating and Alvin continued breathing heavily as he placed the long strands over her shoulders, so that her hair ran down her front, cascading half way down her breasts. Again, he adorned her back with his lips. While his mouth worked, he reached around and cupped her breasts, lightly rubbing the firm tips. Her hair lining his palms, grazing across her sensitive tips, created an amazingly erotic combination.

Jolie gasped, alive with sensation coming at her from the front and the rear. She felt him pressed up and throbbing in the small of her back. She spread her legs and arched herself in silent invitation. She hoped he would hurry and she wouldn't have to take matters into her own hands, literally.

Jolie's cheek lay against the wall, leaving the other exposed. She felt the tip of him at the same time she felt his lips caressing the side of her face. He slid in slowly, resisting the urge to move wildly. All hesitancy left when Jolie reached around with her right hand and firmly kneaded his backside.

"Oh yes," she hissed as he responded to her fingers. Bending his knees, he moved smoothly and swiftly as his lips shifted from her cheek, to the side of her mouth, to her neck, and then to her collarbone. Both hands returned to the wall as she pushed against it to give herself leverage. Instinctively, her feet rolled into an arch as she balanced on her toes, trying to take him more fully.

She knew her release would be fast and furious. His hands traveled all over her front, making her tremble wherever they touched. Then he began moving his fingers in increasingly larger circles. When the calloused tips brushed the tops of her thighs, in her gut and elsewhere, she knew what he was up to. Although she was fully prepared, it didn't stop her from moaning loudly when the hot touch brushed her mound. The next time they passed, they pressed a little harder. The third time, Jolie risked losing her balance and grabbed his hand to keep the tip were it was most wanted. Alvin let one finger travel through the folds to the center of Jolie where he lightly stroked in time with the movements of his hips. Again, Jolie whispered an affirmation right before he felt the wonderful clench of her orgasm as it ripped through her.

Triumph was the dominant emotion he felt when he buried his face in the crook of her neck. Then he felt relief, thanking God that she got there before him because he was ready to blow. Placing his hands at her waist, he let his body have its way. It wasn't long before he was using his last vestige of control to pull from her and release into the small of her back.

Jolie felt the hot spurts and realized what had happened. She stood limp against the wall, more than satisfied physically. Somewhere deep inside, she was grateful for his thoughtfulness. Lord knows, now wasn't the time to start another life. Besides, she knew she'd caught him completely off guard. Without further thought, she said what was on her mind, "I see you're still thinking about almost being a daddy."

"What?" He staggered back from her. "Jolie, what the

hell is going on?"

She felt contrite. She turned to face him and said, "I'm sorry," right before water began streaming from her eyes.

Alvin muttered an oath before gathering her in his arms. He carried her to the couch and settled her in his lap. Her long legs hung over his hairy thighs. As he soothed her with gentle sounds and soft strokes to her head, he found himself mesmerized by the differences in their limbs. Her bronze skin was smooth and supple against his dark brown. Like warm caramel poured over chocolate.

Jolie's sobs graduated into weeping, and then just hiccups. She kept her eyes closed through most of the cleansing process. When the hiccups were few and far between, Jolie whispered another apology. "I'm sorry, Alvin. You must think I'm nuts."

"Hey, I'm confused here, but one thing I know is that was buck wild! You don't need to say sorry for that!"

Jolie sat up and lifted her face from his wet neck. She felt too shy to look directly at him, so she focused down and away. She surprised them both by laughing. The hiccups started once more. Alvin was beginning to wonder if maybe he should call a doctor until she spoke. "You're still wearing your socks." Jolie giggled again.

Alvin gripped both her legs and leaned over her breasts to look at his feet. Jolie seriously doubted that his face had to be so close to her nipples to determine the truth of her words, but she wasn't in the mood to complain. Alvin wiggled his toes and gazed more at Jolie's front than at his calf high, white tube socks.

"Somebody didn't give me a chance to take them off! We're lucky I didn't slip and make us bang our heads on that wall. Ty would have come back to find us both lying on the floor with concussions."

Jolie quickly glanced at her watch.

"Uh oh. Did I say the wrong thing?"

"Uh, uh." No longer timid, Jolie kissed his forehead. "My brother shouldn't be home for another hour and a half, according to the message he left on my cell phone."

"Hum, a lot can happen in that amount of time if you don't feel like talking." He hugged her close. "We've waited this long. Another hour or day for that matter shouldn't make too much of a difference."

Jolie felt a small stirring in her belly. It surprised her because she was so recently satisfied. Usually, one was definitely enough for the day. She removed herself from Alvin's lap. "I think we need to talk, but I want to shower first. Wait here."

Alvin stood and Jolie couldn't help laughing. He looked so funny, standing there all lean muscle, semi-aroused, with his big feet encased in white socks that barely made it past his ankles.

"I think I need to join you," he said in a husky voice.

All laughter died. The small stir had become a full-fledged ping. "Alvin, if you get in there with me, the last thing we'll do is talk. It'll probably create an embarrassing situation where we'll lose track of time, and Ty'll come home and get the shock of his young life."

"Uh huh," he said. Her luscious body had more of his attention than her words. How could she expect him to think straight when she stood there in her birthday suit? And, Good Lord, what gifts had been bestowed on her. Her full breasts, wide hips, and toned thighs had him wiggling his toes for a different reason. Jolie's next words stopped him dead in his tracks.

"I've used you once tonight. I don't want to do it again."

What the hell? he thought as she retreated down the hall. Mesmerized by her bottom, he found himself yelling at her back, "Come on and use me then. I'm Bill Withers so just go on 'Use Me Up'."

She smiled over her shoulder and kept on walking. She came back in a robe with towels.

"There's a bathroom down the hall you can use . I'll take a shower in my room. I'll meet you back here in ten minutes." It was Jolie's third shower of the day.

Chapter 12

Approximately two hours later they sat at the Offbeat sipping espressos. After the showers, Jolie had asked Alvin to just drive. She didn't care where they were going, she just wanted to relax her body and feel the comforting motion of the car moving beneath her. Alvin didn't ask questions. He did as she requested, deciding she would tell him what was bothering her in her own time. Jolie settled into the plush seats of the Mercedes, turned on the seat heater, and focused on thinking of nothing. Fifteen minutes into the drive, she was fast asleep. Alvin drove for another forty-five minutes before her eyes opened.

"Where are we?" she asked through a yawn.

"T-town."

"We're all the way to Tacoma?" Jolie sat up straight and looked around. It was dark outside and they were on kind of a funky street with lots of lights and people milling around. "This place looks way too lively for Tacoma."

Alvin chuckled. The city of Tacoma had been trying to revive itself for the last thirty years. They were finally having some success on Sixth Avenue. "I can tell you haven't been down here lately. This street has been kicking for about a year now. See Jazz Bones?" Alvin pointed to his left. "It opened about six months ago. There're a couple of Starbucks, new restaurants and now, the Offbeat." Alvin pulled into a parking spot underneath the huge sign.

"Is this a club?" Jolie frowned and looked sideways at Alvin. "I'm not up to dancing tonight."

Alvin shut off the car. "Clubbin' starts around ten-thirty. Before that, it's an espresso bar, restaurant, and art gallery." Alvin turned and smiled at her. Jolie's insides fluttered, reminding her of the first time she'd experienced butterflies. It was in her VW bug when Alvin had kissed her. "You want to go inside and have a cup of coffee?"

How could she resist such a smile? And so they went inside, and now they sat at a table, both waiting for Jolie to talk. Alvin sipped his latte with his long legs stretched out. Then he rested his cup on the Formica and tried not to stare at Jolie. He wanted her to feel comfortable enough to speak. Jolie envied Alvin's peace of mind. He looked so relaxed. With a heavy sigh, she reasoned that peace would come after she did what needed to be done.

"Which do you want to hear first: pregnancy, or the jaguar?"

Alvin's brows rose. "The baby."

Jolie focused on the hot chocolate she cradled between her hands as it sat on the table. "I knew I was pregnant that last time you came to see me. Remember how we both said we had news, and you wanted to go first?"

Alvin didn't recall, but he nodded anyway. He'd hated what he was about to do and he was taking his father's approach. Alvin Senior always said, "When you dislike something you have to do, that should be incentive to do it fast. Quicker you do, the quicker it's done." It didn't surprise him that Jolie said he had wanted to speak first.

"After you let go of my hand. I didn't want to tell you." Her tone was resentful. "I lost the baby a few months later."

"Would you have ever told me?"

Jolie briefly looked into his eyes before returning to the murky brown of the chocolate. "I don't know. Being fair to you hasn't been high on my list of priorities."

"Do you do that on purpose?"

"What?"

"Say things that cut me to the quick. You can stick a knife in my gut faster and deeper than anyone I've ever known, including my mother. I just wondered if it came naturally or whether you have to work at it."

Jolie felt herself getting angry. "I'm not working at anything. Maybe it's your guilty conscience that makes you too sensitive." Jolie remembered the letters her mother had blocked and regretted the words. It was too easy to slip into the old pattern of hating him. Clearly, he didn't deserve that. Now was the time to stop prior bad habits and see if the truth could make things better for them.

She reached across the table and rubbed Alvin's hand. "I'm sorry." She could see that she'd surprised him. He closed his mouth and sat back. Jolie chuckled, "It took me fifteen years to develop this bad attitude. It's going to take me a second to realize that it's no longer necessary." Jolie took another deep breath. "My dad sent me a box of my mom's things. In them, I found a stack of letters that I'd never seen before." She looked into the wide brown eyes. "Letters from you."

Alvin was quiet, digesting what she'd said, then he leaned forward a little. "You mean you never got them? I sent over a dozen letters that first year and you didn't get any? You weren't just ignoring me all those years!"

Jolie shook her head.

"Did you know that I called almost every day and dropped by when I came home for Christmas break?"

"No, I waited for weeks for you to show up and tell me you'd made a mistake. I planned to make you wait about five minutes and then fly into your arms. When it didn't happen, to say I became bitter is an understatement."

"Is that why you nearly took my head off when I saw you at the park that summer."

"Yes, by that time, I'd lost the baby and ..." Jolie shrugged her shoulders. She knew he'd gotten the point.

Alvin threw his head back and released a little sigh. "God, we've wasted so much time, Jolie." He reached forward and grabbed her hand.

"Wait right there, Alvin. It's been a while. We've both changed. Who knows if we'll like who each of us has grown into. Also, you hurt me." Jolie looked down with the confession. They both knew it was true, yet the actual words had never been voiced.

"Look at me, Jolie."

Honey eyes met dark brown eyes.

He thought the L word would scare her off. What they were accomplishing was too fragile to move too fast. So he said, "Jolie, I am so sorry I caused you pain. I'm not the insecure boy I once was, and I will never intentionally hurt you again. Can we put the past behind us?"

Jolie nodded, believing that now she could, but that didn't mean she was sure about their future.

Alvin squeezed her hand. "I've always cared for you."

Why isn't he saying love? The question roared through Jolie's mind. It was instinctive and immediate. Jolie appreciated the irony. She wanted the man to mention love, yet she was unsure about them being together.

"And from what I've seen, you're still a wonderful, unique person. Not everyone would care for family the way you do. Not everyone would follow their dream and become a zoo keeper like you have. I'll bet you're the only black zoo keeper."

"No, there's one more."

He smiled and kept talking, "From everything I've seen, you're still a wonderful person that I want to see more of."

Jolie pondered why she felt as if she'd been given a backhanded compliment. His words sounded good, but it was like getting the cake without the frosting when he didn't say love. Then she chastised herself. How foolish of her to expect the man to be in love just because they'd cleared up the past.

Alvin didn't understand her expression. The smile pasted on her face reminded him of the fake stuff kids throw out when they're told to smile for the camera. Didn't she like compliments and hearing that he wanted this thing between them to move forward?

Jolie removed her hand from Alvin's and began to talk to fill the rapidly becoming awkward moment. She shifted topics. "The reason I was so...well, so out of it earlier was that I got into a tussle with the jaguar and...and he tried to make me the morning enrichment exercise."

The subject change stunned Alvin. First, she didn't even acknowledge his words, and second, she was talking about fighting a wild animal!

Jolie delivered the story in a sort of nervous prattle. Alvin sat back and listened, his system going through a gauntlet of emotions. He went from confusion to shock to fear and then his brain settled on anger. The thought that he could have lost her permanently today sent shivers through his soul. He felt like insisting that she quit her job, but he knew how well that would go over. He doubted the caveman tactics would work. Instead, he calmly asked, "How did it get out?"

Jolie's voice lost its nervous edge and became clipped and even toned. "Geez, that's why I was so angry earlier. Our zoo gets some city funding, but a large portion comes from private donations, so if you give the powers that be enough money, they're inclined to let you do almost anything. Some rich guy's son wanted to see the inside enclosure for the big cats. So, for the kid's fifteenth birthday, daddy gets him behind the scenes. According to the poor zoo keeper who had to escort these two around, the kid was messing with everything, and daddy was talking her ear off. She couldn't ignore the old man, and she was too intimidated to keep yelling at the kid."

Jolie stopped to breathe and then continued speaking. "The cat's inside enclosure is fifty years old and twenty-five years out of date. A thick, heavy padlock is really the only thing between the cage and the interior of the building. As you can imagine, these locks get pretty banged up and after a while, they fail. Every night, the zoo keeper pulls and tugs on the lock," Jolie demonstrated with her right hand, "to make sure it's not broken. Then the keeper places the lock up, so it rests on the shelves of the bars. If a lock is hanging down during the morning inspection, someone's head will roll because that means things haven't been checked properly."

Jolie sat back and crossed her arms. Her lips pinched, her even voice became hard. "Apparently the kid starts pulling on the locks and one breaks. Instead of telling somebody, the kid just puts it back on the shelf. When I came in this morning, I didn't suspect anything because the locks were all where they were supposed to be."

"How do you know it was the kid?"

"The kid's a punk, but at least he's honest. After I escaped being lunch, the head of the zoo called daddy. Everyone who had been in the building in the last two days was contacted. Daddy talked to his son, and the kid admitted it. Daddy's donating a half a mil Monday. Nice to know I have fundraising capabilities with the zoo."

Alvin didn't find her joke funny.

Jolie yawned. Suddenly she was exhausted. "I think the endorphins and whatever else the fight or flight syndrome released into my system are wearing off. Do you mind taking me home?"

Alvin stood and escorted her to the car. The Offbeat had become crowded as they talked. Neither of them had noticed as people started filtering in and the employees began transitioning for the night crowd. They made it to the car and Alvin began driving. Not much was said in the forty-five minutes it took to get Jolie home. During the ride, Alvin decided he wanted some resolution before the night ended. Jolie was about to leave the car when he said, "Before you go, what about you and me?"

Jolie sighed. "I'll be truthful, Alvin. I still have feelings for you, but I'm scared. First time it didn't work, shame on you, but if this doesn't work again, it's going to be shame on me for making the same mistake twice."

Alvin grabbed Jolie's hand and squeezed. The fact that she admitted that she still cared had done wonders for his spirit. "There won't be shame between us, Jolie. I promise you that. There's still a spark there that could bloom to full fledged happiness for both of us if we let it."

His smile was infectious and Jolie found herself returning it. "I hope you're right," she whispered as he lifted her hand and kissed it.

Chapter 13

Sunday morning, Jolie awoke to a wonderful aroma, one that she hadn't smelled in a long time. "Bacon!" she whispered to herself in excited glee. Then she made a big mistake and moved. "Ohhhhhh," she hissed. "Dang, I'm sore." Her arms and legs felt like rusted metal. Jolie eased herself back into lying still, waiting for the crisis to pass. She couldn't help wondering if it was the cat, or Alvin that was responsible for her current condition. Even though she lay frozen, her muscles remembered her attempt at mobility. They throbbed and stung in protest. Blinking was the only thing that seemed bearable. After a time, Jolie concluded that she couldn't lie there all day. Taking a deep breath and gathering her courage, she rolled towards the side of the bed. Gritting her teeth, she managed to swing her legs over the side and force her aching body to sit up. She sat there a moment, grimacing. Then, she glanced at the clock on her nightstand, she groaned for a different reason. It was ten-thirty and she'd missed the ten o' clock church service. She disliked going to the noon mass because of the crowd. Jolie knew she'd have to show up at least fifteen minutes early or be resigned to standing at the back or leaning on a sidewall.

Moving like an old woman with a bone density problem, Jolie donned the red terry cloth robe that lay at the end of the bed. Tying the belt over her white nightshirt, reminded her of the stitch in her hand. She moved it gingerly as she shuffled to the kitchen. It didn't feel too bad compared to the rest of her body. Following her nose to the bacon helped her ignore the feel of stinging needles that accented her every move.

Tyrese looked over his shoulder as he stood at the stove. He saw her slightly bent form and thought nothing of it. He didn't notice how her right arm was firmly braced against the doorframe. "This is the first time since I've moved here that you've missed ten o'clock mass. If this bacon didn't wake you up, I was going to check your pulse and call the National Guard."

"Uh huh." She barely heard her brother because she was maintaining laser beam focus on the dinette chair. I can make it. I can make it, she told herself as she revved up to move. She moaned slightly with the first step.

Tyrese turned around and the smile died on his lips when he saw her hobbling. "Damn sis, you moving slower than Ms. Ethel." He helped her to the chair. "What in the world happened to you?"

Jolie moved her neck experimentally. It made unnatural noises. "I'm just sore," she uttered.

Tyrese turned back to the stove. "What? Did Sensei go nuts and make you do a hundred fingertip push-ups in karobics?"

Tyrese thought karate and aerobics were for woman and short men. He loved to tease her about it. "No, smarty pants. I got up close and personal with a jaguar. That's why my body feels like it's been bounced around in a dryer." That shocked him into silence. As Tyrese quietly served her bacon and eggs, Jolie told him about her near-death experience. She tried to convince him to come to church, telling him that they both needed to thank the Lord for her deliverance.

"Geez, sis. I hear ya, but if I go, I'll be late for work. I have to be there in an hour." He stood behind her and gently massaged her shoulders. "Ya know, the best thing for sore muscles is aspirin and stretching. It'll take the woodenness right out of your system."

Jolie smiled. At that moment, she could feel her mother in Tyrese. She'd heard her tell him that many times when they were younger. "I'll get you some." He disappeared and returned with two small white tablets and a glass of water.

"I'll straighten up my room and vacuum before I go."

Jolie blinked, stunned that the boy had volunteered to do housework. Usually, it took a battle royal to get him to do his share of the chores. Jolie sipped her orange juice and ate while reflecting on how the horrific experience had bridged a gap between her and Alvin and caused a metamorphosis in her brother. She released a cynical chuckle because she suspected the change in Tyrese would be very temporary. Would her and Alvin's tentative reconciliation be as brief?

A loud gagging sound dragged Jolie from her thoughts. After being momentarily startled, she thought nothing of it, assuming that Tyrese had caught one of his socks in the vacuum cleaner brush again. Her mouth dropped open when he came into the kitchen carrying a pair of underwear with a pencil. It was Jolie's turn to gag on her drink, and then she remembered the priest's message from a few Sundays back, "The Lord doesn't give you more than you can handle."

With a smirk on his face, Tyrese said, "These aren't mine! Are you sure your being sore doesn't have something to do with these?"

Jolie blushed deeply.

"Has the little angel been indulging in more earthly pleasures?" If Jolie's face got any hotter, she knew the skin would melt into her robe.

Seeing her acute embarrassment, Tyrese continued to tease. "As little as you date, I know your body isn't used to such extracurricular activity. I hear it's hard on the muscles after a long absence. I'm curious, though. Did you get the pants off the guy before or after the big cat showdown?" There was a brief pause, and then Tyrese's lips were moving again as he studied the underwear. "I ain't touching them, but they look clean. At least the brotha gets points for hygiene." His eyes lifted. "It is a brotha, isn't it?"

That comment unstuck Jolie's lips. "Of course it is…or of course it would be. Where…where did…you find them."

He walked up to her and with a wrist flick, the underwear dropped onto the dinette table in front of where she sat. "Under the couch. You're always after me to vacuum under it and surprise, surprise, the Kirby sucked up some Hanes." Jolie cringed at the laughter in his voice.

She strove for decorum. Chagrin and mortification made dignity hard to find, but she didn't feel remorseful. That hot union had been the start of something wonderful, or depending on one's interpretation, the continuation of something wonderful after a long interruption. However, annoyance still flared through her brain that Alvin had forgotten such an important article of clothing. That combined with anger and irritation that she hadn't determined the time her brother would find out that she was involved with someone.

Tyrese pulled out a chair and sat down in front of her, the offensive material laid between them. "I'm curious, sis. Did you practice what you preach and engage in safe sex, or have you switched to do as I say, not as I do?"

Jolie resisted the urge to lower her head. Safe sex had been the farthest thing from her mind when Alvin's hand touched her back. The Lord finally provided her with enough poise to calmly say, "You're being more than presumptuous. Just because you found these," she pointed to the underwear, "doesn't mean that I had sex. They could be Dad's."

"Come on, Jolie. Dad hasn't been here in over a year. I know I'm bad, but I've vacuumed under the couch since then. No, I think those are a recent addition to the junk that lives under the loveseat. My only concern is that y'all must have been gettin' pretty freaky to be doin' it in the living room."

Jolie gasped, then decided she was an adult and there were certain things she didn't have to explain, or put up with, when dealing with her teenage brother. "Look, Tyrese, I'm full-grown. Your parents finished raising me a long time ago, and I must say they did an excellent job. Now you're my baby brother and I love you dearly, but there are certain areas of my life that you will not be privy to."

"Well heck, you all up in my stuff!" She knew her brother was serious despite the teasing tone.

"You're in high school, living in my house. It's part of my responsibilities to be all up in your stuff. When you leave and are supporting yourself, you can tell me to mind my own business."

All teasing gone, Tyrese surprised her by saying, "Who is this guy? Even though you all grown, I worry about you because you're my blood." Tyrese thumped his chest with the inside of his fist.

Jolie looked down and her eyes met the Hanes. She grabbed them and put them in her lap under the table. Stoically, she suppressed the wince brought on by moving too fast. As she sat there, eyes on the veneer of the dinette, she reasoned that the boy was bound to find out anyway, so it made sense to put her spin on it. Head still down, she lifted her eyes up to look at Tyrese. "You promise you won't laugh and tease me."

"Cross my heart and hope to live."

There was a brief silence before she said, "Alvin."

"The recruiter guy!" Tyrese sat back so hard, the chair scooted. "So, all that hard nose stuff was like the little boy who pulls the girl's hair because he likes her."

"No." Jolie's voice lacked fire. "I was just protecting my baby boo." She got up slowly and stiffly moved towards the door. When she passed her brother, she ran a hand across his corn rows.

"Don't baby boo me. Didn't you two know each other in high school? Did you kick it then?"

Jolie was trying to leave the kitchen and escape the conversation. "We dated, but it fizzled out." Selective truth was all her brother needed.

She was going to exit until Tyrese mumbled, "Shoot, now I know I'll start next year."

She tried to dash back to the table, but all she could manage was a rigid, awkward walk accomplished with slightly bent knees, chest and butt poked out. "Wait one minute, Ty. This will in no way affect what's going on with you. You're going to have to earn playing time. He's not going to give it to you just because we like each other. So get that nonsense out of your head right now. Besides, you're so good, you won't need any favoritism that comes from me."

Tyrese threw his hands up. "Chill, sis. I got ya. You just tell him to treat me fair. He also can't make me ride the bench because he digs you."

"I'm sure Alvin wouldn't do that. You just keep working hard and you'll get what you deserve."

"Cool, cool." Tyrese put his hands down. As Jolie was leaving, he had to have the last word. "Just don't be bringing no babies home without a ring on your finger."

Jolie did a slow whirl to find Tyrese doubled over with laughter. "You're really enjoying this, aren't you?"

"Come on, sis. How often do your size eights leave the straight and narrow? This is the only legitimate thing I've had to tease you about in years."

"Just finish vacuuming, boy, before you leave for work."

Still chuckling, Tyrese got up and went to the Kirby. Jolie's shoulders didn't relax until the drone of the vacuum cleaner drowned out her brother's cackles.

Chapter 14

Three days later, Jolie was checking on the reptiles she used for community service events when her name was announced over the loud speaker. "Jolie Smith, report to the main entrance receptionist immediately." The message was repeated several times before she managed to grab her cell phone and dial the number.

"This is Jolie."

"Hi, Jolie, report to the main receptionist immediately."

"Okay, but what for? Is something wrong?"

"No, are you doing something where we need to send out relief?"

Jolie looked fondly at the cages filled with lounging snakes. "No, I'm just checking my babies."

"All right then, go see the main receptionist."

All sorts of things flashed through Jolie's mind as she rushed to the location, her slightly sore muscles protesting a little. She knew it probably wasn't about Tyrese and the baby because he would have called her cell directly. She finally decided that it was probably just more officials who wanted to talk about the jaguar incident. She looked at her hand as she rushed along. A couple of normal-sized bandages covered the area that barely hurt now. Jolie sighed.

"I'm tired of talking about that," she muttered.

She'd been on the other side of the zoo when she heard the page, and her fast walk became a squishy jog as her hiking boots met the pavement in the light drizzle. By the time she got to the door of the main area and threw off the hood of her coat, there was a slight sheen of perspiration on her face. Breathing a little heavy, Jolie approached Tammy at the reception desk. "Hi, what's up?" she said. Later, she would reflect that if she hadn't been so focused on Tammy, she would have noticed the large object to her left.

"Geez, don't you see?" Tammy's grin was pushing her checks into big, joyful mounds under her eyes.

"See what?" Jolie's voice didn't reveal the tinge of frustration she was beginning to feel. She was safe, the jaguar was fine, and she wanted the whole thing to be a distant memory. Nothing more than something to wow the grand-kids with. Children. A sense of Alvin shot through her body, and she struggled to suppress the quiver that came along with it.

Tammy's exasperated, "Those!" helped her to squelch the feeling. She looked at the receptionist who was pointing a slim, white finger at the object to Jolie's left. Jolie turned and saw a big bouquet of white roses resting on the counter. She looked back to Tammy.

"They're for you, silly!"

Jolie moved over a couple of steps and sniffed the fragrant blossoms.

"There're twelve," Tammy informed her. "I know

because I counted twice. I've been working here since forever, and this is the first time someone's gotten flowers. It's so romantic."

Jolie couldn't agree more. She plucked the card from the flowers. Printed in block lettering were the words, "Just because...Sincerely, Alvin." Jolie recognized the writing and it touched her that he'd signed the card personally instead of leaving it for the florist to do. But still, she hesitated at the actual words. *How am I to interpret that?* She read the two words again and asked herself, *Just because you're nice? Just because I like you? Just because I was thinking of you? Or maybe, just because I love you?* The thought made her breath catch.

"Oh, this is wonderful." Tammy clapped her hands together, making Jolie look at her briefly. "I can tell by your face that you didn't expect this, and you must really like this guy."

Jolie's eyes had drifted to the card, but they flew back to Tammy. "What do you mean?"

"Oh Jolie, it's in your expression. That surprised wonder mixed with joy."

"Humph! I guess my face is showing stuff that I didn't even know I was feeling."

Tammy laughed, "Yeah, you like him. That sarcastic tone is a dead giveaway. You are definitely sprung. Oh, new love is fabulous. So, who is he?"

Her tone was so sappy that Jolie chuckled as she answered, "Just a friend."

"A friend, huh? I'd say he's a pretty special friend to send you a dozen white roses. If I'm not mistaken, I think white means everlasting friendship, but don't quote me on that."

Jolie's heart thumped with disappointment. She refused to analyze why as she said goodbye to Tammy. It took her fifteen minutes to go up a flight of stairs and walk the short hallway to her office. The large bouquet drew questions, congratulations, and smiling comments from everyone she passed. Her phone was ringing when she placed the vase on her desk. For the same reason she didn't want to analyze her disappointment, she didn't want to focus on why she expected Alvin to be on the other end of the line.

Joan's booming voice yelled a jubilant hello. Because of all the background noise, Jolie knew she was calling from her car phone. "Hey, girl, I had an appointment in your neck of the woods. Can you leave animal kingdom long enough to have lunch?"

Nose to the flowers again, Jolie said, "Yes, I can go. Pick me up outside the main gate in five." She hung up the phone still admiring her flowers. She decided she didn't care what the reason was. She had beautiful flowers from an attractive man, and darn it, she was going to be pleased about it!

§§§

The two sat at the table in Indochine. Jolie ordered garlic chicken and Joan got heavenly beef. "So." Joan sipped her Thai ice tea. "You've been cheesin' since you got in the car. What's the reason for this new inner glow stuff?"

"I just got flowers. Nothing like a dozen roses to make a sister shine."

"You ain't never lied." Joan threw up her hands, then grabbed her purse, and started rummaging inside before she caught herself and gave Jolie a sheepish look.

Jolie sighed as if the world's weight were pushing the air from her, and then she flashed a smile. "Go ahead, girl. I feel so good that I can probably tolerate one."

Joan pulled out a pack of Benson Hedges, menthol ultra lights. Seconds later, she turned sideways and released a huge cloud of blue gray smoke. She looked at Jolie who was shaking her head. "Hey, I'm getting better. Give a sister some credit. Didn't you notice that I didn't even try to light one up at Esquire?"

Jolie nodded.

"I'm down to only four a day: one in the morning and night, one at lunch and one at dinner. But forget that." She paused to take another drag, releasing smoke from the side of her mouth. "So, who's the Romeo?"

Jolie sat up straighter, preparing to be teased. "Alvin Guillory."

Joan's eyes cut to her and she slowly put her treasured cigarette in the ashtray. "Wait a minute. You're beaming from ear to ear about getting flowers from Mr. Not Dark Enough? Don't tell me you tasted the forbidden fruit and it was sweeter and riper than you thought?"

Jolie blushed.

"Ahh haa!" Cigarette back in hand, Joan took a self-satisfied drag.

"Now Joan, why did you have to go there? I discovered some stuff independent of...tasting...that made me rethink my position." Jolie filled her best friend in on her and Alvin's checkered past. She withheld the pregnancy, figuring that was only her and Alvin's business, but she did explain how her mother had blocked their access to each other. The food arrived and Joan was crushing out the butt when Jolie came to the end of the story.

Her friend picked up her fork and held it midair with her head to the side as she said, "Sounds like lost love found, or maybe love interrupted."

The smile melted from Jolie's face. "That's more than a little premature, Joan."

Joan waved her fork at her as she chewed. In between bites, she said, "Shoot, y'all been wanting each other all this time and now you can just go with it. Let nature take over and see what happens."

Jolie tried to voice her concerns. "Joan, we were great together a long time ago. I'm scared that we're living in the past. You know, we're different people now, and we're being foolish trying to recapture lost moments."

Joan looked at her through a haze of smoke. Jolie frowned. She hadn't even seen her light up. "Hey, I'm skipping the one at dinner." She shrugged. "We're talking about

serious stuff here." She waved the newly lit cigarette.
"These help me think."

Jolie just shook her head.

Unperturbed, Joan continued. "The answer really is
simple, though. Both of you obviously have the hots for each
other. Get to know one another."

Jolie looked down and studied her twisting hands.

Joan stubbed out the half-smoked cigarette, sensing her
friend's deep discomfort. "Jolie?"

She looked at Joan and there was moisture shimmering
in her eyes. "When I look into my heart of hearts, Joan, I'm
scared. I poured every good feeling I was capable of into this
thing fifteen years ago. When it failed, I wanted to die."
Jolie didn't mention how the loss of her child had enhanced
the turmoil. "I don't know if I can survive this round if we
strike out again. I'm terrified, Joan."

"Oh baby." Joan scooted around to her side of the
bench, and wrapped her front to Jolie's side in a fierce hug.
"All of this is about taking chances, sweetie. If you don't take
the risk, you may regret it the rest of your life. The fact that
you two found each other again must mean something.
Have courage, give it a try, and run like hell if it doesn't work
out, but at least you will have given it your best effort. And
remember, I'll always be here if the pieces of this puzzle
don't exactly fit." Joan's arms tightened into another hard
embrace before she shifted back to her place.

"You know what?" she said once she was settled in her
seat. "You can deny love, but it'll still be there. It's as invis-

ible as air, and as unconscious as breathing. You can try to ignore it and pretend it doesn't exist, just as you can hold your breath and try not to breathe, but eventually you'll faint and your body will overcome your will and make you breathe while you're out. You can keep denying it, Jolie, but I think this guy's in you in more than the biblical sense. He's going to pop up every time you relax."

Jolie replied blandly, "There you go, taking gigantic leaps forward. We're talking about dating, getting to know each other again, not love and being inside folks."

"Are we? Well, no matter. Let's eat. You know this Thai food is nasty when it's cold. Just remember my words if you find that you're beyond liking what you're getting to know."

When Jolie got back to her office, there was a message from Alvin. His smooth, deep voice cooed to her from the machine, "I have a couple of back-to-back home games, but keep Friday free. I have plans for you. If you can't make it, give me a call. Until then, bye my little rose."

Chapter 15

What to wear for an official date? Jolie didn't have a clue. Hands on hips, she stood in front of her closet glaring at the clothes. Glancing down, she saw the boots with the ripped up soles. They rested side by side with her spanking new hiking boots that her boss had bought her the Monday after the incident. Even though the ripped up ones were retired, they still had a prominent place on the floor of the closet to serve as a constant reminder, but not of the jaguar. No, the shoes brought waves of heat because they were a souvenir of the wild, passionate aftermath with Alvin and a wall.

Looking back up, Jolie tried to focus on the problem at hand. What to wear? Nothing seemed appropriate for a real date. Her eyes settled on a raspberry spaghetti dress. Jolie fingered the five thin straps that highlighted each side, and decided to put it on over her red bra and panties. The button front dress was the perfect choice because it was comfortable, dressy, and a little funky with the novel straps and daring front split. Black, strappy heels completed the outfit. Jolie looked in the mirror, deciding that she needed something else. Opening the jewelry box, she pulled out her mother's diamond stud earrings and gold, bangle bracelets.

As she put the items on, she spoke. "Momma, you may be fussing in your grave that I'm wearing your good stuff on a date with Alvin, but I'm going to give him another shot. I have to see how this goes for myself."

Turning from the mirror, she left the bedroom and headed down the short hall to the living room. She faltered when she saw Alvin already sitting on one of the chairs, facing her brother and Robyn who were sitting together on the couch. Jolie leaned against the wall momentarily reeling. Alvin looked good in a pair of sharp, crisp slacks and a silk mock turtleneck. However, Jolie knew what lay beneath those fine clothes, and that knowledge made her pulse pause. Alvin was nodding his head as Tyrese said something with a tight, stern face. Robyn sat back listening as she absently rubbed her very round belly. Both males stood when they noticed Jolie standing in the doorway. She walked over and bent to hug Robyn, and then ran a hand over the baby. Next, she looked at the two men. Alvin's lips were upturned slightly as if he were amused, and Tyrese wore a very plastic smile.

"Hey sis, I was just about to come and tell you that Coach Alvin's here."

"Uh huh," Jolie said, suspecting that her brother was being less than truthful.

"Have a good time tonight. Don't do anything I wouldn't do."

Geez, that means I can do just about anything. With great restraint, Jolie kept the comment to herself. She smiled and moved towards the door. Alvin took the hint, said his goodbyes, and followed Jolie.

When they were settled in his car and on their way, Jolie said, "Oh, goodness. What did he say?"

Alvin laughed. "Nothing you have to be concerned about. He's just ensuring my intentions are honorable. This may surprise you, but your brother worries about you also."

"Oh no, I believe. I'm just not sure how far that boy will go. He didn't step out of line, did he?"

"No, he very politely told me he'd kill me if I messed over his sister. A strong desire to protect you must run in the family." Alvin glanced over in time to see her stricken expression. He reached over and massaged her leg. "Don't worry. I'd do the same thing in his position. Take pride in the fact that he cares for you so deeply."

Jolie managed a nod he couldn't see. Her eyes were drawn to the strong, long fingers that were creating a wonderful sensation in her thigh. When that feeling was just starting to creep upwards, he placed both hands on the steering wheel. She defied the impulse to yank the hand back to where it had been.

"So, my lady, you have options this evening: intimate and intense, or remote and elegant."

"Don't I get more clues?"

"Nope, that's it, but if I were you, I'd pick option number one."

Laughing, Jolie said, "All right, intimate and intense it is then."

"Good. I knew you'd make the right choice."

Jolie didn't realized how edgy she was until she began to relax. Alvin's light, teasing style left her slightly off guard and pleased. She was puzzled when they pulled into his neighborhood and parked underneath his building.

"Did you forget something?"

"No," he took the keys from the ignition and looked at her with soft, warm eyes. "Are you ready to be pampered?"

"Depends on who's doing the babying."

"Oh, I suspect that it's a guy that you're going to like very much."

"Oh yeah, this guy is pretty confident, huh?"

"Yes, but only because his motives are pure."

The softly spoken words negated any spicy response that sprang to Jolie's lips. They both got out of the car and Alvin showed Jolie the way by gently guiding her with a hand just above her elbow. In no time, his palm had slid down to catch her hand in a loose grip as he led her past the doorman, up the elevator, and into his condominium. Soft jazz emanating from hidden speakers caressed Jolie's ears as soon as they entered the apartment. Will Downing. She'd recognize his rich, deep voice anywhere.

Alvin was pleased to see her head gently bobbing. He hung her coat in the closet near the front door and turned to her. "Have I told you how wonderful you look?"

Smiling wide, Jolie shook her head.

"I love it when you show off your broad shoulders and long neck. And your hair, damn, it looks so good out and wild all over your shoulders."

Jolie laughed. "Alvie, wild isn't exactly a compliment."

"You know what I mean, girl." He sidled up and took her in his arms. Swaying gently, he steered them across the short distance to the living room. Feeling her body lightly held against his, and, at times enjoying a brush from her breast or thigh, Alvin was happy. He expressed it by twirling Jolie around before he whispered a kiss on her cheek and released her. "Make yourself comfortable. I'm just going to check things in the kitchen."

Jolie continued lightly swaying to the music as she wandered over to the stereo system. She picked up the open compact disk case. "Will Downing and Gerald Albright," she read confirming her suspicions. The title sent quivers through her torso, "Pleasures of the Night." Closing her eyes, she realized she was listening to the title track. Will sang about warm breezes blowing and other erotic things. The words, combined with Albright's seductive saxophone play, made Jolie feel surreal. As if she'd snuck into someone else's love affair because this was way too idyllic to be hers.

She sensed his presence right before sturdy arms slipped around her. Keeping her eyes closed, Jolie willed the fantasy to continue. The weight of her hair was lifted, shifted to the side, and then soft lips began barely touching her neck. The gentle touch became kisses that developed into a full caress that traveled from ear to shoulder and back again. Jolie found the famous words of Lauren Hill sashaying into her consciousness. "The sweetest thing I've ever known is like the kiss to a collarbone." Good God, Lauren had it right; Jolie's legs began to feel about as strong as wet paper.

Alvin perceived her dilemma and tightened his arms to hold her firmly. "Would you like a drink before dinner?" His lips traced the shell of her ear.

"Dinner?" Jolie was thinking about other delights beside food. Maybe we should eat later."

"Yes, dinner. Think of it as an appetizer before other…indulgences." The last word was murmured into her ear. The hot, moist air toying with the canal had her sweltering. "How about a nice glass of white wine or maybe a merlot as rich as your lips."

Firm hands journeyed up her sides, underneath her arms, and rested on the top of her shoulders. From there, the tender hands slowly turned her into an electric embrace. An intense kiss followed, one that had Jolie crushing the silk of Alvin's shirt as she pulled, trying to yank it from his slacks. Alvin grasped her hands and pulled them to his lips for a kiss. "Perhaps a nice glass of Absolut vodka, I have a bottle chilling in the freezer for you. I've got shot glasses, but if you prefer, I don't mind if you drink straight from the neck."

Jolie knew he didn't drink and she was touched by the obvious attempt to please her. Through her chuckles, she said, "Thanks, but no. I only drink hard liquor when I've been chased by wild animals."

"Perhaps a coke or 7-Up then?" She found it hard to answer because he lifted her hand, pressed his lips to the Band Aid, and then began kissing the webbing between each finger. Recognizing the longing, he really didn't expect an answer. When none came, he transferred the hand he'd loved into two of his and led her into the dining room.

Jolie stopped and stared. Although her feet weren't moving, her heart raced. A large bouquet of white roses rested on a formally set table for two. Candles on the table and on the surrounding counters were the only light in the room, and the muted glow accented the whole experience. "Alvin, this is wonderful, simply wonderful, but..."

"What, honey? Don't you know you can ask anything?"

"Doesn't white mean everlasting friendship?"

Alvin chuckled. "No. According to the florist where I bought them, white means two things. It can stand for heavenly, that's you, and it can also mean I'm worthy of you, that's me."

"I like that a heck of a lot more than being buddies." She arched on her tiptoes and kissed his cheek. Choosing to enjoy whatever he had in store, she said, "I'll take the merlot."

Alvin's eyes were drawn back to her mouth. He was tempted to dabble there again, but he knew all his well-laid plans would be aborted. He wanted this to be special, a thing of beauty that they'd have fond memories of until death did them part. Gazing at her admiring the table setting as he poured the wine, he knew that what he wanted with all his heart was to be with this woman for the rest of his days.

Jolie suddenly looked over her shoulder and caught the look on his face. The intensity of it struck a chord in her immediately. She didn't know exactly how to intepret it, but it was magnetic, pulling at something deep in her belly. He walked to her, holding the half full glass that he lifted to her lips. Jolie's fingers wrapped over his hand as she drank.

Together, they lowered the flute. Alvin didn't resist the urge to touch her this time. He lifted his free hand and explored the contours of her face: the depth of her cheekbones, the hollowness of her cheeks, the subtle strength of her jaw. He watched her, closely as he let his fingers relearn her. Her eyelashes lowered and her breathing became steadier, heavier. Next, his fingers whispered across her full mouth, over the ridge of slightly lighter skin that outlined the succulent, brown lips.

Jolie released a shaky hand, letting him have full responsibility for the wineglass. She clenched her fingers into a fist and said in a raspy voice, "If you continue with this, I'll have to insist that we skip the lovely dinner that I know you've prepared, or had prepared."

Alvin chuckled, a deep sexy sound that was different from his usual laugh. His hand floated down her neck and the front of her dress before leaving her body completely. He could have sworn she swayed after the departing fingers, trying to prolong the touch.

With an almost imperceptible shudder, Jolie said, "What's for dinner?" The memory of his gentle touch was still vibrating softly through her system, making the simplest question difficult to articulate.

"Oh a little of this and a little of that." He dipped his

head and warm lips stroked her forehead. Then he handed her the wine. "Have a seat, my dear, and the first course will be served."

"Oh, there're courses, huh?"

"Uh, not really. Just dinner and some sweets I cooked up." He paused in thought for a moment. "And then more dessert, until your every appetite is satisfied." He disappeared into the kitchen, leaving Jolie with the distinct impression that the more dessert had nothing to do with food. She would surely be disappointed if her premonition was incorrect.

He returned with two plates and Jolie discovered that the food was truly wonderful. He'd prepared shrimp scampi, garlic bread, and a Caesar salad. Despite how good the food was, it was difficult for Jolie to eat because she had a good idea of how the evening would end. And Good Lord, she was looking forward to it! Trying to concentrate on the food, Jolie took a bite and complimented him.

Alvin confessed his love of the culinary arts. "At first I hated it, but Mamma insisted that I learn how to be self-sufficient, so I wouldn't have to marry to eat. She wasn't impressed when I told her I'd be rich enough to hire a cook." They both chuckled. "But over the years, I began to enjoy it, and it became a stress reliever. When things got rough, I'd just settle down and find the time to cook. It felt like I had control over something, and regardless of anyone else, I could make it come out good."

Jolie was lifting her wineglass for a sip when she stopped

and looked at him quizzically, "Was it difficult being a star?"

Alvin chuckled. "The term star is relative. I'm proud of my accomplishments, but I was never a household name like Michael Jordan or Magic Johnson. People usually didn't recognize me outside of the city I was playing in and that was generally okay by me because it's no fun living in a fish bowl. One thing I credit myself with is the fact that I'm realistic and you know what? I owe that to you."

He saw the look on her face. "I know, I know. I see the confusion in your eyes. You don't think I'm making any sense, but hear me out. When I went through my freak-out and it resulted in me doing the dumbest thing in my life, breaking up with you, I decided something: I wouldn't let anything else get into my head and mess me up like that. If I couldn't do something, I would find out after I'd worked damn hard at it. It wouldn't be because I got scared and panicked. I lost you because I couldn't handle my fears, but because of that experience, I was no longer scared to face my fears. I was able to stare them down and confront them because the worst had already happened; I'd already lost you. This is the first time I've actually said this stuff out loud." He looked directly at her. "Does that make any sense?"

"Yeah, a lot."

"Good. I faced each challenge with determination and eventually found myself in the pros. I'm only 6'2", kind of short by NBA standards. I have a quick first step, and I've got a decent jumper. I was an incredibly hard worker, but I rarely started. The culmination of all my diligence is that I was an excellent sixth man. Do you know what that means?"

"You were the first to come off the bench to relieve the players who had started."

"Yes!" Alvin put down his fork in surprise. "You've learned a lot following Ty."

Now it was Jolie's turn to make a confession. She looked him in the eyes as she spoke quietly. "No, Alvin. I've been following you. I remember when you were being considered as the sixth man of the year. I thought they'd robbed you when you didn't get it."

His eyes softened. "You followed me?" He sounded like a little boy who'd just gotten the toy that would make him the envy of all his peers.

She nodded.

"Ahh, you deserve a kiss for that." He stood up, and leaned towards her while bending down. His head tilted to gently rub lips with hers. Jolie's mouth opened slightly, and Alvin glided inside to softly tease her tongue. Then he slipped away and returned to his seat. Once he had settled, he continued speaking. "I was a slightly above average player who had to work his butt off to get there. Now your brother, on the other hand, has the potential to be great. He just gets things that it took me years to develop, and he has an instinctive feel for the court, something you're born with that's almost impossible to teach. I've snuck in and watched a few of his games now. The boy's a leader, the others naturally follow him. If he stays in gear, he's gonna go big time."

His overall words gave her a new sense of him, and his praise of Tyrese filled her with sibling pride. "Thanks, I'm very pleased with him most of the time."

Alvin nodded his head and said, "Eat, so we can move on to more delights."

Jolie regarded her full plate, and then she looked at Alvin. His sensuous lips were just closing around a fork holding shrimp. The movement reminded her of high school and the cookie. Alvin caught her looking, and maybe he thought of that moment also because he began eating the piece slowly, with lips and tongue, as if he were enjoying some part of her anatomy. At least that's how Jolie's erotically charged imagination interpreted it. She lost track of time and space as she watched him consume more pieces in much the same manner. She sat, mesmerized, captivated by firm, brown lips enjoying seafood. At last, he cleared his plate.

He looked at her and innocently asked, "You don't like my cooking?"

Jolie blinked. It took her a minute to come out of the fog and understand his words. Then she chuckled. "You know good and well this food is excellent. And you probably know I have so many butterflies in my stomach right now that I couldn't eat even if I'd just come off a hunger strike."

Alvin threw back his head and laughed. "Okay, I'll put you out of your misery." He stood and took her plate.

"Would you like dessert?" Jolie shook her head. What she wanted had nothing to do with sweets. She steepled her arms and rested her chin on the back of her interlocked fingers. Alvin put down the plates and ran a finger from the top of her forehead to her chin. He repeated the light touch on the other side of her face. A perfect heart and you have my heart, he thought.

Jolie closed her eyes, savoring the light touch, gravitating towards the palm when it moved into a full caress of her check. She murmured, "Alvie." His knees buckled. She might have laughed or smiled in wonder if her eyes had been open. Jolie, you just don't know your power. "One day I'll have to tell you."

"Hum, did you say something?" She whispered a kiss across his palm and opened her eyes, looking at him over his hand.

He didn't realize he'd spoken the words out loud. "Nothing important, babe." Later, when he was surer of her feelings, he would let loose with words that he kept locked in his chest. Tonight only his actions would show how he felt. His knowing fingers began a gentle massage at the point where her jaw and neck met. Seemingly of their own accord, her lids slowly lowered. His intent was to make her ache from want and then take her slowly and deliberately. Looking at her, he concluded the time was right because he sure as hell couldn't wait any longer. He pulled her to her feet and said, "Why don't I freshen your drink, and show you how good I am at lighting a fire."

Jolie allowed herself to be led into the sunken living room. She accepted the wineglass full of red liquid from Alvin's hand. Their brief touch produced a small electric shock. But how could it be otherwise? There's so much energy charging between us we could probably light a small city. The thought produced a slight smile that turned into a chuckle when Alvin opened a cabinet by the huge fireplace and pulled out several Presto logs. "That's not the manly way to start a fire. All you need is a match."

Alvin put the logs on the grate. "Oh, don't worry. I'll show you the manly way to heat things up in a couple of minutes."

That wiped the smile from her face, and she took a strong sip of wine to calm the anticipation. A funky, Brazilian jazz song filled the speakers just as the flames began licking the Presto wood. Alvin stood, dusted off his pants, and stretched out a hand to her. "I love to dance, but I don't know how to do that salsa, samba stuff," she whispered.

"Just flow with me." Jolie put her glass on the coffee table. Alvin placed large hands at her waist and settled her long form into his body. Jolie relaxed and just let him guided her through the twisting forward and back motion. After a time, she tilted her head and said in slight wonderment, "I don't want to jinx myself, but I think I've got it."

"Yep, you're all that plus a bag of chips." He felt her merriment against his chest. The lively music changed into a slower, more haunting tune and Alvin said, "Do you mind if I just hold you?" His voice was low and gravelly.

Heck no! Why in the world is he asking? Her hands transferred from his shoulders to his flat, hard chest. She leaned back and looked up at him, searching his eyes. Her fingers felt his heat and the steady pump of his heart. My goodness, she thought, what is the man waiting for? A blatant invitation? Something flickered in his eyes, and Jolie instinctively knew the time had come. Her lids lowered, and she released the barest of whimpers when his mouth pressed to hers. She yelped when, without a word, he lifted her in his arms and carried her into the bedroom.

"Thank you." Her tongue touched his ear as she spoke.

"For what?" He laid her down on the mattress.

"For finally deciding to have your way with me."

His chuckle was hoarse as he ran his fingers down her torso. "We did it your way last time. Now it's my turn." He teased her lips, not giving in to the warm cavern that lay just beyond, preferring to let his mouth travel down her neck, across the V of her dress, before slipping the straps off her shoulders. His nose and cheeks moved against the red lace bra, tantalizing the smooth skin underneath. While his head occupied her upper body, his hands pushed the dress down. Jolie managed to do the rest, and soon she was partially nude. Alvin's hands never stopped moving as he rubbed the flesh below her belly button, just grazing the cloth that covered her mound.

"So beautiful," he sighed as his right hand joined his mouth and undid the front clasp of her bra. Jolie withered as he painted almost every inch of the flesh revealed with slow, lavish strokes from his tongue. He avoided the nipples that had grown into rock hard nuggets, choosing instead to nuzzle the valley between the peaks as if he'd find gold there. His hands weren't idle as they removed her underwear, then dallied along the tops of her thighs and wandered into crevices that surrounded her most secret self.

Jolie lifted her fingers to caress the back of his head. She felt need coursing through her, but there was also something else. She was...fearless. Yes, that was the right word. She was going to give this man her all tonight, take the risk, and travel along the potentially dangerous path to unbridled joy. Her body arched uncontrollably when she felt the stroke of his finger near her center at the same time his lips closed around her left nipple. Her arms jerked out, flinging her outstretched fingers.

The heat began to rise and swell in Alvin as she responded to him. He continued his labors as he kicked off his shoes, socks, and undid his pants. Then he moved both hands up and captured a breast and gave it his complete attention, sucking it in a leisurely, drawn-out motion before stopping to rip his shirt over his head. The movement was so quick, he was back before Jolie noticed. He treated the other peak to similar attention before he rose up and removed his pants.

Jolie opened her eyes and gasped at the sight. He wasn't built like a body builder, but more like a panther. Strong, lean, athletic, but not overdeveloped. His smooth, sleek muscles played peek-a-boo as he removed his pants.

"No socks," he said, making her laugh as she continued to watch the muscles move under his skin. She wanted to reach out and trace their shape. However, she couldn't help comparing it to the body she once knew. The height was the same, but the thin frame had firmed up in all the right places. One thing about him hadn't changed though. His manhood stood out as proud and long as it had when he was nineteen.

He placed his body over hers and rubbed his entire length against her lightly before capturing her mouth completely. Not holding back, his tongue filled the opening Jolie gladly provided for him. His hands encircled her hips as he lightly ground against her. He followed the same path he had before, tongue and lips over neck, shoulders, and breasts. Then he continued even farther, stopping to investigate her navel with his nose and mouth before moving on to run the length of her legs. Quivering flesh and soft moans followed his every touch.

And then he journeyed back up.

As he moved, he glanced at her face to gauge her reaction. He craved to be the first to show her every joy, every nuance, and side road of lovemaking. He was disappointed. As he reached the apex and positioned himself, he realized that her expression was far from surprised. No, what he saw was expectation. Obviously, this delight wasn't new. Jealousy made him pause.

Jolie assumed this was more teasing. Her fingers itched to grab his hair and pull him to where she wanted him most.

Instead, she reached up and stroked his cheek.

Closing his eyes, Alvin turned to the fingers and kissed them. Her presence was a strong magnet that helped him push the troubling thoughts aside. He opened his eyes to see Jolie's thighs separating. Alvin was mesmerized. He decided right then and there, that he might not be the first to provide this particular pleasure, but he'd damn sure be the best. He started on the hair that covered her. He treated it the same as her breasts, lavishing it with his tongue. The hair lay flat before he ventured into the wet crevice. Jolie gripped the sheets as he vibrated her center excellently. And then she lost it when she felt his thumb enter and leave her body rhythmically. The release brought tears of sheer joy.

As Jolie's tense body slowly relaxed into the bed and Alvin's waiting hands, she remembered her cousin Kisha's words. Kisha had dated a man that was less than good for her. In frustration, Jolie asked why she put up with the bum. With an innocent, wide-eyed look, Kisha said, "He licked me, boo, and I just haven't been the same since." Jolie remembered dying with laughter, thinking there wasn't a technique out there that was so fabulous a woman would lose her common sense. Now she knew better as she leaned up and looked down at Alvin. The lower half of his face was still covered as he continued gently stroking the area near her hot spot. She squeezed her eyes shut and knew that she owed her cousin an apology.

Jolie flopped back on the bed enjoying what he was doing too much to make him stop. Deep in her heart, she knew it was more than the act. The feeling she was scared to name was the real culprit. His wonderful ability combined with that feeling made her reach unheard of heights of pleasure. Feeling extremely decadent for lying back and only enjoying, Jolie sat up and looked down into his smiling eyes. "That…was…nice."

"Nice?" he murmured against her. "Maybe I should keep this up if I only accomplished nice?"

Jolie chuckled, "If you get me to that again, I'll have a heart attack right here in your bed. A woman can only take something that strong once a night! Come here." She reached out to him. He couldn't resist the husky command. With a parting kiss, Alvin rose and went to her. She urged him to keep coming forward until his hips were near her face. Then she sat up and wrapped a hand around him. Before she began her magic, she asked, "Protection?" Alvin reached into the nightstand, retrieved the requested item, and placed it in her open palm.

The situation seemed unreal to Alvin as Jolie's mouth closed over him, filling him with more pleasure than he thought he could feel. Disappointment and regret battled with the bliss of feeling Jolie's tongue move up and down his length. The sight was too much, and he closed his eyes. The Jolie he knew before would never think of doing such a thing. Their adventures in high school and college hadn't expanded much beyond the missionary position and now, here she was working him as he'd never been worked before. He hated the fact that she'd been with, learned from, anyone other than him.

With a gentle caress to the sacs that lay beyond his length, Jolie lay back. Alvin's lids rose to the wonderful sight. He was surprised that he was fully prepared. He wasn't aware that she'd opened the protection, much less slid it on.

Alvin stared as Jolie spread her legs wide. Her aura was enough to chase all the bad feelings from him. He adored this woman he was about to enter, and if he did this thing right, she would hopefully learn to feel for him again. The past was the past, and he only wanted to look to the future with Jolie.

Both inhaled sharply when their bodies joined. Alvin slowly rose and descended, while Jolie's fingertips ran along his sides and across his buttocks. Her touch deepened as he moved faster, and her eyes drifted closed as the wild rhythm began carrying her away. Large, warm hands gripped her backside; knowing and bold, they helped to move Jolie along to passion's heights. This time there were no tears, but the air was pierced with a good old-fashioned holler when she reached the summit.

Alvin murmured something unintelligible against her straining neck. The sheets sprang from their mooring as Jolie raised her knees and lifted her hips slightly. "Yes, baby." His eyes shut tightly as the delightful, spiraling vibes carried him over the edge.

§§§

They were completely content to lie and do nothing more than stroke each other. Every once in a while, one of them would release a soft groan or murmur. Jolie was slipping into that place that was somewhere between sleep and wake when Alvin whispered, "So, how many lovers have you had?"

The question jerked her just like her mother's ear pulls when she drifted off during mass. As she adjusted to the query, her eyelashes fluttered against the crook of his neck, teasing the sensitive flesh, and making him squirm softly. In a throaty voice she said, "I'm quite sure it's been considerably fewer than you."

There was a slight edge there that let him know he should tread lightly. "Were you ever in love?"

"Yes," she answered without hesitation. "A very special man brought me to those highs." There was a short pause before she added, "And those lows."

Alvin held his breath and croaked out a small, "Who?"

A husky chuckle, then a playful thump to his chest, and a nipple tweak before she said, "You, silly! I loved you."

Alvin's breath was released in a joyous laugh. He rolled her onto his chest before he realized she'd used the word loved, past tense. He couldn't resist digging just a little deeper. "Who was that guy at the Esquire?"

Jolie rested her forearms on his chest and lifted up. "Paul? We were living together when that stuff happened with Ty. He tried to make me choose." Jolie shook her head. The bulk of her hair had been resting on her back. Now it slipped over the sides and tickled Alvin's face and shoulders. "I could never love someone who was that selfish. Besides, he was too much like my father; same issues, different face."

Alvin remembered a leftover remnant from some psychology course. "Isn't that what women look for in a man?"

"Yeah, I've heard that, too. Who knows? If I hadn't had a woman-to-woman chat with my mom before she died, maybe I'd be with Paul now."

Alvin's arms tightened, crushing her face to his neck.

"Relax, Alvie. This is all theoretical. I'm lying naked on top of you with juices from your efforts dripping out of me."

"Oh, babe." The arms loosened as he began trailing kisses along her collarbone.

"Alvie...if you want me to finish explaining, you've got to stop." The last words were a whisper.

Alvin wasn't sure if he wanted to face this Pandora's box he'd opened. Out of respect for her, his lips stilled.

"Thanks to Mom, I understood my dad. Hardships he'd faced in the South left him with issues. My mother loved him despite his shortcomings. I still get frustrated, but I love my father, too." Jolie breathed deeply before continuing. "Once that stuff happened with Ty, I realized how much my dad and Paul had in common. Except there was one big difference. Paul didn't have my dad's history to explain his lack of emotion, his failure to empathize. After I recognized the similarities, I ran from him. I didn't want to be with that side of my father." Jolie leaned up and pecked his lips. "So what about you, Mr. NBA? You had your choice of women."

He grasped the back of her head and drew her in for a kiss that surprised her with its intensity. He devoured her lips and explored the opening beyond with knowledge and passion. Jolie's toes wiggled and the soft mounds pressed against his chest were jolted back into hard peaks. She was breathless when he eased up just enough to mummer against her lips, "I knew the real thing. I spent time searching, but none could compare to perfection."

Jolie trembled out of delight and concern. "Alvie, I'm a real woman. Don't put me on a pedestal, 'cause I have faults."

Alvin trailed his lips down her upturned neck before whispering against the warm skin, "We've all got those, babe. What I meant…" He drew the sentence out as she slowly lifted up to give him access. Right before his mouth closed over a nipple, he said, "Is that you're perfect for me."

No other intelligent words were said as their passion drew them into another bout of lovemaking. Afterwards, they lapsed into the gentle strokes again. Silence dominated as touches became slower, kisses became more languid, and they nestled into each other and drifted into a light sleep. A little while later, Alvin's lids lifted. He had a crick in his bicep and his throat felt parched, but he wouldn't have moved for the world. Jolie's head rested on his arm and her long, auburn tresses tickled his nose.

She seemed to feel his gaze, and he watched her slowly waken. Sleep gave way to a look of peace and tranquility as she lifted up and kissed his nose. She noticed where she rested. "Your arm must be killing you, I'm sorry." She kissed lightly on his tricep as he wiggled his fingers and flexed. "You know what?" She raised her eyes shyly.

"What, baby?" Her manner disturbed him.

"I'm hungry." A smile played with her lips.

He wrapped her in a bear hug. "So, you want more of me, huh? Okay, baby, eat away."

Jolie chuckled and jokingly pinched his hard chest. "You should be so lucky. How does the scampi do in the microwave?"

"It should be fine." Alvin stood up and stretched. Watching him made Jolie rethink her eating options. "If you keep looking at me like that, I can guarantee you that you won't be eating shrimp and noodles any time soon." Jolie's stomach growled, helping her to decide. She accepted Alvin's outstretched hand, and together they walked into the kitchen. "I'll fix it," Alvin said. "Why don't you make yourself comfortable."

"Okay." Jolie wandered into the living room where the last embers of the fire were struggling to stay alive. Going on memory, she reached into the cabinet, grabbed a Presto log, and placed it on the cinders. Afterwards, she lifted the wineglass she'd set down earlier and took a sip. She was completely happy, almost overjoyed to be standing naked in Alvin's condo sipping wine. She turned to see him leaving the kitchen with a plate of food in his hand.

He placed it on the coffee table. "I've tested it for you and in my humble opinion, it's still delicious, just like you."

He pecked her lips.

She put the glass down and said, "Oh God, Alvie, I'm really beginning to fall for you again, and it scares me. I'm starting to believe that maybe we can work. Please don't prove me wrong."

Her words made his heart thump with joy. He gathered her into his arms and was about to confess his love when the scrape of the door opening made them pull apart.

"Alvin?"

"Shush, baby." He placed her behind him and turned to face the door, taking up a defensive posture. "Stay behind me," he hissed, readying himself to dive at whoever came into his place.

There was a clanging noise and a female voice said, "Damn," as the door swung open. Alvin stared wide-eyed in disbelief, and Jolie peeked over his shoulder as the crouching woman picked up keys from the floor, and straightened to face a naked Alvin standing about ten feet away.

Jolie recognized her as the woman she'd seen in Alvin's condo. She stood in the hall light wearing a pair of tight, black Capri pants that ended right before her ankles. Her feet were encased in black suede, high heel mules, and her heavy breasts were captured in a sweater that was short enough to reveal a flash of toned stomach when she moved. Jolie uttered an oath of her own as she cowered behind Alvin.

"Well, well," the woman said in her husky voice as she twirled the key ring on a finger, the other hand was firmly planted on her shapely hip. "A naked...hard man in front of a roaring fire. What else could a sister ask for?" Jolie jerked straight at the words. Alvin reached behind and placed a steadying hand on her thigh. Sophia strolled into the condo, shutting the door behind her. "Oh, maybe this joy isn't for me, huh? Who is that hiding behind you?"

"None of your business, Sophia. Please leave, now." His voice sounded much calmer than he felt.

"Oh, sugar. This won't take long. I believe I forgot my gold evening gown here. I need it for a show. After I'm gone, you can go back to...whatever and whomever you're doing tonight."

By the self-satisfied look on her face, Alvin knew that there wasn't a contrite bone in Sophia's body. For some unknown reason, she'd planned this situation. When he'd run down to the market earlier that day to buy fresh scampi for the meal, he'd bumped into her. She'd seen the wine in his basket and said, "You don't drink."

He'd told her the wine wasn't for him. He was having company for dinner and she'd raised her eyebrows and released a long, drawn-out, "Ooohhhh!"

He'd quickly forgot the encounter. He hadn't spoken to Sophia since that day she'd come by to retrieve her things. Her behavior was a complete mystery to him.

Using both hands to hold Jolie behind his back, he said, "Wait outside. I'll look for your dress."

Ignoring his words, Sophia sauntered over to them. "Oh my goodness, I had best hurry. Your...excitement, shall we say, is rapidly...deteriorating."

That comment had Jolie glancing over Alvin's shoulder, and the two women's eyes met. Jolie didn't know what she expected, but what she saw truly startled her. There was an odd sort of glee captured in the other woman's cynical smile. *She knew I'd be here.* The thought was a neon sign blinking in Jolie's mind. *Apparently this is some sort of challenge.* The audacity of it pissed Jolie off. She removed Alvin's hands from her person and stepped to the side.

"Oh, it's you." Forefinger to chin, Sophia boldly observed Jolie. "I don't think we were properly introduced last time. My name is Sophia Mack, and who might you be?" Sophia abruptly stuck her hand out.

As ridiculous as it seemed, Jolie shook her hand. "Jolie Smith. I can't say it's a pleasure to meet you. As a matter of fact, it's downright disheartening."

Sophia clapped her hands and laughed. "Oh, I like her, Vin. She has spirit much like me. I'm sure you two have hotly contested games of one on one. Yes, I believe I can see the evidence on your skin, Jolie."

Jolie balled her fists and Alvin stepped between the two women and spoke. "I will not tolerate you insulting my guest, Sophia. As I said before, what is happening here is none of your business. Get your stuff and go or I will put you out by any means necessary. Leave the key and if I never see you again, it will be to soon."

Sophia took a small step backwards. "Ohh, there's no need to get nasty, Vin." She looked from Alvin to Jolie. "We're all adults here, handling a ...revealing situation.

Jolie, Jolie," a finger tapped her forehead. "Oh, yes, such a unique name. You're the one with the brother that Vin's recruiting." Sophia stepped back and once again, Jolie stood to the side so she could meet the glare face to face. Sophia looked Jolie up and down once more. Jolie stood proud and refused to recoil or flinch in front of the woman.

"Well, she is certainly a beautiful girl. Auburn and copper just like a shiny new penny, and probably worth about as much. You'd sleep with a dog to get the boy, wouldn't you? I can understand why you'd be willing to take such a hit for the team."

Furious, Jolie slapped Alvin's hand when he reached out to detain her. She walked to Sophia and stopped when their noses were almost touching. "Hit for the team, huh? At least I'm a part of the team. It sounds like your membership was revoked some time ago. You're just an interloper who has trouble understanding when she's not wanted." It was Jolie's turn to let her eyes travel up and down Sophia's body. "You've been cut, baby. Maybe this time you'll get the point, gather all your stuff, and leave the keys when you go, or do we need to have the locks changed? I know how you player wannabees sometimes have trouble getting the point when you've been dismissed."

With that, Jolie spun on her heels and walked into the bedroom at a slow, steady pace. She remembered something when she reached the entrance. "I believe you'll find the dress in the closet where you put it." She pointed to where she'd seen Sophia place the "lost" article when she had come there to take Alvin to dinner. "And as far as worth, at least this penny is intact. Your…game has so many holes I can see right through it." Back straight, Jolie walked through and shut the door softly.

§§§

Alvin was so angry, he was scared to get near Sophia because of what he might do. His fingers bent and straightened with the urge to wrap around her neck and choke until her body was as feeble as her mind. Instead, he held out his hand and she understood. Removing the key from her ring, she tossed it into the open palm. In a tight, controlled voice, he said, "You have exactly one minute to get your things and get out. If you're not gone in sixty seconds exactly, I will pick you up and throw your ass out." Alvin wanted her to leave as soon as possible, so he could do damage assessment. He had to reach Jolie before she shut him out for another fifteen years.

Unperturbed, Sophia walked to the hall closet and pulled out the dress.

As Alvin watched her move towards the door, he asked one question. "Why?"

Sophia cast a look over her shoulder, and said, "Because I can." Then she stopped, turned as if she had an afterthought. "You know, Vin, gum and men are alike. For me, they last about the same amount of time. I love Bubble Yum, but as soon as the flavor's gone, it's garbage time. I wasn't done chewing on you yet." Sophia's shrewd, dark brown eyes hardened into black onyx. "You tried leaving my mouth a chomp before I was ready, and now we're even. You've been officially spat out."

His fingers actually ached with the desire to throttle her. He wiggled them until she was gone, and then he threw the security bolt.

Jolie was completely dressed by the time he opened the bedroom door. The cold, hard woman he'd seen at Tyrese's first basketball game was back. Disdain flowed when her steely gaze rested upon him. Looking at her, Alvin wouldn't have believed that she'd squeezed her eyes tight and sunk to the floor with her back against the door when she'd first entered the room. She'd sat there, remembering Alvin's praise of her brother earlier. At the time she'd thought nothing of it. All she'd felt was sibling pride. However, now the conversation took on an ugly tint. Did Alvin's interest extend beyond Tyrese? In front of Sophia, she'd held her ground and acted as if the allegations were false, but were they? Embarrassment fired through her blood, and she knew her face was crimson as she sat on the floor. Recalling how the woman moved around with so much entitlement, as if she belonged there, had made Jolie's blood fire for a different reason. She'd picked herself up off the floor and begun yanking her clothes on. Alvin opened the door, just after she'd flicked her hair out of the dress.

"Please don't leave. Let me explain."

Her face was emotionless as she moved to pass him

without speaking. He reached for her arm. She bumped into the dresser, trying to avoid him. She ignored the pain as she hissed, "Don't touch me!"

A picture on the dresser fell. Jolie glanced at it, and the force of what she saw made her halt abruptly. It was the sketch of the horses that she'd given Alvin on their first date. Slightly dazed, she stared at the picture lying flat on the dresser. Out of the corner of her eye, she could see Alvin putting his hands out with the palms up as he said, "Okay, okay, I won't lay a finger on you, but please don't go, Jolie. I didn't know she would come by tonight. In fact, I didn't expect to see her in my space ever again."

Anger supplanted confusion. Jolie whirled on him. "The woman had a key, Alvin! You're so full of ...bull."

Frustrated, Alvin threw up his hands, "She was supposed to leave it, Jolie. Remember, I was in the shower, rushing to get ready for you. I expected her to leave the damn key."

Jolie remembered how she'd watched Sophia put the dress back in the closet. Even though she knew the woman was devious, she was livid that she'd been put in such a position where she could be so thoroughly humiliated.

"Jolie, please, please trust me on this."

She saw a basketball resting by her feet. She picked it up and rolled it between her fingers before responding. Lifting her head, she glared at Alvin and said, "Why should I, Alvin?" Then, taking lessons from the jaguar, Jolie hit him hard and fast. "I gave you all of me fifteen years ago. Do you hear me, Vin? I gave you everything that I was, and you threw it back in my face when times got tough. You left me to deal with the death of our child alone! I repeat, why the hell should I trust you now? So you can finish me off? Just make my heart stop from all the pain that you've caused me! No, thank you. Just stick with the damn orange ball and the likes of Sophia, and leave me the hell alone!" She threw the ball. Alvin was so stunned he didn't even attempt to stop it from bouncing off his chest. Before he could grunt in pain, Jolie was moving. She grabbed her purse and coat from the closet right before she released the security bolt and slammed out the front door.

She dashed down the stairs and out the building. The yellow of the cab across the street shone like a beacon. Barely glancing for traffic, Jolie flew across the road and into the taxi. She maintained her composure until after she checked her sleeping brother. However, the wall crumbled when she took off her mother's jewelry and put it away. The tears were flowing by the time she stepped into the shower. "Bastard!" she hissed into the warm water pelting her face. It washed away tears of embarrassment, frustration, and red-hot anger. The spray was so effective that Jolie could almost pretend she wasn't shedding tears over that fool at all.

When her shower was over, she yanked on underwear and a T-shirt. Just before the soft material passed her face, something in the open closet caught her eyes: the ripped sole hiking boots. A gasp escaped as remembered herself between a wall and Alvin. Furious, she grabbed the shoes and went into the garage where she dumped them into the garbage.

Chapter 16

"Hey, sis. It's the big game tonight. You gonna be there?" Tyrese asked in between bites of his raisin bran.

Jolie had just finished pouring hot water over a teabag. "Have I missed any of your play-off games thus far? Why would I wait until the championship to stop coming?"

Tyrese shrugged his broad, thin shoulders. "I'm kinda hyped up, ya know?"

Jolie could hardly understand him as he spoke through a full mouth. She was about to reprimand him until she looked. His foot was tapping at a hundred miles per hour while he consumed the cereal with mindless gusto. It occurred to her that her brother was nervous. "Ty, you're going to do great tonight. Just like you did last night and the weekend before." She sat down across from him and sipped from the steaming cup.

He looked at her right before he slurped the milk from the bowl, a disgusting habit that Jolie hated. Her eyebrows became one line as she sucked in her cheeks. "Sorry, sis. I forgot you were here."

"Gee, thanks. What else do you do when I'm not here?"

Shoulders hunched, he smiled.

"Forget I asked." Then she said, "Don't be worried about tonight. Just focus on the game and go with the flow."

Tyrese nodded. "You know what, sis? I'm not worried about playing, that's the easy part. It's all those other folks that get to me. The evil R people from planet X."

Jolie smiled at the playful tone in his voice, but she sensed his underlying seriousness. "Who are the R people?"

"The reporters and recruiters. Somebody's always up in my face, asking for a quote, or telling me to go to join their program. I thought the schools would back off once I told the newspapers I'm going to WAM, but they still come at me in sneaky ways."

WAM! Mentioning the university was enough to invoke Alvin. Jolie's thoughts made her jump and sit up a little straighter. Tyrese was too busy fussing to notice. " Big Mac slipped me a note from a Nevada school after practice yesterday. Telling me the world would be mine if I came to Vegas. I need a suspension like I need a hole in the head. This Vegas school is always having problems with the NCAA. I'm trying to get a degree and make it to pro ball, not get kicked out before I even start. And Mac, he's another one. He keeps ragging me to play on his summer league team. He acts like I owe him something just because he saw me in the park last year, and I talked to him about playing high school ball. He's telling the whole world that the only reason I'm playing now is because of him, when it was really Ms. Ethel and Robyn. I'd still be hearing gunshots every time the ball left my hand if it wasn't for Ms. Ethel." He paused to breath and then continued venting. "I love hoop, but I need to work and be with Robyn this summer. He just wants to ride my back to a trophy, jockey my name to glory, and I ain't having it." Tyrese crossed his arms and stared defiantly.

Jolie didn't know what to say. She waited for her mother's presence to fill her and help her pop out some words of wisdom that were perfect for the situation. It didn't happen. Guilt filled her instead. She'd been too busy obsessing and moping about Alvin to see what was happening with Tyrese. She watched her brother unwind his arms, and then he started twirling the breakfast bowl like it was a giant worry bead.

Her lips started moving and she sure hoped they would say the right thing. "Look, Ty. Your job in all this craziness is to play basketball and keep your grades up. The only ones you owe something to are yourself, Robyn, and most of all, the baby. This is the last game of the season, so the media attention should die down after this. But you're good, so we are going to have to figure out ways for you to be respectful, yet still maintain a distance for your sanity."

"Hey, I bet Coach Alvin can give me advice since he's been through this himself." His look turned mischievous. "And now that you two are closer, you can ask him to school me."

Jolie took a long drink of the now lukewarm tea.

"Hey, do you think he'll be there tonight? It's the state championship."

"I don't know, Ty."

He cocked his head, "You don't track him like you do me?"

The teacup was empty. Jolie cradled it as if the answers were concealed in the hollow of the porcelain. She didn't want Tyrese to resent Alvin, especially since a very small part of her knew that Alvin's only crime was negligence. Sophia was a woman scorned with a key, and that allowed her to cause all kinds of havoc. Her anger had died down to irritation, but she'd made such a grand exit at his condo that she didn't know how to come back from it. She'd hoped that he would call and they could ease back to where they'd been before, but she'd had no word from him in the last two weeks. She looked at her brother and knew she'd better say something or her lack of expression would tell him all that he needed to know. She repeated what she'd read in the paper last night about Alvin's team.

"He's been busy, Ty. I'm sure that's why he hasn't been at the other playoff games. WAM's had a heavy game schedule, and they've been preparing for March Madness as well."

Tyrese enthusiastically started talking about the college playoffs, unwittingly providing her with a way out. "I know. Isn't it great! They're going to the first round of the big dance, and some analysts are saying they're going to make it to the Sweet Sixteen! That's somethin'. With my help next year, we could go all the way!"

Jolie nodded, enjoying her brother's exuberance. She also remembered Alvin's revelations about the athletic director. He'd have a hard time getting rid of Alvin and his friend if they did well in the playoffs.

Tyrese stood and went to the sink to wash his bowl. Jolie spoke to his back. "Look, baby bro', don't get wrapped up in all the extra noise and let it interfere with what you've set out to do. Always be respectful and hold firm in your convictions, okay?"

"All right, sis. I hear ya."

§§§

Later that evening, Jolie watched her brother do pre-game warm ups with his team and knew that she was more nervous than he was. He effortlessly did a 360 dunk and received high fives from his teammates as he ran to the end of the line. This was the last game of the evening and their section of the Tacoma Dome was packed. The large arena had been sliced in two by a ceiling to floor curtain. The girls' game on the other side had ended and most of their crowd had wandered over to the boys' game to see firsthand who would win the classic battle between big city and small town. The game pitted the Rainier Beach Titans, Tyrese's team, against the Eastern Wolverines. The Wolverines came from a tiny farming community in the eastern part of the state, and according to the paper, they were on a mission to humble the arrogant city boys.

Jolie wasn't an expert on the game, but she could see what the problem would be. Height. She counted, and from her seat three rows up, she could see that the Wolverines had four boys that were taller than any Titan player.

Despite her vow not to, Jolie found herself scanning the crowd for Alvin. She was well aware of his game schedule, so she knew that he was in town and that his team didn't have a game that night. She hadn't seen him at any of the playoff games, but this was the championship. He had to be somewhere checking out what could be the best talent in the state.

Even though she was looking for him, she still felt surprised when her eyes found him. He sat across the court about five rows up, almost directly in her line of sight. For several moments, Jolie just studied him. It was an easy thing to do because he hadn't noticed her. He looked good, crouching there with his hands on his knees as he watched the players. He kept the horse sketch! The memory coursed through her brain, bringing the pain of regret that things weren't right between them. The picture she'd given him on their first date was captured in a frame that sat on the dresser in his room. That, more than any words, showed her that he had indeed cared for her, deeply, over the years that they'd been apart. The buzzer sounded and Jolie tore her eyes from Alvin and tried to concentrate on the game.

As expected, the big boys on the Wolverines put on quite a show. The Titans' smaller players couldn't stop them once they passed the ball inside to their larger boys. They made easy shot after easy shot. On offense, the Titans couldn't get an inside shot because their players would reject the ball like a deformed toy. Tyrese seemed to be the only one who could hit an outside shot, and soon the Wolverine guards' were double- teaming him, attempting to shut him down. By the end of the half, the Wolverines were up by ten.

Alvin and Tyrese had eye contact as he headed into the locker room for half time. The Titan coach nodded his way, and Alvin returned the gesture; he sure hoped the man would see the adjustment he needed to make, so that Tyrese could experience his first championship.

He knew that Jolie had to be there, yet he refused to look for her. Looking at her meant longing for her, and he was damn tired of aching. Maybe that mess with Sophia was the Almighty's way of saying that it wasn't destined to be. Who was he to defy such a higher power? Besides, she'd said such ugly things to him. Did she really think he was the type of man who would abandon his child? How could she pass judgment when she'd had the nerve to not even let him know she was pregnant? He reminded himself that he didn't need to be with a woman like that. So he kept his head down as he walked to the concession stand because he knew that all his arguments would fly out the window once he saw her.

Jolie was determined to make it so. As she watched the game, she kept him constantly in her periphery. When she saw him stand up at halftime, she zeroed in until she was pretty sure where he was going. Then she made a beeline for the concession stand.

It was packed. Although Jolie was tall, she couldn't see over the crowd enough to figure out where he was. Then she caught a glimpse of a pair of hips. It was a long shot, yet something about how they swayed as they moved through the crowd reminded her of Alvin. Jolie cajoled and wheedled her way through the crowd, trying to follow the elusive pair of dark gray slacks. There was an opening in the mass, and Jolie was pleased to see the hips expand into a back that she knew intimately. She followed Alvin until he was near the bleachers, and scared she'd lose him, she yelled his name.

He recognized the voice, and his strong, confident stride hesitated briefly. He wanted to continue walking, but he couldn't. As he turned, he heard a different voice call his name. He stood there, holding his hotdog in one hand, a pop in the other. He watched as the two women who didn't know each other approached, coming from different directions.

Latisha, Rock's wife, reached him first, and he held his items to the side as she locked her arms around his middle and gave him a big hug. He saw the misunderstanding in Jolie's eyes and he did nothing to correct it. Let her think what she will. She'd already painted him the villain, and he was sick and tired of trying to correct her. Jolie spun on her heels and was disappearing back into the crowd by the time Latisha released him. Desire, craving, and maybe even need burned a hole in his stomach, causing an ulcer for sure as he used incredible will power to not run after her like a rat chasing a piece of dangling cheese.

Latisha looked at his face and stopped short. She turned to see what he was looking at. The throngs of people milling around didn't give her clue. "You look like a number one recruit has just told you to go to hell! Did this Tyrese kid change his mind?"

Alvin sipped his pop before answering, "No, Tisha. I'd never have this look over basketball. It's not Ty, it's his sister who's giving me fits."

"Ohhh. So, you two talked."

"Yeah, it's too packed to discuss it here." Alvin didn't want to converse about it at all, so he changed the subject. "Where's Rock?"

"We got here late. He's sitting up there." She pointed into the crowded bleachers. "I had to go to the ladies room and I spotted you. Come and sit with us." Latisha beckoned with her hand, and Alvin followed her up the stairs.

§§§

On her way back to her seat, Jolie's quickly wiped tears from her eyes. When she'd seen that woman surge into Alvin's arms, she'd literally recoiled. The pain of that old, recurring wound being torn open again had made her take a step back. Now her feet shuffled forward as she followed the many shoes in front of her and tried to bury her shame and anger. However, her head lifted when she heard her name screamed. Joan was waving frantically and shouting for her to come join them. She wanted to suffer in isolation, in that special loneness that comes from being in a crowd and not really knowing anyone, but it wasn't to be. Joan was making such a scene, she knew she'd better go or the woman would follow her to her seat and drag her back.

Jolie was familiar with the crowd of parents that sat with Joan and her husband, Robert. She answered greetings, shouted hellos, and agreed that the boys needed to get going in the second half. She said a polite hello to Robert and waved up in the stands to Robyn who was sitting with a group of her friends. After she hugged Joan the best she could standing between the narrow bleachers, she sat down, flanked by Joan and Reverend Thompson. Reverend Thompson's son, Ricky, played guard for the Titans.

"Girl, I knew you were here somewhere. Why didn't you sit with us?

Because I'm tired of the cold war between Mr. Congeniality and me. Jolie had seen Joan walk in with her husband earlier, and she'd avoided them like a child shunning a bath. Robert had boycotted the previous games, and Jolie was mildly curious about why he'd decided to show up now. Perhaps it was as the newspapers claimed, the championships drew the whole state together.

Jolie was infinitely happy that Joan sat as a barrier between her and the yucky man. She had never mentioned her conversation with Robert at the Esquire Club to Joan. She didn't think it was appropriate to tell her friend that she thought her husband was an elitist snob, so she kept her feelings to herself. She preferred to see her friend when her husband wasn't around. A part of Jolie wondered if she would attempt to kill the friendship or let it die out if they didn't share a connection growing in Robyn's belly. Regardless of Robert's and her feelings for each other, they would interact because of the baby, so in the long run, it seemed silly to Jolie to end the friendship with Joan just because of her husband's bad temperament.

Despite Joan's endless chatter, Jolie's eyes were drawn to Alvin's previous seat like a motorist who can't resist looking at an accident, even though it's causing a traffic jam. He wasn't there. She was stricken motionless by her thoughts, paralyzed in her seat as all sorts of scenarios ran through her brain, pulling out chunks of her heart as each thought passed. Did he leave with the attractive woman who was hugging him? Were they in the car this minute, making out furiously, or maybe ignoring the speed limit as they rushed to the closest bed. Jolie released a soft groan.

"What?" Reverend Thompson asked. "That's just one basket, only two points. We've scored the last three times we got the ball. Our boys are coming back."

Jolie forced herself to pay attention to the game.

§§§

Across the court and sitting in the left corner, Rock was helping Alvin keep his mind off Jolie. By the time the buzzer had sounded, he and his friend had thoroughly discussed what Tyrese's coach should do with the towering farm boys as they affectionately called the team from Eastern

Washington. To their delight, the Titans' coach was on their wavelength. He stopped playing the slow, plodding game that favored the taller players. All of the Titans ran, ran, ran, and then ran some more. Their defense was scrappy, full of double and triple teams that produced a multitude of turnovers. They grabbed every loose ball, which they turned into quick shots in transition before the bigger Wolverine players had time to run the floor. The style of play was rough on the Titans though. The coach frequently substituted to allow for rest. Everyone took a turn on the bench, except Tyrese. Alvin and Rock got to see how well conditioned he was as he played continuously through the third quarter and into the fourth.

By the middle of the fourth quarter, the bigger Wolverines were beginning to show signs of wear. They were tired and becoming sloppy on defense, which opened up the world for Tyrese. He kicked it into fifth gear and began slicing and dicing through the middle of the key instead of settling for a jump shot. At the last minute, while in the air, he'd change the direction of his arm, body, head, and flick the ball through the hole with ease. After a couple of circus shots brought the crowd to its feet, the small town boys began to lose composure. The Wolverine coach called a time out with one minute to go. The Titans had their first lead; they were up by one.

"Oh, gosh! This is too tense for me," Joan hissed excitedly. "Did you see Ty's last shot, honey? I didn't know a person's body could do that in mid air."

"Humph. Neither did number 24. That poor boy looked confused."

Jolie looked at Robert out of the corner of her eye. Did that man just compliment my brother? She turned and her gaze met Robert's behind Joan's head. He smiled at her. Wonders never cease.

The last minute had Joan peeking through the fingers that covered her face. Jolie looked at her, and was too anxious to laugh. It was the Wolverines' ball after the time out. They worked their slow, plodding offense to perfection, and their center made a reverse lay-up, despite the fact that Tyrese was hanging on his arm. He also made the extra point and the Wolverines went up by two. The Titans' coach called a time out with twenty seconds to go.

"I got ten bucks that says they go for the kid." Rock pretended to reach for his wallet.

"I'd be crazy to go for that. Of course, they're going to give it to Ty."

Rock laughed.

The Titans got the ball at half court. The guard passed the ball to the forward and then ran full speed at an angle toward the basket. "Uh oh," Rock said. "It looks like we were both wrong. They're going to give it back to the guard and go for two under the basket. The Coach wants a tie and overtime."

"No, I don't think so," Alvin said. He noticed how Tyrese was setting up a little away from the action. The dashing guard got the ball back and executed a daring, blind pass over his shoulder to Tyrese who stood a little beyond the three-point line. Tyrese was just about to release his patented jumper when a Wolverine player all but tackled him. The final buzzer competed with the crowd's roar. There was no time left, but Tyrese had three foul shots. With two he could tie the game, and with three he could win it.

The three referees conversed briefly before one of them motioned for Tyrese to come out. He was the only player on the court as he stood at the foul line. Jolie angled her head so she could see his face. It was blank, giving her no clue as to how he was doing. His body seemed relaxed though; he wasn't fidgety, or anxious as he stood patiently waiting for the referee to give him the ball. A bounce pass later, and Jolie watched with a pounding chest as her brother set up to take the shot. The Wolverine fans released a deafening roar in an effort to distract as Tyrese dribbled twice and released a beautiful arc that swished through the basket. Jolie sat with fists clenched and didn't celebrate with the rest of the Titan fans. Tyrese had two more to go.

Nor did her brother react. He stood impassive and waited for the ball. He caught the pass from the referee, two dribbles, and another elegant shot that whistle through the hoop. Tyrese turned in a tight circle, and Jolie could feel him hissing, "Yes!" The game was tied, and he could win it with the next basket. Jolie made the sign of the cross and whispered a silent prayer. The Wolverine fans were jeering, taunting with all their hearts as her brother took the ball, bounced it twice, and released it off his fingertips. Jolie's heart stopped as the ball hopped around the rim three times before falling through the net. Joan jumped and spilled her popcorn all over Jolie, who could have cared less. The buttery stuff was mashed between the two women as they hugged furiously.

"I don't believe it! I don't believe he made all three!" Joan hugged her husband and then ran up the stairs to make sure her daughter was crushed against her bosom as well.

Jolie had forgotten all about Robert until he said, "The boy can play."

Her smile faltered, then returned full force as she watched her brother being buried by his teammates. Jolie turned to Robert. He had moved so that he was right beside her. "Yes, he can," she answered.

Robert sighed and said, "It's hard to be perfect. No human can achieve it all the time, and it's a wonder that a few can get there at all. What makes people like Tyrese special is that they have the potential to be great. The treat for the rest of us is that we may catch him in that moment and be lucky enough to see pure excellence. Your brother reached that level tonight, and I feel privileged to have seen it."

Jolie nodded.

Robert continued, "Parenting is very similar. We work hard to raise our children, and if they grow into well-adjusted, contributing members of society, well, to me, it's just like watching Tyrese make three foul shots to win the game." Robert coughed a little and looked towards the ground before meeting Jolie's gaze again. "According to my good wife, this...situation our families are in has been a test of my flexibility. She claims that my thinking is stagnant because I ignore the positives and look only for the negative. I've come to the conclusion that she may be right. I was looking for a scapegoat, a party to blame, and you were the easy target because your living arrangement is...unconventional.

"I did what you suggested and took a hard look in the mirror. I wasn't happy with all that I saw there. I feel that I must apologize to you, so that I can smile at the person I see in the looking glass. Therefore, I say to you that I am truly sorry for the harsh and unjust things said." He bowed his head, "Please forgive me."

Jolie looked into the narrow, stern face, and for the first time she understood why her friend had been married to this man for twenty-five years. Bowing her own head, Jolie said, "Apology accepted." She shook the outstretched hand. The bony grip of his long fingers was firm.

Joan was back, holding Robyn's hand. Her smile dimmed a little when she saw their faces.

With an "excuse me," Robert stepped across Jolie to peck his wife and daughter's cheeks. Jolie heard his whisper, "Not to worry, my dear. I have righted what was wrong." Joan's smile returned full strength.

The four of them stood, then sat as they enjoyed the celebrations and congratulations that were floating through the air. The only time Jolie's happiness wavered was the moment she saw Alvin leaving the stands with the woman who'd embraced him close behind. When Alvin reached the bottom, he turned to help the woman with the last step. The woman slipped and Alvin caught her in his arms. Her tunnel vision didn't allow her to see Rock grabbing for his wife, also. Jolie's heart pounded and she angrily twisted away, preventing her from seeing Rock wrap his arms around Latisha's waist and nuzzle her neck from behind.

§§§

The Titans had received their trophy and the ceremonies were at an end. Jolie stood waiting to congratulate her brother as he completed his last interview. Tyrese, now dressed in jeans and a Titan T-shirt, came over and wrapped Robyn in a heartfelt bear hug. The two were leaning into each other, and wrapped up so tightly it looked as if they'd fall without each other's support. Robyn clung to Tyrese and Jolie could hear the whispered, "You did it, babe."

"It's all for you," she heard Tyrese whisper back.

Looking over their heads, Jolie noticed that Joan was teary-eyed. Robert was avoiding the scene by looking at the departing news crew. A long arm pulling her into a hug brought her attention back to her brother. He whispered, "I saw Coach Alvin. He was with a short guy that I think is the head coach. At first, I was wondering why they didn't sit with you, and why they didn't say hi, but then I remembered. There's too much attention here with all the media and the other recruiters, right?"

Jolie nodded. Let him provide his own excuses about

me and Alvin.

"I'm so pumped to go to WAM next year."

Jolie managed something close to a smile, she hoped.

§§§

As they headed to their cars, Jolie heard Tyrese asking Robyn to a dance. Jolie chuckled when Robyn saucily replied that she was eight months pregnant and all she wanted to do was go home, get her last paper of the quarter done, and put her feet up. Tyrese offered to go with her and rub those feet.

Robert released a loud, "Ahem," and everyone turned to him.

Ignoring her father, Robyn told Tyrese, "Go have fun with the gang. I'm just tired. I know you're still on an adrenaline high from the win, so go dance away some of that excess energy."

After asking if she was sure about a million times, Tyrese kissed her passionately and bounded away to catch the bus that would take him back to the school. It was Friday night and Tyrese had a one o'clock curfew. Jolie shouted a reminder to his retreating back. He waved an acknowledgement.

Robyn and Joan gave Jolie a hug at her car. Robert shook her hand and the three left. Jolie was just about to back out of the parking spot when a knock on the window almost jolted her into heart failure. She spun to see a flash of gold in an ear, and then a round bald head.

"Hey, Joe Lee. Don't be scared. It's just me, the Big Macster." The big man stopped crouching and stood straight.

Jolie removed the hand from her chest and took deep breaths. She put the car in park before rolling down the window.

The man bent into the opening and started rambling before she could say hi. "I just wanted to say congrats on how your bro' played tonight. Baby boy's got crazy skills!"

Jolie leaned back. "Thanks, Mac."

"I was just Einsteinin', ya know, thinkin', and I believe it would be a beautiful thang if Ty ran for my summer team in June, seeing how I did hook y'all up by spreadin' the word."

Jolie remembered Tyrese's comments about Mac and irritation started flaming in her belly. She cut him off. "Leave my brother alone, Mac. He doesn't want to play in the summer."

The coldness in her voice had Mac standing straight again, and it was now Jolie who leaned out the window as she forcefully got her point across. "Don't call him, don't write him, and don't give him notes from anyone, especially other colleges. Okay, Mac?"

"Well, damn. Don't kill the messenger, baby. I was just tryin' to do y'all a favor!"

"Thanks, but no thanks. Just let us be, Mac!" With that, Jolie threw the car in reverse and revved out of the stall.

Chapter 17

"Now this is a party!" As he stood near the door of the Seattle Convention Center, Tyrese's head nodded to the beat.

"Damn right, old dude!" His teammate and friend, Ricky, clapped him on the back. "You gonna have to come outta that grandpa shell tonight and get with it 'cause we's about to get funky up in here!" Ricky danced around in a circle. "Did you know that this place holds nine thousand people and at least half of them are probably babes? We just won the state championship. We can have our pick, ain't that right fellas?" Rick was preaching to the choir. He rubbed his hands together as the others murmured, gestured, and hissed their agreement.

"You know I ain't with that, Rick. I like being the old dude 'cause I'm quite happy with my honey and my mature ways. I ain't looking at these skanks." A girl in an orange mini skirt and halter-top cruised by, eying the group of boys that Rick and Tyrese were among.

"All right, Mr. Married with Children. You be the saint, but I'm about to have some fun." After a couple of steps, Rick turned and came back to the group of boys. "At least roll with us tonight. Try one of these." He pulled his hand out of his pocket to reveal two tiny white capsules resting in his palm.

"No, man." Tyrese shook his head, truly offended. "You know I don't do that shit. Get outta here."

"What do you think this is, huh? It's not crack or some illegal junk, old dude. I wouldn't try to mess you up with that. Come on, dude, you know me. This here is ecstasy! It's as harmless as caffeine. All it will do is wake your ass up, so you can dance. It's like drinking a lot of coffee or pop, dude!"

Tyrese looked at the pills skeptically. His brow rose as he leaned away from the hand and shook his head.

"What's up with you, man? You deserve to have some fun. All you do is study, work, and be the devoted boyfriend. You're wasting away your youth, and I'm here to make sure you have at least one night of fun, dude. You just won the state championship by making three foul shots in a row! You're a hero, dude! Let loose and have some fun for once. You can go back to being Mr. Boring tomorrow. You feelin' me?"

Tyrese turned to get some support from his boys. Instead, he got Marcus who stepped forward and downed both pills. Rick's hand disappeared into his pocket only to reappear with two more capsules in his palm. Marcus picked them up and stretched a hand to Tyrese. "Go on, Ty. We've all taken it. All it does is make you feel good and give you energy."

"No!" Palms up, he waved his hands. Someone tapped

him on the back. He twisted to see a petite, brown-skinned girl. He accepted her offer to dance to get away from his trippin' friends. Two songs later he left the clinging girl, proclaiming he was tired. Rick was waiting for him at the edge of the dance floor.

"Hey, old dude, I'm sorry 'bout hassling you earlier. You know you're squarer than my daddy, the reverend, but you my boy, and I'm just glad you're here. So, I bought you this." He handed him a cup. "You were jammin' out there. I thought you might be thirsty. It's pop."

"Thanks, Rick. I'm kinda thirsty. That water at halftime was a long time ago." Tyrese drained the small plastic cup his friend handed him. He peered into the empty container. "Taste funny."

"Man, you know how they always trying to make a buck. They probably cut it with water or put in less syrup."

"Huh." Tyrese tossed the cup in a nearby garbage can. Two girls approached and asked the boys to dance. They both agreed. A few songs later, Tyrese was still dancing. A strange joy was coursing through his system. He assumed it had something to do with the fact that he was the man. Half a year of organized ball, and he was a state champion. The world was his, and all he wanted to do was groove to the beat with the endless throng of women. Something caught his eye. He turned to see beautiful colors slashing through the air. Reds, purples, oranges drew him like a gnat to light. Leaving the girl he was dancing with, he drifted towards the color sticks waving through the air. He bobbed his head and wormed his body as some unknown person moved the sticks in an intricate pattern in front of him.

Tyrese became dimly aware of an irritating buzz, an annoying drone coming from his right side. "Come on, old dude. Sit down a minute and chill."

Tyrese pushed the irksome hand away and turned back to the euphoric lights. He didn't notice that he was sweating profusely and his movements were becoming sluggish. All he wanted to do was follow the bright sticks.

۞۞۞

It was one in the morning and Alvin wasn't asleep. He lay in bed staring at the ceiling trying to will sleep to come. Slumber avoided him because there was an inner war being waged in his body. The cause of the civil war was his decision to stop pursing Jolie. The shrill of the phone was a relief. He answered it on the second ring with an alert "Hello."

"Hey, dog. This is the Macster. Meet me down at the new Convention Center pronto. Your boy's in trouble."

Instinctively, he knew he was talking about Tyrese. "What is it?" His heart began to pound as he yanked off the covers and sat up in the bed.

"Don't know yet. Gotta call from one of my summer league boys, Rick. Kid was freaked out and crying on the phone, beggin' me to come down. I got here to find Ty drenched and talkin' silly. I put 'im in the car. Rick's trippin' too much to tell me what happened."

"Take him to Harborlake Hospital. I'll met you there." Alvin slammed the phone down and threw on jeans and a shirt. He grabbed his cell phone, wallet, and ran out the door. He lived about fifteen minutes away from the best trauma center in Washington State. On the way, he called the team physician. Without a greeting, he said, "This is Alvin. I have an emergency. You can't come down because the kid hasn't signed with us yet, but call our contact, Dr. Graves, at Harborlake, tell him I need this to stay out of the papers."

He got there before Mac. Dr. Graves met him at the emergency entrance. He'd already alerted the staff, so everyone was ready. Alvin had just stepped back outside when Big Mac's immaculate 1973 Coupe Deville Cadillac pulled into the emergency center driveway, wheels squealing. The big man threw open his door and yelled, "He can't walk."

Alvin ran and got the staff. Dr. Graves led the way, yelling questions as they maneuvered Tyrese onto a stretcher. Big Mac answered. "Ecstasy, man." He glared at Rick, who was cowering to the side of the action. "The kid was slipped some ecstasy."

"Shit!" Alvin hissed.

"How much!" Dr. Graves yelled.

Rick sniffed and ran his hand under his nose. "Four pills. I opened 'em up and put 'em in his pop."

"All right. Let's go." Dr. Graves led the way. He yelled

over his shoulder to Alvin. "I'll let you know as soon as I know."

Alvin debated whether to call Jolie now or after he knew something. He decided to wait a half hour and then call her regardless of his information. While he waited, he called Rock and let him know what was up.

ӍӍӍ

Jolie rolled over and uttered a curse. "Corporal punishment for all who call after eleven," she mumbled as she grabbed the phone off the nightstand.

She sat up straight and knocked the base over when she recognized the voice. The falling cord jerked the receiver from her hand. She reached down, fumbled for the phone, and mumbled a quick apology once she put it to her ear again.

"It's all right," Alvin's smooth voice reassured her. "Jolie, I'm at the front door. Please, let me in."

"What?" She knew she must have heard him incorrectly.

"I'm standing at your door. Let me in and I'll explain everything."

Jolie looked at the bedside clock. "Alvin, it's two in the morning. Whatever you have to say can wait."

"Trust me, baby. This is important."

Jolie was about to answer with the biting retort that all trusting him did was cause her pain. However, something in his voice stopped her. Some pitch that she'd never heard before reached around her neck and made the hair stand up. "I'll be right there." The words rushed from her mouth seconds before she tossed the phone. Instinct made her run to Tyrese's room. Her hand flew to her throat when she saw the empty, well-made bed. "Don't panic, don't panic!" she whispered as she dashed to the door. Tears of frustration threatened as she struggled with the bolt and the chain lock. Once the obstacles were removed, she hurled the door open.

Alvin's heart jumped into his vocal cords, preventing him from saying his prepared speech. She stood before him in a pink tank top and matching panties. He closed his eyes and when he opened them, he refused to look below her neck. It didn't help. Her ruffled auburn hair reminded him of lovemaking. It fell around her face in attractive whorls, making him want to run his finger through it and draw her forward for a hell of a lot more than a kiss. Her slightly parted lips seemed to be inviting him, but her eyes killed the notion. He read the dread in her wide stare and felt remorseful for not immediately putting her at ease.

"My brother?" Her tone was high and tinny.

"He's had a scare, but he's fine," Alvin said as he eased past her to enter the house.

"Then what..." Her brow began to fuse together and the dimple suddenly appeared.

To avert the rising storm, Alvin rushed into an explanation. "One of your brother's so-called friends decided to slip a drug into his drink."

Jolie gasped.

"He's all right." Alvin tried to take her into his arms. She pushed against his chest. His heart ached. Shoving his hands into the pockets of his jeans, he gave her what she wanted: space and an explanation. "Your brother was at a Rave party. Do you know what that is?"

Jolie shook her head.

"Parties where the main focus is dancing. The kids get so obsessed with it that they gulp down energy drinks or take drugs so they can keep grooving. Usually, the Raves are held in out-of-the-way places, but this one was at the Convention Center. That place holds thousands of kids!" Alvin shook his head. The doctors told me that about thirty were rushed to emergency tonight.

"Anyway, a guy named Rick decided to loosen your brother up by slipping some ecstasy in his drink. The drug can be lethal if you don't get enough water because it causes dehydration. Ty lost a lot of fluids during the game, and apparently, he didn't drink enough to replace them. That combined with the drug... Well, he was near collapse. We got him to the hospital, and he's going to be okay, but they want to keep him overnight to make sure."

"Which hospital?"

"Harborlake. I'll drive you." Jolie was running to her room as he said the words. Alvin took a deep breath and uttered a silent prayer as he watched her bottom wiggle underneath the thin material until she disappeared from view.

She came back wearing black tennis shoes, jeans, and a white zoo T-shirt. She grabbed her coat, and as they rushed to the car, a gray head poked out next door. The door opened wider to reveal Ethel dressed in a gold lamé sweat suit. "Jolie!" she yelled in a raspy voice that carried far in the earlier morning hours.

Both Jolie and Alvin turned. Taking a deep breath, Jolie strove for calmness in her voice. "Hi, Ethel. What are you doing up so late?"

"The boy's not home yet. I don't turn in until I hear him pull up. And you, leaving at this hour, I know something is cockamamie; something wrong with my boy?"

Alvin chuckled, "She's a wise one, isn't she?"

Jolie nodded and said in a low voice, "Yes, she's very astute. No sense in lying, she'd pull my ears when she found out later." She yelled to Ethel who was now leaning on her cane near the edge of the porch. "Ty's going to be fine, but he's in the hospital."

Ethel's chin jerked up and down and she commanded, "Wait. I'll grab my purse and coat and be right with you." Unless she'd seen it, Jolie wouldn't have believed that Ethel could move so fast. The cane thumped loudly as she disappeared inside. When she reappeared, Alvin ran up the steps to help her lock the door. She shooed him away. Jolie offered Ethel the front seat, but she went straight for the back. "I'll be more than comfortable right here, thank you very much." Once they were all seated, Jolie turned sideways to make formal introductions and quickly told Ethel what had happened. Ethel made hissing noises through her dentures and shook her head. The three of them lapsed into silence, and Jolie shifted to sit forward.

At every opportunity, Alvin glanced at Jolie. He'd expected more drama and a staunch denial of any help. Instead, she was stoic and stone-faced, clutching her purse a little tightly, but that was about it. He had to admit that he admired her courage. No tears, hysteria, or antics. She got the information and reacted to it by rushing to the aid of her sibling. This was the type of woman he wanted by his side. Caring, yet able to act. He could never imagine Jolie being a wilting flower; nervous maybe, but never collapsing.

§§§

Alvin led the way through the hospital corridors. As soon as the three entered Tyrese's room, Jolie said, "What's he doing here?" The words were said with so much venom Alvin was taken aback. Ethel ignored them as she continued to Tyrese's bedside.

"Whoa, Nelly," Big Mac said with his hands up. His large silk shirt and matching pants billowed as he moved. "I'm the hero here. Don't go yapping at the big dog." His thumbs pointed to the purple material covering his chest.

Big Mac sat in the chair beside the bed where Tyrese was resting comfortably. Jolie chose to disregard him, and Big Mac scooted his chair back so both women could stand by the bed. Ethel moved towards Tyrese's feet, so Jolie could assure herself that her brother was fine. He appeared to be sleeping, despite the IV that was administering fluids into his arm. Jolie ran a gentle hand across his forehead, letting her fingers travel in between his corn rows. Next, she bent as if to assure herself that he was breathing.

"Doc was just in here. Said little dog is gonna be fine, he just needs to chill for a while."

Jolie turned long enough to glare at him. He retaliated with a gold-toothed smile.

"Jolie," Alvin said. "Mac's the one who rushed Ty to the hospital. This would have turned out much worse it he hadn't acted so quickly." Mac smiled wider, revealing at least two more shining teeth. Jolie shifted her eyes to Alvin. The glare had been replaced with a questioning look. "Rick, the kid who snuck Ty the pills, called Mac when Ty started having a problem. Mac called me and rushed Ty here."

Jolie spun back to Mac. After appraising him for a few more seconds, she extended her hand. "It looks as if I owe you an apology." All that was visible was her lower forearm as Mac swallowed her up in his meaty grasp. His bracelets jingled as he pumped her hand vigorously, and then held on longer than necessary.

"Just 'cause little dog don't wanna play for me doesn't mean that I wish 'im ill will. I made Rick call his parents and tell 'em what went down. They picked 'im up about five minutes ago. From how they was lookin', I think ole Rick's in some trouble."

Jolie thanked Mac again and pulled her hand from his

grip. Alvin began speaking, and Jolie shifted her focus back to him. "I have Dr. Graves treating Ty under an assumed name. This should stay out of the papers."

"Papers?" The issue hadn't even occurred to Jolie. At first she felt relief, and then an ugly suspicion slunk into her brain, making her furious. Her eyes narrowed and she said, "Protecting your star recruit, huh?" On a roll, Jolie walked up and spoke in a low tone for Alvin only. He bent to hear the whispered words better. "I suppose if the media does find out, we're supposed to say you were never here. We wouldn't want the NCAA coming down on you. But, oh yeah, we have a story for that, don't we? Too bad you didn't tell the other women that we were dating."

Alvin straightened, and the look on his face killed her doubts and filled her with guilt. Pain slackened his facial muscles and dulled his soft brown eyes for a few seconds, and then his jaw hardened and those same eyes crystallized into granite. His nostrils flared as he took in air in what Jolie assumed was an effort to calm himself. "I won't dignify that with a response." He walked away from her to the side table and picked up a pencil and pad. As he wrote, he spoke in short, terse phrases. "I'm sure the doctor will be here shortly. He will update you. I believe Ty can go home tomorrow. I'll call. There will be a taxi available when you leave." He ripped off a sheet of paper and placed it on the table alongside the pad. "Here's my cell and pager. Call if you need me." With a twirl, he was gone.

"Damn, sista." Big Mac rose up. "I bet you're the star

of the cut a brotha quick club." Mac used his arm as a sword and waved it around. He possessed surprising grace, and the purple fabric floating through the air was almost majestic. "Slice 'em, dice 'em, and throw 'em away. I'm gonna split before you aim that weapon at me again. Tell little dog I said be good, and if he feels like a little ball this summer, look me up." With that, the big man eased out of the room.

Ethel lowered herself into the chair Big Mac had vacated. She tapped her cane enough to make a light thud, but not so loud that it would disturb Tyrese. Jolie looked at her and knew the old woman had done so to make sure that she had her attention.

"Oy vey, dear, you certainly made a fine mess of that, I tell you." She pointed with her cane in the direction of the door. "That large man made my eyes hurt with all that purple. And, oy, the gold was strangling his neck and fingers, but he sure summed you up." The cane was now aimed in the opposite direction. "So, okay, never mind that. Pull up a seat, and let's sit a minute until that doctor comes by."

Jolie grabbed the chair and placed it next to Ethel's. She did as told and sat down.

Ethel started with a familiar refrain, "Your brother talks to me, you know?"

"Yes, I know, Ethel." Jolie angled her chair and body, so she could look the grand old lady in her upturned face. It was three in the morning and Ethel's bun was immaculate, not a hair out of place. Jolie felt self-conscious about the wild briar patch she knew was crowning her head. Ethel's brown eyes were still bright, surrounded by the wise lines that criss-crossed her features. She laid the cane across her lap and began to absently stroke the lovely polished wood. "He not only talks about himself, he talks about you."

Jolie inwardly cringed and averted her eyes.

"Look at me."

Jolie did so.

"Have I told you I buried five husbands?" The way she continued speaking clued Jolie to the fact that an answer wasn't required. Ethel looked up in the air. "A principal ballerina, I was. Got more than my fair share of attention, you know? Unfortunately, I was heartier than the ones I chose." The old lady cackled briefly before going on with the monologue. "Listen to me. Me, I'm not ashamed to say that I've had a few men: some good, some not so good. The tall, handsome one that left before the large one is good, I think." Her eyes shifted back to Jolie. "Like I say, me and the boy talk. He tells me that first you push this man away, then he finds his underwear, and now you shove him away again. Why's that?"

Ethel saw the red rising up from her T-shirt. "Oy, goodness girl! There is no room for embarrassment. This is mild compared to me. It's good you let someone in. Only the old should be as alone as you, and that's only after a very full life, I tell you. Oy, my memories are bittersweet, but they keep regrets away. So, back to you, why do you push this man away?"

Jolie didn't want to get into it at three in the morning, sitting in a hospital, at her brother's bedside. The piercing brown eyes demanded an answer. Sighing, Jolie gave in, determined to only give the barest of details. "We knew each other in high school, and he...he dumped me. I don't trust him."

"High school! Why, you were both so young. Was he mean to you? Did he have other women?"

Jolie shook her head.

"So, I should think his only crime is breaking up with you when he was but a mere boy?"

"I was pregnant." Jolie's hand covered her mouth. She stared at Ethel wide-eyed and shocked that the secret words had slipped from her mouth.

Ethel's eyes got just as big. "Don't tell me Tyrese is the son?"

"No, no. Ty was three when we were dating."

"Oy vey, goodness, I think I read the *Inquirer* too much. Where is the child?"

"I...I miscarried."

Ethel clicked her tongue and grabbed Jolie's hand. "I too know this pain. I would not allow myself to be with child, a career woman ahead of my time. Only twice I conceived: once at forty and at forty-two." Ethel's eyes drifted back to the ceiling. "The doctors, they gave me some medical reason for my failure. They claimed I couldn't carry a baby regardless of my age, a leftover result of those nasty camps, but still I wonder, what if had tried when I was younger? Oy, so, what can I tell you? In life, there's... disappointments." She focused back on Jolie. "Yet, the behavior you tell surprises me. That man doesn't seem the type to run from hard times."

"He didn't. Well, he didn't run from the baby. I just told him a couple of weeks ago."

"Ah ha!" Ethel let go of Jolie's hand, lifted the cane, and thumped it back down. "So, he's not the only one who behaved badly. It wasn't right for you to keep this from him."

"Oh, Ethel. It is so much more complicated than that." Jolie ran her hands over her face.

"Why is it so complex? You people today look for too much gray. Sometimes it can be black and white. He broke up with you and hurt your feelings, and you didn't tell him something that he had every right to know. Listen to me, child."

Ethel waited until Jolie's hands lowered and their eyes met. "I was there with you two for a time and, me, I felt it. That man was looking at you at every opportunity. If my license hadn't been revoked last year, I would have driven, so he could keep his eyes on you. And you." Ethel pointed a bony finger. "Oy, you were very coy, but I saw a look of wonder in your face when his head was turned. You like this man, more than a little, I think." Jolie didn't return Ethel's smile.

Undaunted, the old lady continued. "But what really did it was the look on his face when you accused him. Me,

I know pain, and you caused it with your words. That man was dumbstruck, then very angry, and still he managed to be very nice." Ethel paused briefly. "I'll say one more thing, then I'm through. A foolish action when one's a boy doesn't mean that a man isn't trustworthy. I managed to find quite a few partners during my time on this earth, but let's be honest. You, you're not as outgoing as me. Besides, only two of those five were really my soul mates. Why don't you give the man a chance before you sentence yourself to regrets."

True to her word, Ethel fell silent after that. Jolie's mind buzzed as she tried to discount the advice. What about Sophia? a part of her questioned. She blew that off. The facts were there that burst the Sophia bubble. Hell, she saw the woman intentionally leave the dress! She knew she was being a bit childish about that whole situation, taking it out on Alvin because she couldn't yank Sophia's hair out by the roots. But what about the woman at the game? She could ask him and see what he had to say. A knock on the door drew Jolie from her thoughts. A middle-aged white man with a receding hairline entered the room.

He introduced himself as Dr. Graves and said, "You must be Jolie."

Jolie nodded and introduced Ethel.

He went over and checked Tyrese and the IV. "He's doing fine. We got fluids into him in time, and there is no permanent damage. By late tomorrow morning, he'll be good as new and you can take him home. You ladies are welcome to wait; however, feel free to go home, rest, and come back around eight. I think he's out for the night. Plus, I'll be here until he's released."

Jolie looked at her brother one more time. Then she suggested that they take a cab home, so she could get her car. Ethel agreed. As they left the room, a man in the lobby stood up and said Jolie's name. The man introduced himself as the cab driver and said he'd been waiting to take them home.

"Oy, a man of his word," Ethel whispered as they followed the cabbie out of the hospital.

At the end of the ride, the man refused Jolie's money. He wouldn't even accept it as a tip. His only comment was, "Look, lady, the bill's been taken care of, all right. I can't take your money."

Despite her protest, Jolie helped Ethel to the front door. "I'm just old, not sick. I can walk up my own front steps alone, I tell you!"

Jolie kept a firm grip on the elbow. "I know, I know. It's my problem, not yours. It's dark out here and I believe this rain is mixed with snow."

"What rain? It's snowing," Ethel said. "This weird, fickle Washington weather. It's not supposed to snow in March." They were at Ethel's front door. Jolie waited patiently as she fumbled with the latch. Ethel would probably bite her hand off if she moved to help. Finally, the door yielded. As Ethel slipped inside, she said, "Call me before you go back, and, me, I don't want to hear from you for at least five hours. We both need to rest."

"Yes, ma'am." Jolie hid her smile. Then she turned and took a deep breath of the cold, crisp air and she slowly made her way to her house. She felt fuzzy, kind of hollow as if someone had reached inside her and stirred her innards like a big pot of stew. Ignoring the weather, Jolie stood in between the two houses and looked up. The strange weather reflected how she felt. Seattle rarely got snow, and it was almost unheard of coming so late in the season. Jolie searched for the moon, but the cloud cover hid it from view. However, she knew it was there. That's kind of how she felt about Alvin. She couldn't see him, but he was there, hovering in her mind and body. Maybe Ethel was right. Maybe she should fight against the gray and look for the black and white in her relationship with Alvin.

"Darn," she told the heavens above. "I sure as heck don't know, and I'm too tired to figure it out." Jolie made her way into the house and stripped off the drenched clothes. She saw her cell phone resting on the kitchen table. Naked, she grabbed it and her pants. From her pocket, she pulled out the paper that Alvin had put his numbers on. She called his numbers and reached his voice mail. Pushing down her disappointment, she left the same message on both phones. "Alvin, call me. We need to talk."

Next, she called her father. She didn't want to, yet she felt obligated. He picked up on the fifth ring, and after the sound of much fumbling, she finally heard him say, "Hello."

"Hi, Dad."

"Jolie? My goodness, what time is it?" There was a

brief pause and more groping noises. "Geez, Jolie, it's the wee morning hours! Is everything all right?"

"Sort of. Ty was slipped some drugs at a party. He's in the hospital for observation, but he's all right."

Silence.

"Soooo, you coming out here, Dad?"

"No...um ...it sounds like you have it taken care. I mean, you said he's okay."

Now it was Jolie's turn to be mute.

"I'm going to call the hospital and see how he's doing, then I'll come if it's necessary. Where's he at?"

"Harborlake. Ask for Dr. Graves and tell him that you're his father. He was admitted under an assumed name to keep it out of the media."

After saying goodbye, Jolie pressed the off button. She put her cell phone back on the table and drifted to her bedroom. Disregarding her wet hair, she climbed into bed and waited for sleep to come. She thought she'd have to struggle to find rest. When she couldn't sleep in the past, she would go through a ritual of making her whole body relax. She'd lie flat on her back and start with her fingers, work up to her head, and back down to her toes. She'd usually fall asleep before she reached the end of her body. However, this time was different. She curled into the fetal position and was asleep before the sun replaced the moon.

Chapter 18

Jolie eyes flew open and her hand landed on her chest. Her head was pounding. No, the sound was too distant. Wide-eyed, her brain fought desperately to make sense of the situation. Seconds later, she hopped up to find the source of the hammering. Disoriented, Jolie was almost to her bedroom door when she realized she was nude. Rushing back to her closet, she grabbed a white, fluffy robe, then followed the banging to the front door. "Robyn!"

Her black hair was untidy. Jolie could see that a brush hadn't touched it recently. The long strands looked as if they'd been hastily captured and haphazardly thrust into a rubber band. The white snowflakes glistening in it made it appear even wilder. Robyn waddled in and yanked off her big coat to reveal maternity pants that were pulled up crookedly along her belly. Some of her large, long shirt had been caught in the pants. Her appearance would have been comical if not for the worry lines marring her face.

"I've been calling this house and Ty's cell all night and all morning. Ty always calls me before he goes to bed and he didn't call! I've been worried sick!"

"Oh, honey. I'm sorry I didn't phone. It didn't occur to me." Jolie moved to hug her and the agitated girl wiggled in her grasp.

"Tell me! What's happened to Ty?"

Jolie spoke quickly. "Nothing serious, he's all right. Some kid slipped ecstasy into his pop. He became severely dehydrated, but now he's at Harborlake and he's going to be fine."

"Oh my God. I have to get there."

Jolie grabbed Robyn this time. "Stop. I said the boy's okay. Let me get dressed and we can go over there together." She sat Robyn on the couch. "Promise that you'll wait for me."

Robyn nodded.

Jolie stripped off her robe as she ran into her room. She was dying to take a quick shower, but she was scared that Robyn might bolt on her. Taking time only to brush her teeth and wash her face. She slipped into her underwear and yanked her hair into a ponytail. Without really looking, she hauled out the first T-shirt she saw in the drawer and pulled it and cargo pants on. Then she sat on the bed to fight with her feet. She yelped in pain when the edge of her sock caught between her toes. Clothes never seemed cooperative when she was in a rush. As she finished dressing, she noticed that the phone was off the hook. Fussing at herself, she fixed it and then rushed out to Robyn.

She was lying on the couch, her whole body coiled inwards, her features drawn into an awful grimace.

"Robyn!" Jolie ran to her side.

"Oh, God! I think it's coming!"

Jolie tried to talk, but her tongue was stymied by her thoughts. It was too early! The girl still had a month to go. Besides, Joan was supposed to take care of this. Not her! She ran a hand over Robyn's hot forehead. "It's going to be okay, honey. We have lots of time to get you there because this is the first pain."

Robyn's grimace was softening. She took deep, long breaths as she entered the place between the pains. "That's not the first. Now that I've had that mega one, I think they've been happening all night. I've gone in a couple times for false labor and I thought that's all it was. I thought my body was trippin' 'cause I was so stressed 'bout Ty."

Oh, no! Jolie ran for her cell phone and both their coats. "Let's go, hon. We can call your parents and the hospital as we drive."

She helped Robyn to her feet but stopped when the girl shrieked. "Wait! I feel another one. Wait until it passes!" Jolie sat with Robyn and held her hand as she fought through the pain. She'd helped and seen plenty of animals be born, but the knowledge seemed insignificant. Animals didn't use Lamaze, so she had no idea how to coach Robyn through it. She let her squeeze the heck out of her left hand and rubbed Robyn's back with the right. Once the pain began to recede, Jolie helped her to stand, got both their coats on, and they started the infinitely slow walk to the door. No, no, no! her mind screamed. There was at least seven inches of snow on the ground. She turned to Robyn. "Your parents let you drive over in this?"

Robyn laughed.

Jolie failed to see what was so amusing. Her expression must have made her feelings clear.

"Your face is so serious. It's kind of funny. My parents were asleep when I left. The snow was only a couple of inches high when I drove. I only skidded a few times and no one else was on the road. It's…a lot…worse…now."

Robyn's face was drawing back in, and Jolie knew another serious contraction was fast approaching. The laboring girl turned and leaned both hands against the door-jamb. Jolie stood there rubbing her back, whispering soothing words, and feeling completely helpless.

When she could talk again, Robyn said, "Don't worry about the snow. I'm not going to make it to the hospital. My baby wants out! My water just broke!"

Jolie helped her back to the couch. As they walked, she spoke to the Highest Power. *Lord, I know that you never give more than we can handle, but I'm going to need a lot of help with this one!*

A loud pounding started at the door. Robyn ignored it. She seemed very determined to make it to the couch. Jolie's head turned to see the wood vibrating from the force of the blows. She helped Robyn to lie down before she rushed to the door. "Please let this be a paramedic," she whispered fervently.

"Oh, it's you!" Despite the situation and her voice tone, her heart leapt with joy as she looked up into his brown face.

"Don't get too hyped up. I might think I'm welcome."

Alvin's long frame filled the doorway. "First, you ask me to call, and then you drive me nuts because the phone was out of order. I thought something had happened to you in all this white stuff." Alvin didn't mention how he'd disturbed his neighbor and given the guy fifty bucks, to borrow his Bronco and come check on her. The thing looked like crap on the outside, but it drove like a charm.

Jolie heard the concern behind the frustrated tone. "Alvin, I'm really sorry."

The sincerity rung in his ears, but what was she sorry for? Not answering the phone, or the ugly words she'd hurled at him early that morning.

Jolie looked at him quizzically. Lord, is this what you're sending me? If so, you truly do work in mysterious ways!

A loud moan made Jolie run back to the couch. She kneeled beside Robyn. Alvin shut the door and followed. He needed no explanation for what he saw. His eyes stretched so large he felt a twinge of pain at the corners. He wanted to do the manly thing and throw open the door and run as far as possible from this situation. Instead, he said, "I'll drive."

"No, you won't." Jolie didn't look at him as she said the stern words. "There's no time." She lifted her chin towards the end table. "Try the phone. Nine-one-one can walk us through this."

Alvin grabbed the receiver. No dial tone. His eyelids reached for the ceiling again. He hung up and tried again. Same result. Silence greeted his ear. "Damn!"

Robyn was coming out of the pain. Both women looked at him. "Phone's dead. A snow–heavy tree limb probably fell and knocked out a line."

"Try my cell." She ripped the clipped phone from her waistband.

Alvin tried. "There's a fast busy signal. No service."

Robyn's eyes were focused on him, and she missed Jolie's look of sheer panic before Jolie lowered her head. Seconds later, her head came back up. Her eyes were clear and determined. "It's okay, Robyn. I've been around animals most of my life. I've experienced the miracle of life from conception to delivery."

Robyn reached down and Jolie put her hand in the outstretched grip. "I'm scared. I don't want to lose my baby!"

Oh, God! Those were the exact words I said to my mother when I lost my child! Jolie squeezed back. She remembered how powerless she'd felt when she'd miscarried. There hadn't been a darn thing Jolie could do to keep that embryo inside her womb. Well, she could sure as heck do something for Robyn. Another baby would not die as long as she could do something about it. "Don't worry, honey. You're not alone and I will move heaven and earth to make sure you and my niece or nephew are okay." She angled her head towards Alvin. "Go get the down comforter off my bed and lay it on the floor." Her voice was calm. It had lost the breathy, nervous edge. Alvin's eyes were bright with admiration as he left the room.

Jolie was surprised herself. Robyn's words that were her

own so long ago and having Alvin there were making her feel more in control. She removed Robyn's shoes and socks, and then struggled with the wet, stretchy maternity pants while Alvin moved the coffee table and laid the covering on the carpet. He averted his eyes when he saw what Jolie was doing. "I'll get towels and hot water," he uttered as he backed up.

"Get the towels from the hall closet, then come back and help me move her to the floor."

She looked over and smiled at him. Really smiled at him: eyes warm, lips wide, and teeth shining. Some of her hair had escaped the ponytail and lay in loose tendrils against her cheek. She was the most beautiful thing that Alvin had every seen. He would have walked through quicksand to keep that look on her face. He rushed to do her bidding and then found himself thanking God that Jolie lifted Robyn's legs and he only had to contend with the shoulders as they moved Robyn to the floor. Jolie positioned herself between the girl's legs.

Alvin needed a break. "Should I go boil water?"

Jolie didn't answer right away. Going on instinct, she grabbed a throw pillow and placed it under Robyn's hips. "Does that feel all right, honey?"

Robyn nodded.

Looking at the standing Alvin, Jolie said, "Why?"

He shrugged self-consciously, "They always do in the movies." Even Robyn smiled at that one.

"Okay. But you don't need to boil it. I have a hot water

tap right next to the faucet. Wait!" she yelled before Alvin turned away. "Stay here a second. I want to wash my hands." Jolie hopped up and disappeared down the hall. Although, Alvin worried that Robyn would have a contraction and he'd be forced to do something, Jolie dashed back just as Robyn began the heavy gasping.

Alvin escaped to the kitchen. He prayed that the power wouldn't go. What the hell would they do then? Just in case, he poked his head through the doorway to ask where the candles were. Robyn was gasping and puffing. Rather than interrupt, he began searching the cabinets. He found a whole stack of candles in the one above the refrigerator. Right next to them were matches and a flashlight. He smiled at Jolie's organization. He returned to the battlefield with a pot of water and his other treasures. He placed the items and himself out of the way, just above Robyn's head. He refused to go any lower unless it was absolutely necessary.

Jolie saw the additional items and understood instantly. She hadn't even thought about the power. She nodded to Alvin and whispered, "Thanks."

Then she looked at the clock above her fireplace. Robyn cried softly in between the pains. Jolie ran a soothing hand along the girl's thigh. "Honey, the contractions are less than a minute apart. I think this will be over soon, and you're going to have a gorgeous baby."

Robyn groaned loudly and bit her lip when another pain hit. "Hold her hand and rub her head gently," Jolie said softly.

A little hesitant, Alvin did so. Robyn clung so hard, Alvin thought his fingertips would pop. His lips pursed and he struggled not to react to the death grip. With supreme control, he stoked the moist forehead with his free hand.

Jolie glanced at him with surprise and appreciation. This man is nothing like my father. Her dad would run through the snow naked rather than face an emotion-packed situation like this.

The top of the baby's head made Jolie forget about her father. "Okay, Robyn. I see what I think is the top of precious' head. Push really hard with the next one. You're almost done, honey." Jolie continued a steady stream of gentle instructions and compliments as Robyn cried, cursed, and pressed down with all her might when the pain came.

Jolie didn't share with Robyn that the baby hadn't moved. "You are doing so great, honey. I just need you to push a little harder."

"I can't! I'm trying, Jolie. I can't do it!"

Alvin cringed at the desperately said words.

"Yes, you can, honey. You're strong and you can do this. Give me all you've got."

Robyn screamed so loud when the next contraction began that Alvin jumped. Robyn's grip on his hand pulled him back.

Jolie spoke over the scream. "That's it, honey. The head is out. All we have is those shoulders. Oh, there's black hair, Robyn. It's beautiful." While she talked, Jolie stared intently at the head she held in her hands. She looked for a cord wrapped around the neck. When she didn't see one, she whispered a silent thank you to above and then prayed she didn't drop the gift from God.

Alvin was ready for the blood-curdling scream this time. Jolie was prepared, too. Robyn bore down, and Jolie braced herself when she saw the shoulders force their way through. She caught the slippery bundle and yelped with joy. "It's a boy, Robyn! We have a boy!"

Alvin helped the struggling Robyn to rise a little further up. Before she could put the baby on his mother's stomach, the little tyke let loose with a loud wail. Alvin was alarmed.

"It's okay, Alvie. That just means he's breathing."

They both watched Robyn lie back. The girl was exhausted, still she cooed to the life resting on her. Soothed, the baby quieted.

Alvin wiggled his recently released fingers. His eyes met Jolie's and he forgot the pain in his hand. Something special was passing between them. Together, they'd helped bring life into the world. If Robyn's body hadn't been in the middle, he would have crushed her to his chest.

Jolie whispered, "I know." Robyn caught the words and looked at Jolie. Wide-eyed, she turned her head sideways and saw the same expression on Alvin's face. Grinning, she didn't say a word.

"Oh, goodness." Jolie drew herself from the trance. From her experience with animals, she knew that the afterbirth needed to come out. Alvin looked at the baby as Jolie gave instructions to Robyn. After a time, she stood and placed a large towel over Robyn's lower body. "I'll be right back."

She returned with scissors, dental floss, and a plastic bag. Turning the baby on his back on Robyn's stomach, she used the floss to tie the cord. "I poured rubbing alcohol on these." She lifted the scissors and cut a little above the knot. Jolie gave the scissors to Alvin and put the afterbirth in the bag. "It looks complete; however, the doctor may want to see it to make sure all is well." Next, she reached for her nephew. "I have the privilege of bestowing the first bath on this angel."

Full of emotion and a bit faint, Alvin stood and went to the window. After lifting the curtain, he turned back to the ladies. "You won't believe this."

"What? The snow's to the roof?"

"Nope, our weather is schizophrenic today. The snow's turned to rain. The stuff's already becoming mushy." He watched Jolie wrap the baby in a towel and hand him to his mother. "Okay, guys, I believe it's time to go see daddy."

Chapter 19

Hours later, the proud parents talked to Ethel on the phone in Robyn's crowded hospital room. Despite learning the good news, her neighbor fussed so loud about being left that Jolie heard her even though she sat clear across the room. Finally, Tyrese asked her to be the godmother, and that quieted her.

"Whew," Tyrese said as he replaced the receiver. Robyn smiled as she lay in the bed with rings around her eyes that a circus animal could jump through. When Joan suggested that everyone leave, with the exception of herself of course, Robyn raised her hand in protest. "No, Mamma. It's so neat to see everyone here and happy. Don't kick them out just yet. This is tight!"

Laughing, Joan told the room, "Okay, all of you can stay a little while longer, but the three members of this family need some rest soon."

Jolie couldn't agree more. Tyrese was practically lying in Robyn's bed. His long legs hung over the side, leaving his big bare feet resting on the floor. His head lolled on the pillow above Robyn and his lips frequently met her head and brow as he stroked the back of the baby that slept on her stomach. Jolie had tried to get him to wait until check out, but once he heard he was a father, he'd sprung out of bed and rushed to Robyn's room, three floors up, still garbed in the hospital blues.

Her brother was a father. Jolie shook her head in wonderment. Her father had called Ty. After being told he was a grandfather, he'd promised to see the grandchild when he came out for Ty's graduation. That was three months away. Strangely enough, Ty was unperturbed, only Jolie seemed to be irked by his lack of excitement.

Jolie glanced over at Alvin tucked into the other corner of the room. Robert stood beside him talking about who knows what. Alvin listened attentively; however, his eyes were on the scene in the bed. A slight smile toyed with his lips as he watched Tyrese, Robyn, and the baby. Somehow, Alvin had worked his magic again, and Dr. Graves had come to Robyn's room. From there the doctor examined Tyrese once more and then cleared him for release. Although a nurse had brought Tyrese's belongings, he had yet to change into his street clothes.

Suddenly, Jolie's heart warmed with appreciation. Because of Alvin, this entire situation had been so much more bearable. The man across the room was nothing like her father. He didn't run from emotional situations. He stood his ground and dealt with them. The depth of Jolie's feelings was so strong and unexpected that she felt tears spring to her eyes. Alvin looked at her and a small line creased his brow. He leaned away from the wall. Jolie shook her head, and he stopped his forward motion.

She felt too vulnerable to face him. The Lord only knew what she'd confess to if she spoke to him now. They needed to talk, but it had to be at a time when she could hold her feelings closer to the vest. She had no desire to let him know that he had the power to crush her.

Robert talked on, oblivious of their contact. Jolie had never seen the man so animated. First, he'd made a grand speech about how momentous the occasion was, and now, he was cornering each of them separately and droning on about a wide range of topics.

Running a quick hand across her eyes, Jolie announced to the room, "I'm gonna get a cup of coffee from the machine. Anyone want a cup?"

Robert was the only one who raised his hand. "But why don't you go to Starbucks? There's one right in the lobby of the hospital."

"Good idea." That would give her even more time to think.

"I want a grande, two pump almond, latte."

"Got it, Robert." Jolie smiled to the room and headed out.

"Why don't I come with you?" Alvin's words stopped her in her tracks.

"No. That's not necessary. I can handle two cups on my own." Jolie thought quickly. "Besides, didn't you say the head coach was dropping by? You should stay and wait for him since you're the only one who really knows him." Jolie was grasping at straws.

Her brother lifted his head. "Coach Rock is coming?" He leaned up and looked down at Robyn. After pecking her forehead, he said, "I better get dressed then." As he slowly left the bed, Jolie slipped from the room. She could see the question on Alvin's face. The slightly narrowed eyes and head tilt seemed to be saying, why are you running now, Jolie?

She kept self-reflection to a minimum as she bought the coffee and made her way back to the room. She'd allow herself to think only when she had the luxury to let the emotions flow. Then she'd sit down with Alvin and work this thing out. If he had a plausible explanation for the girl at the game, and if he promised there would be no others, then they could take it slow and see what happened.

The noise coming from Robyn's room drew Jolie from her thoughts. She entered the doorway and almost dropped the hot coffee. With supreme care, she settled both cups on the counter by the door that served as a sink as well. She flushed blood red as a fire radiated out from her belly, through her veins, and settled in her brain to burn brightly.

Alvin and the woman from the game stood side by side with their arms around each other. Both of their backs were to Jolie as they faced the bed, and the sight of the woman reaching up and kissing Alvin, actually struck her; like a physically blow to her gut. All of this happened in slow motion, and Jolie squeezed her eyes shut before the lips reached their destination. In her mind's eye, she saw tongues thrusting. In actuality, the woman's lips barely grazed Alvin's cheek. Jolie's lids flew up to face the woman's eyes. Her arm continued to adorn Alvin's waist as she looked over her shoulder at Jolie. The woman looked surprised, and then a slight smile of curiosity formed on her face. Jolie refused to be part of a scene on such a day. She turned and fled from the room.

Alvin glanced down at Latisha when she removed her arm from his waist. "You never told me Jolie was so gorgeous."

"What?" Alvin turned to look at the empty doorway.

"A stunning woman with auburn hair just fled with an anguished look on her face. Me thinks she misunderstood that peck on your cheek."

Jolie hadn't gone far when her body was thrust back by a narrow chest. Wiry arms reached out and stilled her.

"Whoa, sis. Where are you rushing off too? The bathroom? I just went."

"No, Ty. I'm exhausted. Call me at home when you're ready to leave."

Ty's hands still held her shoulders. He saw something in the face that Jolie was struggling to keep blank. "You sure you're straight?"

"Yes, Ty. It's just hard work delivering a baby."

His expression instantly turned sappy. He drew his sister into a hug. "Thank you so much, sis. I trip thinking about what could have happened if you weren't there. Now I have a beautiful baby to go along with my beautiful woman." He leaned away from her, "And my beautiful sis. Robyn and I want to name him Joseph Alvin."

Jolie didn't know what to say. Her nephew sharing her name with Alvin's name! Finally, she pulled her brother into another hug and managed to say the expected. Thanks, Ty."

"Hey, coach."

Jolie looked back to see who Tyrese was talking to. Alvin was standing just beyond the room looking at them. Jolie pushed away from Ty. "Call me at home when you're ready." With the force of a fugitive rocket ship, Jolie rushed to the elevator. She looked back to see Alvin following her and shifted direction towards the stairs. He caught her before she'd gone down a flight.

"Jolie, this is ridiculous. Why are you running from me?"

She ignored the truth in his words and focused on the part that matched the blaze raging through her blood. Ridiculous! How dare he judge her! She whirled around to face him. The way he calmly walked down the stairs irked her more.

"This is truly silly and borderline childish."

"Silly? Childish?" Jolie's arms formed a line across her chest. "You have some nerve criticizing my behavior."

Alvin stopped very close to her in the small space between the stairs.

"I can't help it. Good thing I had my tennis shoes on so I could catch up with you." Alvin put his hands in his pockets. "You know, it's odd. You were never such a track star before. You stood and faced things. What are you fleeing from now, Jolie?"

"Floozies! That's what I'm running from, Alvin. Every time and everywhere I see you, it seems as if some cheap woman is hanging off your arm! I can't believe you had her in Robyn's room!"

"I don't think Rock's wife would appreciated you calling her a loose woman."

"Rock?"

"Yes, Rock, Jolie. I've known them both since college. She writes children's books and she loves kids. When she heard about a new baby," Alvin shrugged his shoulders, "she wanted to come. Rock was supposed to be here, too, but then he thought better of it. Said I was breaking enough rules for the both of us."

The new information hit Jolie hard. "The game...the hug."

"Yes, she was there with Rock. She's an affectionate person. She'd hugged everyone in that room before the introductions were made. If you had stayed in the room just now instead of taking off, I'm sure she would have hugged you too."

Jolie looked into the steady warmth of his eyes, still scared to let go.

Alvin's hands lifted from his pockets. "I would really like to hug you now, but I'm not sure that you won't bite. Oh, what the hell, we all have to take risks in life. It's time for you to surrender, Jolie." He wrapped her in his strong arms. Before she could decide if that was okay, his lips were touching hers in a long, slow kiss that obliterated any lingering bitterness and self-doubt.

Unwilling to hold back any longer, Alvin laid it all on the line in the stairwell at Harborlake hospital. "I love you, Jolie. Damn it, I have always loved you. From the first time I saw you in our high school lunchroom, I've wanted to be with you. I watched you blush when I ate your cookie, and I watched the red creep into your face again when the horses were doing their thing." His fingers slipped into her hair as his palms cupped her face. "Your strength amazes me. The way you care for your brother, how you handled delivering that baby." Alvin's lips briefly touched hers. "I'll never forget the way you smiled at me after we moved Robyn to the floor. You stole my soul with that smile, Jolie." The breathy words said softly against her lips set off a different blaze in Jolie. "I knew then as strongly as I know it now that you are the one and only woman for me. It's time for you to give in and allow that to happen."

Jolie gripped the sides of his T-shirt when his mouth covered hers again. She couldn't part her lips fast enough when she felt his tongue toying with her plump lips. She reveled in the way he explored her mouth before inviting her do the same. So much passion and tenderness intertwined, Jolie felt as if she were caught up in an undertow, her senses drowning in this man who kissed her so expertly. And when he stopped kissing her, she reached up with her hands to cradle his face and kissed him. After a time, she drew back. Not because the hunger had eased, but because she knew there were things she needed to say. Her hands slipped down his long neck and rested in the crook of his shoulders.

"Oh, Alvie. I've been so foolish and...well...you said it best, childish."

Alvin was about to interrupt, but she held a finger to his lips.

"No, honey. Now it's my turn." She took a deep breath. "No more misunderstandings or letting other people get between us." She reached up with her right hand and trailed her fingertips along his cheek. Enunciating each word, she said, "I love you." She pecked his lips. "I was wrong to hit you with the ball and with my words. I know you would have never left my side if you'd known what was happening back then. I will no longer let anger be my default reaction. I'm ready to trust you, communicate with you, and yes, baby, I surrender to you."

Alvin's eyes were bright. "Jolie, can I have your hand back. I promise to love, cherish, and protect it."

Jolie chuckled.

"I promise to hold it tight and never let go."

Jolie slid her hands from his shoulders to interlock with his. "Oh, baby. You can have both of them for a lifetime or two." She reached up and brushed her lips against his. "By the way, you were right about the toad thing."

"Hum?" Alvin was focused on capturing the teasing

lips.

"I've kissed you hard and often, and you've become a beautiful, black prince. I think if I lay a few more big ones on you, you're destined to become a king."

"Oh yeah?"

"Yeah."

"All right, let's put your theory to the test."

Epilogue

Three years later.

"And now you may kiss the bride." The crowd cheered as the groom wrapped his arms around his new wife and kissed her deeply. The cheers turned to snickers as the kiss lasted much longer than necessary. The groom finally moved back and pumped his fist as the audience went nuts.

"Me too, me too." A three-year-old ring bearer dashed between his parents' legs. His father bent and lifted him so he could be showered with pecks from both parents. Jolie stood to the side of the action with the other bridesmaids and watched her brother with his family. Her eyes left the happy scene to look at her husband. In his position as the best man, Alvin was directly across from Jolie who stood as the matron of honor. He blew her a kiss, which she caught, and returned.

Tyrese and Robyn finally lifted their heads and began making their way to the back of the church. The wedding party followed. Jolie waved to Ethel, who blew her a kiss. When they reached the end of the aisle, she found herself engulfed in Joan's arms. "I can't believe it, girl! The day has finally come where we are officially family."

"That we are," Jolie agreed, thinking that the only thing that made the day not quite as bright was the fact that

Tyrese was leaving school a year before graduating. He'd entered the NBA draft early, and he'd be moving to Texas next month to play for the San Antonio Spurs. He'd promised Jolie that he'd finish later, but that didn't make her feel any better. Robyn told Jolie not to worry because she'd make sure he kept his word. She'd graduated a week earlier with a degree in business management. Tyrese joked that he didn't need the paper because his wife could take care of all his money. Jolie didn't find the joke funny.

Turning from Joan, Jolie eased into Alvin's waiting arms. "The ceremony was beautiful, babe. You and Joan did a great job putting it together, but I still think ours was better."

Jolie couldn't agree more. Eloping to Jamaica and getting married at sunset on the beach was definitely the way to go. It had been almost two years, but the memory was just as fresh as yesterday. Her eyes softened as she reached up to meet her husband's lips.

"Don't start," he murmured. "Or else this crowd will be shouting at us next."

Jolie couldn't help herself. She felt as if she'd been on an endless honeymoon; the only damper to their relationship was about to be extinguished shortly. Suddenly, Jolie didn't feel like waiting until later to share her news. She grabbed Alvin's hand and urged him to follow her into a side room.

Laughing, Alvin said, "Don't tell me it's some secret fantasy of yours to get freaky in a church. You Catholic girls are always the wildest!"

"No, you nut. I have news that I want to share only with

you right now." Taking both of his hands into hers, Jolie said, "I'm pregnant!"

Alvin's smile disappeared. He whispered, "Are you sure?" He was scared to believe because Jolie had suffered through numerous false alarms. They were both beginning to wonder if it was in God's plan for them to adopt.

"Yes, honey. It's for real this time. My doctor confirmed the home pregnancy test about an hour before the wedding started. I was going to wait until tonight to tell you, but I couldn't hold it in."

"Oh, God!" Alvin lifted her into a bear hug and swung her around. Then he abruptly put her down. "I'm sorry. Did I hurt you?"

"Of course not, silly. I'm pregnant, not sick. You can still do that for a couple more months."

"Oh, Jolie!" Alvin caught her face between his hands and expressed himself with his tongue and lips.

The click of the door opening drew them apart. "Oh, I'm sorry," Jolie's father said. He'd flown in yesterday for the wedding and he was leaving the next day. "Everyone is headed to the cars, and they sent me to find you two."

Still beaming, Jolie ran over and hugged her father. He stumbled and then balanced himself. "You're going to be a grandfather again."

"Oh, really. Um…that's great news."

Jolie could tell that the poor man didn't know what to say. She was so happy that she didn't care. She pecked her father's cheek, and then turned to Alvin, so she could grab his hand and walk with him to the limousine.

"Wait!" Alvin said. "Mr. Smith, could you tell them we'll be right there. I have something I want to tell my wife."

Her father quietly shut the door. "I made a decision today, too. I'm tired of coaching full time and traveling. I've decided to take the boys' and girls' club job."

"Oh, Alvie, are you sure?" Jolie was scared to believe it. As the director of the club, Alvin would be able to spend so much more time with her.

"Yes," he confirmed with a nod. "I always knew coaching was a temporary thing for me. I'm good at it and Rock needed me. Now the program is so strong he won't have any trouble at all replacing me. I'm excited about working with the kids, giving back to the community that's given me so much. Also, I can still coach the little guys when the urge hits, and the farthest I'll have to travel is across the city."

"Oh, Alvie." Jolie practically jumped into his arms. Neither of them heard the door open and wouldn't have cared if they had.

"Oh, look at this here! Will you two cut that out, and come on." Robert stood at the door with his hand on his hip. "You're holding up the cars and the reception and I'm thirsty."

The two slowly separated. "Be quiet, Robert. I'm asking my husband if he knows how much I love him?"

"Yes," Alvin answered, "you showed me long ago when you responded to my coaxing and gave me a second chance."

"Oh, gosh, you two!"

They both glared at Robert. Jolie chuckled first because he looked so exasperated. Soon Alvin was laughing as well. "We'd better go before he tries to physically remove us." Alvin said.

"That's right. You two have been married too long for this nonsense. Just because it's a wedding doesn't mean that people have to lose their minds. The whole thing is way too mushy for me."

Jolie and Alvin followed the fussing Robert, giggling like teenagers.

They slipped into the limousine, sitting opposite Robyn and Tyrese. Their son, Joey, immediately hopped into Jolie's lap. The newlyweds looked at them. Tyrese said, "Damn! It looks like you two just got hitched instead of us. What are you guys so happy about?"

"We're about to give Joey a cousin."

A wide grin spread across Tyrese's face. He pointed to Jolie's left hand. "I guess that's awright since you got the ice on your finger, and I sure hope y'all didn't leave any underwear in that side room."

Jolie gasped. She couldn't hit her brother with her nephew sitting in her lap. So she kicked his leg. It did nothing to stop his howls of laughter. Everyone was laughing including Joey, whom she was sure had no idea what he was giggling about. Alvin hugged her from the side, and Jolie allowed herself to release a chuckle or two.

Soon, they reached the reception hall. Joey scrambled

out of the limousine with his parents and the three rushed into the building. At a more sedate pace, Alvin helped Jolie out of the car and into his arms. His kiss was so lingering and deep it left Jolie aching for more when he lifted his head.

"Wow, what was that for?" Jolie was still reeling. She was ready to risk humiliation and drag Alvin to the nearest empty room.

"That's for being my past, my present, and my future." Her heart melted. He grabbed her hand and kissed it. Smiling through her tears she reached up and touched her lips to his tenderly and said, "I love you." Then with a saucy grin she added, "Wait until we leave here and go home. The things I see in your immediate future are dazzling indeed. Squeezing his hand, they entered the hall smiling as if they had the secret to the joy of life.

Other Titles By
Edwina Martin-Arnold

EVE'S PRESCRIPTION

The handsome firefighter responds to an emergency medical call. She tries not to notice him. Instant fireworks spark between them, but rumors of his red-hot reputation keep Eve struggling to squelch her own growing desires. The flames are lit, but will they keep burning? Will they withstand Hurricane Eve, or will they be blown out?

INDIGO

Winter & Spring 2002

❧ March

An Unfinished Love Affair	Barbara Keaton	$8.95

❧ April

Jolie's Surrender	Edwina Martin-Arnold	$8.95
Promises to Keep	Alicia Wiggins	$8.95

❧ May

Magnolia Sunset	Giselle Carmichael	$8.95
Once in a Blue Moon	Dorianne Cole	$9.95

❧ June

Still Waters Run Deep	Leslie Esdaile	$9.95
Everything but Love	Natalie Dunbar	$8.95
Indigo After Dark Vol. V		$14.95
Brown Sugar Diaries Part II	Dolores Bundy	

OTHER INDIGO TITLES

Kiss or Keep	Debra Phillips	$8.95
Love Always	Mildred E. Riley	$10.95
Love Unveiled	Gloria Green	$10.95
Love's Deception	Charlene Berry	$10.95
Mae's Promise	Melody Walcott	$8.95
Midnight Clear (Anthology)	Leslie Esdaile	$10.95
	Gwynne Forster	
	Carmen Green	
	Monica Jackson	
Midnight Magic	Gwynne Forster	$8.95
Midnight Peril	Vicki Andrews	$10.95
Naked Soul	Gwynne Forster	$8.95
No Regrets	Mildred E. Riley	$8.95
Nowhere to Run	Gay G. Gunn	$10.95
Passion	T.T. Henderson	$10.95
Past Promises	Jahmel West	$8.95
Path of Fire	T.T. Henderson	$8.95
Picture Perfect	Reon Carter	$8.95
Pride & Joi	Gay G. Gunn	$8.95
Quiet Storm	Donna Hill	$10.95
Reckless Surrender	Rochelle Alers	$8.95
Rendezvous with Fate	Jeanne Sumerix	$8.95
Rooms of the Heart	Donna Hill	$8.95
Shades of Desire	Monica White	$8.95
Sin	Crystal Rhodes	$8.95
So Amazing	Sinclair LeBeau	$8.95
Somebody's Someone	Sinclair LeBeau	$8.95
Soul to Soul	Donna Hill	$8.95
Subtle Secrets	Wanda Y. Thomas	$8.95
Sweet Tomorrows	Kimberley White	$8.95

You may order on-line at www.genesis-press.com, by phone at 1-888-463-4461, or mail the order-form in the back of this book.

Love Spectrum Romance

Romance across the culture lines

Forbidden Quest	Dar Tomlinson	$10.95
Designer Passion	Dar Tomlinson	$8.95
Fate	Pamela Leigh Starr	$8.95
Against the Wind	Gwynne Forster	$8.95
From The Ashes	Kathleen Suzanne Jeanne Summerix	$8.95
Heartbeat	Stephanie Bedwell-Grime	$8.95
My Buffalo Soldier	Barbara B. K. Reeves	$8.95
Meant to Be	Jeanne Sumerix	$8.95
A Risk of Rain	Dar Tomlinson	$8.95

Indigo After Dark

erotica beyond sensuous

Indigo After Dark Vol. I $10.95
    In Between the Night   Angelique
    Midnight Erotic Fantasies Nia Dixon

Indigo After Dark Vol. II $10.95
    The Forbidden Art of Desire Cole Riley
    Erotic Short Stories   Dolores Bundy

Indigo After Dark Vol. III $10.95
    Impulse   Montana Blue
    Pant   Coco Morena

ORDER FORM

Mail to: Genesis Press, Inc.
315 3rd Avenue North
Columbus, MS 39701

Name _____

Address _____

City/State _____ Zip _____

Telephone _____

Ship to (if different from above)

Name _____

Address _____

City/State _____ Zip _____

Telephone _____

Qty	Author	Title	Price	Total

Use this order form, or
call
1-888-INDIGO-1

Total for books _____

Shipping and handling:
  **$3 first book, $1 each
  additional book** _____

Total S & H _____

Total amount enclosed _____

MS residents add 7% sales tax

ORDER FORM

Mail to: Genesis Press, Inc.
315 3rd Avenue North
Columbus, MS 39701

Name _____

Address _____

City/State _____ Zip _____

Telephone _____

Ship to (if different from above)

Name _____

Address _____

City/State _____ Zip _____

Telephone _____

Qty	Author	Title	Price	Total

Use this order form, or call **1-888-INDIGO-1**	**Total for books** _____
	 Shipping and handling:
	   $3 first book, $1 each
	   additional book _____
	 Total S & H _____
	 Total amount enclosed _____
	 MS residents add 7% sales tax